"Shush, I'll help you. I've been through the process," Austin murmured into her fragrant hair, so soft against his face.

He would take it easy with her. He didn't want her feeling alone, mourning and bereft all at once. It was more than he could take, so the offer was easy to make.

Then he wanted to kick himself. What was he thinking? Volunteering for things had always gotten him into trouble, especially with her, from the age of twenty-two. He was one badass marine, but she'd broken him with one soft, shuddering sigh, looking up at him with her blue eyes swimming in tears.

Getting tangled up with Jenna Webb was the stupidest thing he'd ever done. He could only chalk it up to the circumstances. The danger and the adrenaline, the way she looked at him like he was her hero.

* * *

Be sure to check out the other books in this exciting miniseries:

To Protect and Serve—A team of navy military operatives and civilians are called to investigate...

* * *

Dear Reader,

Austin and Jenna found each other a long time ago, but due to commitments in their lives, they weren't able to follow through with how they felt. Now they're thrown together as Austin investigates Jenna's cousin's murder and those sparks are still there ready to explode into flame. What will they discover about themselves and each other as the clues fall into place and Austin makes a terrifying discovery?

Jenna is trying to find her way after her divorce from her former ambassador husband—one who coddled and pampered her until she was ready to scream. Now she's on her own, visiting her only living relative when her cousin is murdered. The only bright spot in her life is the appearance of Austin. He was the young marine who had saved her life. Now he's the NCIS agent who will be on her cousin's case. She has to not only deal with her past, but work at discovering who she really is and finally where she belongs. Will that be in Austin's life?

Austin races against the clock to discover the real killer behind all the murky clues. He wants to not only get the justice Jenna's cousin deserves, but protect a woman who could mean more to him than anyone in his life. All he has to do is keep her alive.

Karen Anders

AGENT
BODYGUARD

Karen Anders

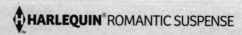
HARLEQUIN® ROMANTIC SUSPENSE

Recycling programs
for this product may
not exist in your area.

ISBN-13: 978-1-335-45648-9

Agent Bodyguard

Copyright © 2018 by Karen Aiarie

This edition published by arrangement with Harlequin Books S.A.

For questions and comments about the quality of this book, please contact us at CustomerService@Harlequin.com.

HARLEQUIN®
™ www.Harlequin.com

Printed in U.S.A.

Karen Anders writes a suspenseful and sexy mix of navy and civilians investigating murder, espionage and crime across a global landscape. Under the pen name Zoe Dawson, she's currently writing romantic comedy, new-adult contemporary romance, urban fantasy, syfy and erotic romance. When she's not busy writing, she's painting or killing virtual mmorpg monsters. She lives in North Carolina with her two daughters and one small furry gray cat.

Books by Karen Anders

Harlequin Romantic Suspense

To Protect and Serve

At His Command
Designated Target
Joint Engagement
Her Master Defender
A SEAL to Save Her
Her Alpha Marine
The Agent's Covert Affair
Agent Bodyguard

The Coltons of Texas

High-Stakes Colton

The Adair Legacy

Special Ops Rendezvous

Five-Alarm Encounter

Visit the Author Profile page at Harlequin.com.

To the Blue Angels and the dedication and precision it takes to become one of them. After all the books that I have written, the navy is very near and dear to my heart, so I salute you all as a symbol of navy pride. The sky is the limit...

Chapter 1

The Embassy of the United States of America
Khida, Ja'arbah, Middle East

*I don't want children, Jenna. I thought you realized
that when we married.*

Jenna Webb walked up the embassy steps on her way
to meet her husband for dinner. The husband who had
dropped the bomb on her just last night: no children.

She spied Sergeant Austin Beck, who must have just
come off guard duty, still dressed in his uniform, short-
sleeved khaki shirt, midnight blue trousers with a red
stripe, and the white peaked hat or, as the military re-
ferred to it, cover. He was a momentary distraction
from her thoughts; every time she laid eyes on him,
even through her current distress and unhappiness, her
heart beat just a little bit harder.

He paused on the stairs to talk to someone and Jenna
looked up the length of the Chancery to the window of
her husband's office building.

She sighed softly, remembering how he'd informed

her in that brook-no-argument voice, as if that was the final word. No children. That had floored her. Of course, he was twenty-five years older than she was. She'd been coaxed into the marriage by her father at twenty. She'd even left school halfway through her degree in architecture, convinced that Robert was the right man for her. She had been...*was* in love with him four years later, but had it been the starry-eyed kind? Was she starting to see clearly for the first time in her life? Could she give up on herself again? She regretted not finishing school, not pursuing her ambition to follow in her mother's footsteps. Jenna had admired her so much.

Her father had meant well, even with his overprotective instincts. Her mother, a renowned architect, had been killed in an insurrection overseas when she was on a job. Her father had been devastated, and she'd found herself giving in to his wishes to save him more pain. But her choice of degree and vocation weighed heavily on him and she could see how it worried him to the point of affecting his health. Had she allowed herself to be blinded by her father's distress, thinking once she was married she would be content to be a wife and mother, especially a mother?

Even as she realized that disappointment was part of life, she felt that Robert had led her on. Emotion welled in her chest, her throat getting thick, tears hovering. She pushed them back. This would be a terrible place to have a breakdown. She couldn't be late. Robert hated it when she was late. That wasn't always the case. Robert had been attentive and sweet to her throughout their courtship.

But if her father, God rest his soul, had known that her CEO husband would become an ambassador and take her to many overseas assignments, he would have never recommended marriage to him. A little nagging voice told her she might have made a mistake.

When she got married, Jenna had every expectation that motherhood was an unspoken promise. But it was a bitter and disappointing pill, that she'd never know the joy of having kids of her own. Children she could give all her unconditional love to without fear of them not loving her back. Losing her mom when she'd been eight left her with loneliness, a keen sense of isolation and a strong desire to give her own children the nurturing Jenna had lost.

She closed her eyes briefly at the pain that thought caused. Her inattention cost her as the right toe of her expensive pair of the-ambassador's-wife heels caught on the stair and pitched her forward.

Bracing herself for impact, she instinctively reached out her hand to break her fall, but instead of striking against concrete, she hit something hard. She looked up into Sergeant Austin Beck's handsome, concerned face.

"Mrs. Webb," he murmured. "Are you all right?"

Without meaning to, she burst into tears. Austin helped her to her feet as she worked at getting herself under control, his muscles thick and firm beneath her palms. He set his arm around her, and she bit her lip. It should have been comforting, but when Austin got anywhere near her, all she felt was hot and bothered. That was so, so wrong.

He supported her inside and when the Post One guard saw them, he buzzed them through. "Mrs. Webb isn't feeling well. I'll escort her up."

The marine behind the glass nodded, giving Austin a *be careful* look. It wasn't lost on some of the employees that she and Austin had a special friendship. The cautious look was a warning to be careful about getting involved with the ambassador's wife.

Mortified, she could do nothing but allow him to help her up the wide marble stairway.

"I can't see him just yet," she murmured. He changed course and led her directly to the conference room just before her husband's suite of offices.

She got a nervous feeling in her stomach when she thought about Austin, and the churning got worse when she thought about her husband. Robert was nothing like him. He was overprotective where Austin was protective, distant where Austin was so approachable, stern where Austin was warm. She felt an enormous amount of guilt at those thoughts, but she had to admit to herself, they were honest.

On her frequent visits to the embassy, she'd had brief conversations with Austin when her husband had been delayed or hadn't remembered they had a lunch date. She and Austin had eaten together a few times. He'd told her all about his work and it had been fun and interesting, being with him in her otherwise mundane day. Austin manned "Post One," the main hub and control center of embassy security. Behind the bullet- and explosion-proof glass he managed and, if need be, could secure the whole embassy, checked monitors for any breaches of the compound, and could respond immediately to any threats or incidents. Post One did ID checks of all incoming personnel, performed roaming patrols and at night looked for any secured/classified infractions.

She could see why Austin had been chosen for this type of duty, and why he excelled at it. He always knew how to connect to the people around him, marine or otherwise. That personable nature of his was just the kind his command would want at an embassy: a big heart, a warm smile and the ability to handle anything that came at him. She found herself thinking about him all too often and wondering what kind of man he was. A flirt for sure. He just about had all the women here wrapped around his finger as he gave them smiles and winks as he buzzed them through the security doors. Marine guards were known for their heartbreaking ways.

Yet she went a little liquid thinking about how he would handle her.

He closed the door behind him and helped her to a seat. "Let me get you something to drink," he said, his voice soft and concerned. He went to a credenza at the end of the room and poured her a glass from the crystal pitcher.

He grabbed a box of tissues and came back to her, sitting down across from her. He offered her the glass and the tissues. She took both, sipping the water, then setting it down on the conference room table. She dabbed at her eyes and finally looked up at him.

"I'm sorry to be any trouble, especially now that you're off-duty."

"I'm never off-duty, ma'am." The concern in his eyes made her wish he would hold her, but that was a dangerous and very inappropriate thought. "Are you feeling better?" She wished she could say that her wishes were silly, but she knew that if given even half a chance, she might find herself in bed with him. She'd taken vows and she wasn't free to indulge herself with another man, no matter how attractive he was. She was vulnerable and hurting from Robert's refusal to consider children.

Her weakness could lead her so far astray without much effort on Austin's part.

She was cold even in this heat and felt that she wouldn't be warm again.

Then he reached out and clasped her hand and heat flooded through her. These imprudent feelings and thoughts were just simply out of her control. She was unhappy in her marriage; she'd be devastated to know that she was nothing but a trophy wife to Robert. She wasn't expected to give him children, she wasn't expected to do any type of work, she wasn't expected to keep the home. All he expected of her was acquiescence and to be impeccably groomed on his arm when he needed her. Otherwise, it was out of sight, out of mind.

Tears welled again and her throat got tight; a small sob escaped her.

"Is there anything I can do?" he said, obviously anguished by her tears and sorrow.

She squeezed his hand and rose, pushing back the pain and the barren feeling in the pit of her stomach. "No, but you're so kind. Thank you for escorting me inside."

This should be oh-so-embarrassing and equally awkward, but there was never any awkwardness with Austin, and his open, gorgeous gray eyes held no judgment or censure, nothing but warmth.

He stepped closer and the air backed up in her lungs. "You would tell me, Mrs. Webb, if I could ever be of service?" His voice was mostly neutral, but there was an undercurrent of heat in his words. His eyes were like hard flint.

The air in the room felt agitated as if the molecules were knocking against each other because of the friction. Her attention narrowed down to Austin. The scent of him, the shape of his lips, the unique color of his hair, the intensity in his eyes.

"Of course."

She went to go, but he slipped his hand around her upper arm, warm and electrifying, halting her. Jenna turned back. "Is he hurting you?" His voice dropped down into the lethal zone, deep and menacing. Jenna realized that Austin might be personable, but he was a marine through and through.

Her voice caught at his touch against her bare skin, her body responding, challenging her will. Her response just short of a whisper, "Yes, but not like you think. I've got to go. He's expecting me."

He let go of her slowly, as if he, too, was fighting his own will, his hand sliding along her arm, causing waves of tingles. She dabbed at her eyes one more time, tossed the tissue in the trash and looked at Austin before she opened the door. "Thank you, Sergeant."

She pushed the door open and let it close softly behind her. Taking a deep breath, knowing that she was breaking her marriage vows by responding to him like this, she couldn't seem to help it. She pushed the guilt and sorrow to a place out of sight to manage a pleasant dinner with a husband who wasn't one in any sense of the word.

Sergeant Austin Beck stepped into the hall where the Marine Corps Birthday Ball was going to be held. It was considered one of the most prestigious diplomatic functions the embassy would host, with dignitaries attending from Khida and foreign embassies. Jenna—Mrs. Webb—had outdone herself with the preparations. He had to stop using her first name in his head. He hadn't been invited to, nor was it appropriate to be fraternizing with an ambassador's wife. He had a longtime girlfriend, but when he looked at Jenna, she captivated him.

The problem was getting her tear-streaked face off his mind. She said he was hurting her and it had bothered him ever since. He was dedicated to his service to the embassy and Ambassador Webb was his commanding officer, so to speak, but the man treated Jenna like she was some kind of freaking possession. If he was physically abusing her, there wouldn't be anything to stop Austin from breaking both his arms so he couldn't lay a hand on her.

He took a breath to release the tension across his shoulders encased in the deep blue dress jacket. As the youngest marine here, he would be involved in the kickoff cake-eating ceremony. It was an old Marine Corps Birthday Ball tradition. The oldest marine cut the cake, ate a bite and passed it on to the youngest, symbolic of the birth of the marine corps.

Without even meaning to, he sought her out. She was talking to another marine and she looked gorgeous. Her deep maroon, open-backed gown clung to her trim body, her shoulders peeking out from the cutouts, the collar high, accentuating her slender neck, the vibrant color making her long, dark wavy hair, now tamed and in an intricate up-do, stand out, along with her clear, stunning, cobalt blue eyes. He caught his breath at the creamy expanse of her back. He searched her face for any signs of unrest, but she was either putting on a good show or she had gotten over whatever had upset her.

He suspected it was the former.

He started toward her, then realized that it was stupid and instead made his way to a large cake with vanilla frosting. The ball got under way then, the music started up and the buffet line opened up. He managed to keep his distance from her, even though she glanced in his direction more than once. He kept telling himself that he was just concerned about her situation, that he wasn't fascinated by her eyes, or thought way too long about her mouth.

Feeling jacked up and restless, as if he could run ten miles, he saw that she was free for a dance. She would be expected to dance with each of them, so this was obligatory.

"Mrs. Webb, may I have this dance?"

She turned to him and stared at him for a moment, as if he was a land mine about ready to blow, then she dropped her thick lashes over those twist-a-man-up-inside eyes and nodded. The waltz was pretty and it felt so right when she slipped her palm against his.

"Good evening, Sergeant. Are you enjoying yourself?"

"I am, ma'am. Very much. You pulled out all the stops and did a fine job."

She flushed at his praise. She remembered her tug of war with Robert's assistant. She oversaw all the planning duties, even though the woman had tried to take over for her at Robert's orders. That had been another battle with him, but this one she had won by sheer stubbornness. "Well, this is all for you. Tonight, around the world, you are all in harm's way, on board ships at sea, at our diplomatic missions, marines are on duty." Her voice got low and fierce. "The amazing men and women of our armed forces serving and protecting right alongside them. You all risk your lives to protect us and our freedoms, many times under circumstances unimaginably difficult and dangerous. So, God bless you all."

"Thank you," he said, dancing her closer to the doors that led outside to the balmy night until finally they were on the patio under the moonlight and the sounds of the party receded.

They parted and she moved away from him, breathing deeply of the air. "It always smells so good here," she said.

He came up behind her; the deep, dark, secluded area made it seem as if they were the only people in the world.

"It does smell good," he murmured, his fingers itching to reach out and capture one of those cascading curls, to feel the heat of her hair, the smooth skin of her back. But he breathed deep of her instead, a floral aroma mixed with her unique woman-scent that made him weak—seriously messed with his badass quotient.

She turned toward him. "Have you enjoyed your billet here, Sergeant?"

"Immensely," he said, caressing her delicate features with his eyes in the moonlight, knowing he was crossing over that invisible boundary against his will—or was he doing it deliberately?

"The people have been very accommodating and so welcoming—warm and accepting. I find that it's been my most favorite post, as well."

"Yes," he nodded, stepping closer to her as her body seemed to soften and sway toward him. "The people are fantastic."

She reached up and drew her finger across his ribbons just below the gold eagle pin. "So many. You must have been in the service for a while."

"Just four years, since I was eighteen," he said, capturing her hand and drawing her closer. She didn't resist and his chest felt full, his groin throbbing. Her lips parted, her mouth looking much too tempting to resist.

With a small gasp that only made his balls tighten, she said, "You're only twenty-two?"

"In man years," he responded, shifting. "But in marine years, I'm like forty-five." Grinning the grin that had got him into more trouble than he cared to think about, he fixed his gaze on her. He'd been having sex since he was sixteen and was quite aware of the opposite sex. Surfer boys got more than their share of female appreciation. But Austin had stayed faithful to Melanie, the girl waiting for him back home. Except there seemed to be a gray fog over that memory of her, as if he couldn't recall her face.

She smiled and his heart flip-flopped, a true, amused smile that did things to his well-organized, completely rational brain. The expression in her eyes glinted, then softened, becoming a little warmer, a little more intimate—the look you gave someone you'd known a long, long time. As if they were old souls.

"Jenna," he whispered raggedly, dragging his fingers through her curls.

Someone dropped a lid off one of the dishes and it reverberated with a metallic sound. She froze, and the dreamy, lost look in her eyes snapped off. "Oh, God," she murmured and pushed away from him. "What am I doing?" She shook her head and before he could stop her, she rushed past him and back into the bright lights of the party.

He watched her get control of herself, march briskly to her husband, and they walked onto the dance floor.

She couldn't have put up a larger or more formidable wall. He wanted to know how she really felt, but he was being a complete fool. She was married to the United States ambassador. She wasn't free and neither was he.

This could torpedo his career in a freaking heartbeat. He had to get control of himself.

The faster he realized that, the better off he would be.

The next day, Jenna was summoned to the embassy and told to pack a bag. She was hoping to catch Austin, talk to him, make it clear that she was married and that she couldn't engage in any kind of an affair with him. She was just…a woman who was desperately trying to handle disappointment.

But, as she came through the gates, there were several pockets of people—angry people. They banged on the car windows when the vehicle slowed to enter. As the gates closed behind her, she noticed that the Khida security force responsible for guarding the grounds were flanking the gates fully armed, the looks on their faces tense and watchful.

Once inside, she forgot about talking to Austin as another marine buzzed her in. The uniform triggered thoughts of Austin, anyway, and a flash of memory chased her up the staircase and into the suite of offices as she was immediately allowed entrance to her husband's.

"Robert. What is going on?"

He looked up from his phone call and murmured something, then hung up. He smiled, but it was the tight one that told her he was going to treat her like a child.

"There is no need to worry, my dear."

"There's a growing number of very angry people outside. I think there's a need to worry," she snapped.

His eyes flashed. It was the first time she'd ever raised her voice to him, and God, it felt good.

"Very well. We are monitoring the situation and the residence isn't safe. You'll stay here until this blows over."

"What happened?"

"There was an incident in New York. Several Ja'arbah citizens, who are attending the university, were victims of a hate crime. One of them was killed after being set on fire and the other two are in critical condition."

"Oh, my God."

He came around the desk and clasped her upper arms, smiling that tight smile again. "They're angry and want justice."

"Have they caught the people responsible for the deaths?"

"The suspects in the case are at large and the NYPD is doing everything they can to apprehend them." He gave her a calming look, but Jenna felt cold and unsettled. She moved away from him, folding her arms across her chest and rubbing at them. "They're protesting. We'll let them get it out of their system."

"Are you sure that's all they're going to do? There are militants everywhere, Robert. Even here."

He looked at her like she had grown two heads. As if he couldn't fathom where she might have heard the word *militants*.

She huffed a breath. "Robert."

"For now. Yes. If things change. We'll deal with it."

He went to his intercom. "Janet, please send up Sergeant Beck."

"Yes, sir."

Oh, no, not Austin. "Why are you sending up a marine?"

"You need a guard."

"Guard? You mean babysit me. I'm not a child, Robert."

"I know that, and this is a precaution."

"He's needed elsewhere," she said firmly.

"I don't know what's gotten into you, but if this is about our discussion regarding children, your petulance can stop right now. I am the authority here, Jenna, and I will do what I see fit for my wife. Is that understood?" He never let her forget he was in a prestigious position, symbolizing the sovereignty of the United States and serving as the personal representative of the President.

She couldn't protest any louder because he might wonder why. She bit her tongue and looked away. "Understood."

"Good. Put this on and keep it on until you're safe." He handed her a bulletproof vest.

No, she thought as memories of Austin's mouth and how much she'd wanted to kiss him shocked through her, this wasn't good at all. She took the vest, her stomach tight.

Two days later, Jenna stood staring out of the embassy window, watching as dusk settled, tension in the air, like it was waiting, breath suspended for…violence. That feeling shivered across her skin, settled like a sick rock in her stomach and sent fear skittering along her nerve endings. Robert had been wrong and the numbers of people only swelled. Angrier people, some carrying weapons, now surrounded the embassy on all sides. The police had tried to disperse them with tear gas. They just surged back once it had cleared. The sound of breaking glass audible above the constant, bone-chilling chant. Suddenly someone grabbed her arm and pulled her away from the view.

"I'd prefer you stay away from the windows, ma'am," Austin said, his voice still professional and neutral. No inflection. She cringed. She hadn't said a word to him about what had happened. He had been the perfect gentleman. Both of them must have wised up. Or had she? She still couldn't get him off her mind and if he called her "ma'am" one more time... Today he was in tan camouflage instead of his more formal dress, a battle helmet on his head, in constant contact with the other marines in the compound and Post One.

She huffed and settled on the cushions of the leather couch in the office where she had been sleeping.

He glanced at her, his posture loose as he leaned against the wall. "What is it? You're staring daggers at me."

"Please don't call me that again."

He stared at her, and she breathed a sigh of relief. That blank look was gone, replaced by a pensive one. "Call you what?"

"Ma'am."

He looked down. "It's necessary."

"Jenna, please. Call me Jenna." He just stared at her. "As opposed to 'ma'am.' It makes me feel eighty." But it mostly made her feel alone.

She felt strangely calm inside, as if she'd emptied everything out and now there was nothing left. It was almost a nice feeling, that kind of hollowness. Maybe, she thought with a touch of black humor, she had to honor Robert's wishes about children. But she didn't have to like it, and she could no longer contain her resentment.

She sighed and rubbed her arms. She had been dodging reality long enough.

He smiled then, and she had to remember to take a breath. Austin in marine mode was lethal, but when he smiled…everything melted. She knew it was inappropriate.

"All right. It's not protocol. I should really call you Mrs. Webb…" She narrowed her eyes and he laughed again. "All right, okay. Jenna it is, but I think you should still address me as Sergeant Beck. That's as far as I can stretch my strict protocol."

This time she smiled. He really was working at keeping his distance. Wasn't that a good thing? "If you insist." It would be a good thing if protocol wasn't already on the rocks.

"I do." He indicated the window with a nod of his head. "Let's just keep our heads down and out of any line of fire." She must have blanched because he looked contrite and swore softly under his breath. "Sorry. It's safer. All right?"

"Yes."

The buzz of the chanting closed in on her, and she turned toward the window just able to see over the sill. It was a beautiful night, with the twilight soft, purple, and oddly welcoming. This…fearful restlessness was building in her. It was as if her brain was telling her to flee, but she knew she had nowhere to go right now.

"What if they breach the walls? Come after us?"

"We have safe haven in the event of the worst-case scenario. But your husband decided this morning that we should all be evacuated until things die down. He didn't tell you this?" Safe haven was a fortified room where they could lock themselves in, but how long could they survive? What if they set the building on fire?

"No." She sighed. He would of course want to spare her the worry. "I'm sure he's very busy handling this crisis."

"The choppers will be here in time. I promise you. Nothing will happen to you. I'll keep you safe."

She stared out at the milling crowd, its cadence never wavering, arms pumping over their heads. She wished she was home. Home in DC, where it was safe. She absently tucked her hair behind her ear, trying to keep the fear at bay.

"Talk to me about something, anything."

His eyes softened a bit. "I'm a surfer. I ride the waves as often as I can."

"A surfer? How long have you been doing that?"

"Since before I could walk. My parents were avid surfers and got me on a board when I was a baby."

She raised a brow. "Really? Just a baby?"

He chuckled and leaned back against the wall, eyeing the door, his M4 pointing to the ceiling, the butt end resting against the carpet. On his hip, he carried an M9 pistol. He stood between a locked door and whatever wanted to come through it. They were in one of the second-floor offices, the stairs barricaded with office furniture. They would be exiting out a side office and heading to safe haven or on their way up to the roof as soon as it became necessary.

"Yeah. I was born in San Clemente, California, and they've got one of the best beaches there to surf. Trestles. Well, there are three distinct spots—Uppers, Middle, and Lowers. Lowers used to be part of Camp

Pendleton until President Nixon decreed it park land.
Little did I know I'd be one of the marines who served."

"That seems…so…strange, personality-wise."

He shifted again and gave her a sidelong glance.
"Why do you say that?"

"Surfers are known for their laid-back, get-in-touch-
with-nature attitudes. 'Go with the flow, dude.' Marines, well, they usually are going against the flow with
a very determined attitude, 'hooyah.' Uniforms and
boots versus flip-flops and board shorts."

His smile returned then, those full lips parting for a
flashing curve of white teeth and wry self-awareness,
sexy-tough handling both her and the weapons he carried with masterful ease. "Ah, that was a nice try, but
it's actually 'oohrah' for us jarheads." He leaned forward, his weapon tilting with him, this lethal man with
a glint in the gunmetal gray of his eyes. "You can't see
me out of this uniform?"

She had to swallow at the mention of anything bare
on Austin and with that one sentence all the sensations
and her reaction to his mouth came rushing back.

His face changed, and he grimaced as if he'd just realized what he'd said. "Not that you'd imagine me without my uniform…" He glanced away, then looked back
at her, capturing her gaze, a soft flush of color washing
his cheeks. Shaking his head, he gave her an exasper-
ated look as if he was, all of a sudden, tongue-tied. He
closed his eyes and tipped his head back. "I meant, in
board shorts and flip flops," he said, tipping his head
back and closing his eyes.

"I know what you meant." He was the most fascinating mix of toughness and grace she'd ever seen, six feet
and two inches of raw, lean power, soft-looking short

brown hair mixed with blond highlights. His eyes were the purest, clearest crystalline gray she'd ever seen, the color of river water with sunlight shooting through it.

He was a very beautiful young man, but he carried himself and acted much older than he looked. When she'd found out he was all of twenty-two, she'd been floored. That for some reason made her feel much older than twenty-six. She felt weary, unhappy, and that was probably the reason for having these very wrong thoughts and feelings for Austin. The risk, too. That was jacking everything up to a danger-zone level.

He was gorgeous, with his beautiful nose and chiseled cheekbones, and those lips, which she couldn't help fantasizing about. Just looking at him made her mouth go dry. The essence of him had the kind of presence that made a woman feel safe, a quiet strength embedded with a sure confidence that was take-charge and steady, but with a demeanor that was warm and true.

For the first time in her life, she had cast her eyes in another man's direction, and she was at a loss in knowing how to make it go away—these inappropriate thoughts or the recklessness of wanting to give in to those desires. Dangerous and wrong. She bit her lip, resenting her father and how hard he'd pushed. She'd been the dutiful daughter and acquiesced to his wishes like she always had. She regretted it now.

She was married to a man who treated her like a glass figurine, had no intention of ever giving her children and didn't think she could handle anything more taxing than a garden party or shopping.

Austin was talking about surfing, and she'd let the cadence of his deep voice wash over her and dissipate the spiraling fear. Then he dropped the big bomb. "My girlfriend likes to ride, too, which is a plus." That made her gasp. She had to cover it up with a cough.

"You've got a girlfriend?" Acute disappointment rippled through her. What had she thought anyway? She was the wife of a US ambassador and he was a young marine. There was no hope for them and yet the discontent was keenly severe.

"Yeah—" He pulled off his helmet and leaned over to show her the inside. The picture showed a pretty blonde woman on a beach, her long hair flying around her face, caught in the wind.

"She's very pretty," was all Jenna could muster, her heart heavy.

He smiled and set the helmet back on.

That's when she leaned into the leather of the couch and closed her eyes, trying to get her emotions back under control. This man was taken, so taken. Not that it would have done her any good if he wasn't.

After that, she lay down and fell asleep until something woke her up. Maybe it was the eerie silence that registered when she opened her eyes, no crowd noise at all. Even the constant bashing from the sledgehammers destroying computers, equipment and anything useful that could be beneficial to the enemy was silent.

She looked to find Austin beside the window, and she wondered when he'd last slept. "Sergeant Beck?" He turned his head and maybe it was the sound of her voice, but he took two strides to the couch and crouched down. "What's happening?"

"Nothing right now. Go back to sleep." The light from the moon illuminated his face. "Please don't lie to me to spare my feelings. I'm sure Robert told you to keep me wrapped up in cotton wool."

"Silk, actually."

"Oh, man." She blinked a few times and sighed. "Just tell me."

"They're resting. I think they're done waiting." He rose, his body tense.

"The choppers?"

"On their way. As soon as they get here, we're moving out. I wanted you to sleep as long as you could."

He went to move back to the window, but she stood and set her hand on his forearm. "I can't sleep now. Why don't you get some rest? Even twenty minutes will help."

He looked at her for a moment. "I'll keep watch. I'll wake you if something happens."

He nodded, removed his helmet, propped his rifle against the desk and lay down on the couch.

Restless after a half an hour of staring out at the quiet, milling crowd now stretched out as far as the eye could see, she turned from the window and walked over to the sofa. He was on his back, the throw had slipped off his shoulders, and she knelt down, pulling it up. His warm hand clasped around her wrist. She froze, her gaze going to his face. His eyes were open, watchful. "I'm going to miss seeing you, Jenna," he said, his voice whiskey soft.

His tone set off a reaction in her that only made her lean forward. She closed her eyes, trying to corral her feelings. "You shouldn't say things like that," she whispered.

He rose and she backed away. "I know." His tone was unapologetic. He stepped closer to her, then cupped her jaw and turned her face toward him, his expression unsmiling, his eyes dark and intent.

"Where will you be going?" She felt desperate and everything inside her rebelled at saying goodbye to this man.

"Wherever they tell me to, Jenna. I belong to the marines." He smiled at her and her heart flipped over. Held immobile by the intimacy of his touch, she stared at him, her gut rolling into a ball of dread. She had to say goodbye.

"Give me something to remember," he said, his voice gruff and very low.

That request did unbearable things to her heart, and she breathed around the fullness in her chest.

Feeling as if she was losing her mind, paralyzed by his touch and his request, she surrendered to the desperate moment as if these precious minutes were carved out of time. He tipped her face up and Jenna made a helpless, lost sound as he slowly lowered his head.

He pressed his lips to hers lightly at first, but the initial contact with her mouth made him stop and his eyes pop open, a dazed, oh-my-God look in them. Then his mouth took hers in a kiss that agitated every cell. Right or wrong evaporated and everything receded.

He worked his mouth hungrily against hers, drawing her hips even closer. She couldn't think, couldn't breathe. Her mouth responded, pliant against his moist and so-damn-hot lips, as a thousand sensations shot through her.

Something new was awakening in her, something that she had never experienced before—this...*this* was passion.

He caught her hips and molded her flush against him, his mouth wide and hot. The feel of him drove the breath right out of her, and she made another helpless sound against his mouth. Austin tightened his arm around her back and dragged his mouth away, his breathing labored. Her heart racing and her pulse thick and heavy, she turned her face against his neck, the warmth of his touch filling her with a heavy weakness, her whole body trembling.

She was trying to process why this felt so good. Was it the danger they were in? Was it because it was the forbidden? Did she just need comfort from the fear? Why did this feel more real than her marriage?

Unable to step away from his body, her breath jamming in her chest, she clutched at him. His breathing ragged, he held on to her. He roughly whispered her name and found her mouth again. She lost a whole piece of reality when he caught her hair and twisted her head back, covering her mouth with a kiss that told her he wanted more. She cried out, her voice muffled against his lips. Adjusting the fit of his mouth against hers, he absorbed the sound, running his hands up her rib cage.

The emergency alarm blared across the compound and they froze, broke apart. The *rat-a-tat-tat* of gunfire galvanized her. Chests heaving, they stared into each other's eyes. For a millisecond, there was regret, pain, longing, fear and desperation in his, which she was sure were mirrored in her own.

Then Austin moved, snatched up his helmet, jamming it on and fastening the chin strap. Then he reached for his rifle. Someone was shouting, the sound of his voice audible through the headset. The sudden rumble outside sent her stomach dropping to her shoes, and she gave Austin a terrified look, her heart suddenly lurching.

"They're breaking through. We've got to bug out."
He grasped her arm.

"Safe haven?"

"No, hear that?" Relief in his voice, he started moving toward the door. "Blackhawks."

She heard the powerful *whop, whop, whop* of the blades mixed with the roar of a crowd that was out for blood, the automatic gunfire unending. They must have heard the choppers, too, and had no intention of letting the Americans get away. Both sounds were getting stronger and louder.

Phones were ringing everywhere and gunfire erupted close, the sound of the crowd surging. Explosions ignited, dulled booms in the room, a fireball flaring up right outside the window. They were blowing up the compound, breaching the front doors.

He took her through the adjoining door, and they stepped out into pandemonium. The barrier was rocking as people were pouring out of the offices all along the hallway, rushing up the stairs in a blind panic. Then *pop, pop, pop* flashes behind the barricade, the sound of whizzing, some people dropping to the floor amid screams and panic.

The fact had no sooner registered than a steely arm wrapped itself around her waist. Before she could take a breath or even register the depth of her alarm, Austin pressed her up against the wall—pressed hard, his whole body flat against her back, immobilizing her.

Adrenaline washed into her veins on a river of stark, icy terror.

"I'm going to take you up, then I'm coming back down." His voice was soft, gravelly and very close to her ear, his breath blowing across her skin as he spoke.

"Do you copy?" She had to focus on him, focus on her breathing and slow it down.

She managed a sharp, terrified nod.

"Good. Don't stop for anything."

It was so darn hard to control her fear. Her heart was racing, totally at odds with the slow, steady beat of his. She could feel it against her back. She was frightened, but he wasn't. He was calm, breathing normally, holding her. She felt shrink-wrapped between his body and the wall.

He released her, turned her toward escape and the waiting choppers. They were caught up in the press of humanity running up the stairs at a breakneck speed. They burst onto the roof, the sky full of helicopters, lights brightly illuminating everything. The screams and shouts of both the civilians and military personnel rushed around her like a chaotic, disorienting merry-go-round. She saw her husband being hustled toward the first helicopter to land. People poured in after him and shortly after that, it lifted off.

Her heart sank. He never even looked back. Never even tried to find her.

Austin set her inside the chopper. "Stay here." He grabbed a headset and bellowed, "There are wounded. Do not lift off until I return." He listened, then shouted, "Ten minutes! Roger that!"

He ripped off the headset, and then he was gone. She heard the sound of automatic weapons and then minutes later Austin was back. He was carrying two women, one over each shoulder. One of the crew leaned past her and took the wounded, crying and hysterical women into the chopper.

"Everyone's out," he said, but his voice was weaker.

Then she saw the blood on his uniform and he stumbled, grasping his shoulder.

The crew member grabbed him and hauled him into the vehicle, straight across her lap, as the protesters burst onto the roof. The chopper lifted off with a whirring, deafening roar as the crowd discharged its weapons, but the guns of the chopper held them back as they ran toward the safety of the building. Austin's gasp of pain brought her eyes to his. She unsnapped his helmet and eased it off, cradling his head, his hair soft against her fingers.

Blood, stark red against her shirt, galvanized her. Pressing both palms over his wound, his blood was warm and wet against her fingers.

Their eyes met again and locked as time twisted out into a slow-motion kind of free fall. The look in his said more than words could ever express. It was a longing that sucked at her very soul. She managed a shaky breath, her chest suddenly aching. She couldn't feel this way, this intensely, about a man she'd just met. But parting from him seemed impossible, and Lord, but it hurt. More than anything, more than her next breath, she wanted…him.

She shivered from all the feelings welling up inside her, and she opened her mouth to speak, to tell him what was in her heart, but his eyes drifted closed.

Chapter 2

San Diego, California
Six years later

The Santa Ana winds were in full swing. Jenna Webb could detect that electric feel in the air as she drove away from the San Diego Valley View concert arena. The dry, eerie-sounding wind gave her the heebie-jeebies, as if the heat it brought were trapped inside her. With that atmospheric phenomenon came the very real chance that one spark could set off wildfires that tended to plague Southern California this time of year. She had been used to a climate where it didn't rain much, at least in the desert where she was living, but lightning was a factor, crackling across the sky in spectacular shows of bright white danger.

Fresh from seeing a concert by Nora Anderson, a jazz piano and sultry blues singer who was very popular, she drove toward home. Nora wasn't exactly one of Jenna's favorites, but the performance had been free. Jenna's cousin, Sarah Taylor, had had tickets to the concert, but she wasn't feeling well and had stayed home. She was scheduled to fly with the Blue Angels, the Navy's elite flight demonstration squadron. They flew in airshows across the country, promoting goodwill and performing feats of skill and precision for awed audiences and wanted to make a good impression, being one of two women on the team. Given the nearly two-hour one-way trip to San Diego from El Centro where the Blue Angels had their winter quarters and training site, Sarah had decided that getting rest was a better idea. She'd offered the tickets to Jenna, but there was no one Jenna really knew that well to ask to the concert, so Jenna had gone alone.

She'd been pretty much alone for the last six months.

Yeah, that's what happened when she went through a traumatic life-altering situation and her husband… *ex-husband*, Robert Webb…had still treated her like a fragile little girl who needed constant pampering. He had no more power over her, now that they had been divorced for several months. But she had separated from him six months before that.

All her life she'd been put on a pedestal, and she really found it so suffocating. The first few days after they had returned to DC, Jenna had thought she might have just imagined any real connection between her and Austin. She had been unhappy and they had been in an intense situation. Austin had never tried to contact her, but she'd inquired through Robert to see how he was doing. He'd been treated somewhere overseas and then had been flown back to the United States to his home state to recuperate.

Austin was the only man who had treated her like she mattered.

But that was six years ago, when she'd been married

to Robert. He was now a retired US Ambassador. But the takeover of the US embassy in Khida had been a blow to him. He'd done an admirable job of reestablishing the mission in Ja'arbah and they had stayed for another year before getting an assignment to Cairo. He could never seem to forget about the takeover, and Jenna held on to the memory like it was a lifeline. Her perspective had been changed then and she couldn't go back, their relationship only eroding more as time moved inexorably on.

As the years passed with more postings, safer ones, their distance grew until they slept in separate bedrooms. Right before the term of Robert's post came to an end and they were to leave Khida, Jenna overheard a couple of the marines talking about Austin. They said he'd gotten out of the marines, and his girlfriend wanted him home. They joked that he would soon be married to the old ball and chain.

But none of that seemed to mar the memory or dim it. It was Austin Beck that stood out in her mind.

The first time she'd seen him, he'd tilted her world on its axis. The first time they made eye contact, she had been breathless. Completely winded as if she'd run a mile. She tried to tell herself that it was because he was so young, but later, when she'd been cloistered with him, she had to admit to herself that it hadn't been his age. She was four years older than him. She was now thirty-two while he was only…twenty-eight.

As she approached the city proper, she gripped the wheel as memories flooded back to her. A horn sounded and she jerked, as the headlights rushed past her. Had she drifted? So lost in her memory? Her divorce from Robert became final months ago, but after Ja'arbah, there had been no going back.

The memory of him stuck with her as she drove into her parking space next to Sarah's car. Sarah should be sleeping, but she hoped she was up. With a T-shirt and CD in a bag, knowing her cousin would be thrilled, she entered the hall that lead to their apartment. Unlocking the door and stepping inside, she froze. It was pitch dark inside. No ambient light from anywhere. Jenna tried the light switch. Nothing happened.

Frowning, she cursed under her breath. What had happened to the power? She would check the breaker box and see if they had blown a fuse. "Sarah?" Jenna called, but there was nothing but an ominous silence. *She must be sleeping like a log after taking her cold medicine. It is late.*

A shiver coursed down Jenna's spine. She pressed the flashlight app on her phone to light her path. Making her way into the kitchen and to the closet, she tripped. That damn rug was a hazard. She opened the door and walked inside.

She shone the light over the equipment and froze. That was odd. The fuse box door was open. When she checked the breakers, they were all off.

She threw them into the on position and lights came on in the kitchen and the hall, then she backed out of the closet, the heel of her foot connecting with something solid. She stumbled backward and swore, but the word crumbled in her mouth on a soft cry. She hadn't tripped over the rug.

Her cousin lay face up, wedged against the counter, her long blond hair spread across the hardwood floor, her open, staring eyes looking up at Jenna.

Jenna let out a piercing, sobbing scream.

San Clemente, California

Special Agent Austin Beck woke edgy and twitchy, as if heat was trapped underneath his skin, a kind of fever that sent restlessness spiraling through him. He hated this time of year. With the winds came the memories, all unwanted. "Damn you, you bleak, bitchy harbinger of change," he mumbled as he turned over. "Yeah, I'm a drama king, so sue me."

He wanted nothing more than to take leave and get out of Dodge, but Derrick Gunn, one of his NCIS team members, had taken some time off and his other co-worker Amber Michaels was nursing a cold, which left them strained and severely understaffed. His window of opportunity had slammed shut.

Cursing at how the Santa Anas made his nerves jump and skin itch, he growled as he flung the covers off his naked body and sat on the edge of the bed, breathing around the discomfort.

For a moment, the heat radiated off him. Running his hands through his shaggy hair, his teeth on edge, he rose and walked to the window. Pushing the drapes open and pulling up the blinds, he peered out. Gray rain fell on the parking lot and on the beach beyond, the ocean full of white foam and an angrier gray. Heavy cloud cover obscured the rising sun, a faint glow tinging the horizon, the wan light unable to penetrate the secluded shadows and silence. As he stood in the gloom, trying to will away the awful sensation in his gut—a sensation comprised of regret and old shame—he took a much-needed stabilizing breath.

The winds had been a part of one of the worst times of his life. After the embassy debacle in Ja'arbah, he'd spent some time at Walter Reed near Washington recovering from the bullet wound to his shoulder. He rotated it in memory of the pain from that day, the pain he'd seen on Jenna's face in that chopper running like the streaks of rain on the window glass into the pain of Melanie's eyes the day she'd walked away from him.

Everything had changed between them when he went home to recover fully, but she hadn't known it. He'd let it go and shipped out again as soon as he was well. He'd tried to convince himself that it was just a moment in time; he'd been lonely and had needed female companionship. He'd resolved to forget Jenna and recommit to Melanie.

Folding his arms across his naked chest, Austin rested his shoulder against the window frame, watching the reflection of the lamplight against the glass. The darkened lot below glistened with the inky puddles collecting along the curb. Rain slashed the surface and rattled against the window, and Austin stared out, his thoughts detached as he watched a gust of wind send rain skittering along the pavement. His apartment was on the third floor and this window offered him an unobstructed view of the dark, deserted beach beyond. All he had to do was open this window to hear the ocean.

He pushed off and headed for the closet, dragging out his full wet suit, especially designed for the fifty-seven-degree water temp. He stepped in and worked the thick neoprene up his legs and over his hips, leaving the top of it flopping against his butt as he grabbed his board. At the door, he slipped on flip-flops and went out into the rain. It was drizzling as he trekked toward the beach, the unseasonably warm, seventy-degree weather feeling good against his still-sizzling skin.

A gust of wind caught his hair and his board, rattling against the building, buffeting the street lamp he walked under.

Yeah, he'd separated from the marines mostly because of Melanie's nagging. He'd tried. He'd even asked her to marry him. They'd made plans. He was going to work and go to school to become a lawyer. She'd already finished her law degree and she supported them. But he'd gotten a contract job to help with finances until he was admitted to school, gotten exposed to NCIS and everything had changed. He'd done a three-sixty and joined, excited about the prospect of using his tech smarts and his mind to catch bad guys, as close to a military group without being active military as he could get.

In the process, he'd broken Melanie's heart.

She'd been livid that he hadn't discussed this major decision with her, was once again in a job that would take him away from her, one where he was again in danger. They had fought bitterly. She'd given him an ultimatum that January three years ago to either go to school and forget about NCIS or she would leave him, and he had to finally follow his gut. He'd told her he wasn't changing his mind, law enforcement interested him more than anything else and she had walked. He'd chalked it up to being too young. Not ready. He still wasn't sure after all these years, and given the time between then and now, why was he rehashing this?

Maybe because he was lonely and felt as if he was in stasis, limbo. No man's land. Sure, he'd dated, but no one had interested him for longer than a few weeks.

He came to a halt near the crashing waves, knowing that the ocean, even angry and wind-tossed, would soothe him.

So he needed to stop standing here, staring out at an empty sea, a caged-cat feeling eating a hole in his gut.

A twist of black humor surfaced, and he watched the rain against the frenetic swells, the kind of waves that made a surfer grin. Maybe he was standing here feeling like a caged cat because he hadn't really understood why he'd made the decisions he had. Why he had trashed their plans. He pushed her to break off the engagement. In hindsight, he'd found his calling, but somewhere in the back of his mind, he had been aware she wouldn't accept his career choice.

A pair of cobalt blue eyes and bouncy black curls broke into his musings. Experiencing a hot rushing feeling to his gut, he clenched his jaw.

He had to stop thinking about Jenna.

Time for some distraction.

"Hold up there, dude."

A female's authoritative voice coming out of the gloom made him whip around. Special Supervisory Agent Kai Talbot, his boss at NCIS, stood in the sand, her hair pulled back in a ponytail, revealing the strong bones of her attractive face.

He groaned and slammed his surfboard into the sand. "I haven't had a day off for two weeks straight."

"I know," she said with sympathy. "I've been right there with you. But turning off your cell is not exactly responsible."

To give credit where credit was due, he couldn't argue with that. She wasn't a slacker. Oh, no. Kai got into the trenches with them and dug around in the muck to shift through every clue.

He sighed heavily. "What do you need?"

"I need you in El Centro, preferably before the Santa

Anas shut down I-8. We've got a murdered pilot, Sarah Taylor."

"El Centro," Austin said, turning toward her. "That's Blue Angels territory."

"Yeah, it's a Blue Angels pilot and this one is priority."

"Why?"

"She was one of few female pilots chosen for the team. She never even got to fly her first show. This comes from high up. Solve it fast before there's speculation that could hurt the reputation of the team."

He chuckled. "Yeah? That's what they're worried about?" He grabbed the surfboard out of the sand and walked past her. "Wherever my investigation leads me is where I'm going." He grinned. "Their reputation be damned."

"I wouldn't have it any other way."

And he thought that again as he raced toward El Centro, his heart beating as if something heavy was sitting on his chest. Like the walls were closing in. He swore under his breath at the Santa Anas. It had stopped raining by early morning, but new storm clouds were again piling against the jagged ridge of the mountains, and the rising sun cast the dark, heavy cloud formations in auras of gold and purple.

His thoughts trailed back to Melanie. He'd thought she had been everything he'd ever wanted in his wife. She was bright, funny, energetic and loved surfing as much as he did. She had been in school, heading toward a law degree, and he'd expected to stay in the marines for another twelve years until he could retire, then school for architecture. Their future had looked so bright. Then he'd been sent to Ja'arbah and nothing after that seemed to make sense to him.

He wasn't going to think about Jenna Webb. She wasn't a factor—something he'd told himself over and over.

After he was cleared for duty again, Austin had ended up at the US Consulate General in Rio de Janeiro, Brazil. A cushy job with lush green jungles was a bold contrast to the heat and sand of the Middle East. It had been Portuguese instead of Arabic and an individual bedroom. The Marine House was posh and included a beautiful vista overlooking the city.

When he'd had a chance to go to the American Embassy in Cairo at age twenty-five, after Rio, his decision to reenlist heavy on his mind, he'd found out that Ambassador Robert Webb was being posted there after his time was up in Ja'arbah. After a heated argument with Melanie about reenlisting, tired of her unhappiness and the separation, he'd gotten rip-snorting drunk and put in his walking papers.

Jenna Webb was not a factor, he told himself again.

He snapped out of his past musings when his GPS instructed him to turn and announced that he was at his destination. An apartment building. He sighed and squared his shoulders. Jenna was old news, and he had probably been reacting to nothing but the adrenaline, the fact that he had been assigned to guard her and her beauty. He really needed to stop rehashing it. Move on.

He got out of the car, but froze as he was reaching for his phone. Through the open window as the crowd of law enforcement officials parted, he caught a glimpse of a woman. Her back was to him, but there was something unnervingly familiar about her sleek, dark curls. A funny feeling unfolded in his gut, and he shook his head, disgusted with the way his mind was malfunctioning today. The lack of sleep was definitely screwing up his head. Now he was seeing old ghosts.

He grabbed his phone, his heart stutter-stepping as he approached the door and walked briskly down the hall. Pocketing his phone and reaching for his badge, he cleared the door frame to the apartment. But right then the woman turned, presenting her profile to him, and Austin froze, the moving bodies turning into a weird blur. He stared across the room, feeling as if he'd just been slammed in the solar plexus. His mind wasn't playing tricks on him after all.

"Jenna," he said in a strangled voice. He saw the shocked look on her face, the sorrow and the glazed pain of losing someone close to her that he'd seen on the countless faces of the loved ones left behind. Only it broke his heart that she had been so ravaged, that she had to be the one to find the deceased. He wanted to do nothing but take her in his arms. But six years and her marriage sat between them.

He'd never realized how much she'd affected him until this moment, when the reality of his feelings from the past slammed into him.

He'd thought he was never going to be the same after that embassy situation, but here, now, he knew that this case, this woman, could break him.

Chapter 3

Jenna was frozen in place, her gaze riveted to the man standing in front of her. Her chest was tight; she could hardly catch her breath.

Oh, God. Her heart was pounding.

Austin Beck. He'd saved her life, been wounded and she'd never heard from him again. He was, of course, married, and probably had children with the woman he'd chosen, Melanie. She felt foolish for what she'd felt for him. But even knowing that, she couldn't stop her heart from breaking or jumping at the sight of him. And it was some sight. Six years had been good to him, six years of maturing but not changing the lean angles of his face, the unique color of his hair, or the aching gray of his eyes that had looked into her soul.

And six years wasn't enough time to assuage her guilt, or her doubts, or the way she'd felt about him. Her pulse was racing with an awful mixture of shock and wariness, and a truly horrible excitement at just seeing him again.

What was he doing here?

Then she saw what he was holding. The badge that told her he was NCIS and a special agent. *The* special agent who had been assigned to Sarah's case. *Oh, my God.* He was here to investigate Sarah's murder.

She would have to see him, interact with him. On top of Sarah's death, this was just too much. She put her hand to her temple and wobbled a bit. Austin reached out immediately and without saying anything helped her to the sofa.

After she was seated, he said, "Are you all right?"

How could she respond to that? No, on so many levels she wasn't all right, the least of them to do with seeing Austin again. She hadn't expected this and the shock to her system was overwhelming.

He went into the kitchen and poured her water, then brought it back. Setting the glass in her hand, he crouched down, his gray eyes both a little disoriented and warm at the same time. This felt like déjà vu and the memories from the embassy came flooding back to her.

"It's good to see you again, Jenna."

The inflection in his voice made her heart jump.

"It's been a long time," she said, taking a sip of the water.

He nodded. "How are you involved in this?" he said, glancing over at the people in the kitchen.

"Sarah Taylor is my cousin—a distant cousin."

He rose. "Let me introduce myself and…check things out. I'll be back."

He had been about to say *look at the body*, but had changed his words to spare her. Draining the glass, her throat parched, Jenna leaned back against the cushions. The woman she was just getting to know, the woman who had opened her home and her arms, the woman who was her only living relative, was gone.

With so many regrets piling up inside her, she inhaled sharply, the cramp in her throat intensifying. Sarah had been a port in the storm. And with the mess her own life was in, coming here had offered her an escape. So she had closed down her house in DC, packed what she'd needed and come here to think, to get herself in the right frame of mind to begin her life again. Her dear family friends, Tom and Elise Sonnet, had been taking care of her to the point where she was feeling suffocated. Tom was a longtime crony of her father and she suspected they were more than happy to help her out.

Money was no object as she had gotten a sizable divorce settlement along with the family money she'd inherited. She'd been actively working at charity functions in DC.

She watched Austin interacting with Detective Jack Morton from the El Centro Police Force. He was a big, burly man with kind brown eyes who had introduced himself when he'd shown up on the scene more than an hour ago almost on the heels of two uniformed police officers. He'd taken her statement, and when he'd discovered that Sarah was in the navy, he'd called NCIS.

The medical examiner was here now and all of them were in the kitchen. Her throat cramped again, and she shifted her gaze, trying to will away the sting of tears, angry with herself. God, she was such a mess. Her life was a mess. But then maybe she had it coming. She never should have married Robert. She'd known it was a mistake right from the beginning. But she'd always been the dutiful daughter, even when she'd wanted to bolt two days before the big splashy wedding her father had organized because, of course, the details would have been too much for her.

He tried to convince her that she had nothing but prewedding jitters and everyone had them. It had been her own unexplored intuition speaking loud and clear, but she hadn't had the self-confidence or the experience to recognize it for what it was. Maybe that was why she'd hung on to that buried anger. That was something she hadn't let go of.

At the deep cadence of Austin's voice, her attention went back to him; was drawn to him was more like it. If he was in the room, she was aware of him in every pore of her heart, body and mind. He was dressed in khaki slacks and a blue-and-white-checked button-down beneath a gray Henley sweater, the same pearl gray as his eyes, the buttons undone. Even though he wasn't in a suit, he looked so competent, solid. His intensity was totally focused on the detective and what he was saying, but she got the distinct feeling that he was very aware of her. Reaction shivered down her spine.

He was still lean but more filled out with wide shoulders and a compact body, muscled, but sleek, like a prize fighter and stood with a relaxed attitude of a man aware of his own strength. Spiked on top, fuller than the sides, his layered hair, with some locks across his forehead, was an enticing mix of brown and blond. His sharp features were defined by his well-formed nose and smooth cheekbones, tapering down to a narrow chin with a cute cleft. The dark blond facial hair, in a neat, trimmed, almost-there beard, accentuated his strong jaw. She was having such a visceral response to him, and it wasn't right, with Sarah dead on the floor only a few feet away.

She straightened when the detective and Austin turned their attention to her. His face gave very little away, except his devastating good looks, and his eyes even less—guarded, unwavering, inscrutable. They were, she realized with a funny flutter in her abdomen a deep, dark, bottomless granite—impenetrable and mesmerizing.

Realizing that she was staring, she shifted uncomfortably and wrapped her arms around her middle.

They crossed the room, the detective talking on his cell. Austin sat down on the coffee table across from her, while the detective took one of the chairs, ending his call.

"I'm deeply sorry about your loss, Jenna." She nodded, grateful for his compassion. There was a strained hesitation, then he said, his voice all business, "Detective Morton is going to search her room. While he's doing that, I'm going to have to ask you some questions about your cousin. Is that all right?"

Sensing his sudden withdrawal, as if walls had suddenly gone up, Jenna avoided his gaze, her voice not quite even when she said, "Yes, that's all right. I want to help in any way that I can."

He exhaled heavily. "Could you go over Sarah's actions today?"

"She was sick. She stayed home to nurse her cold. We watched some TV and talked some, had breakfast and lunch, then I left for my concert at six. I got dinner out. That was the last time I saw her."

"Was there anyone in Sarah's life who wanted to harm her?"

She tightened her arms around herself, bracing to answer these questions, glancing at the now covered body for a moment before she said, "I don't...didn't... know my cousin as well as other people know their family members. We just became acquainted recently in Baltimore. It was for Maryland Fleet Week and Air Show. She contacted me and asked if we could meet up. We hit it off so well, she invited me to stay with her in El Centro for a short visit. I came here the beginning of December to get to know her better. It was just temporary, as I had plans to return to DC in a couple of months. I will say that Sarah had been exacting in her standards, never took any lip from anyone, unless it was a commanding officer, and had nerves of steel."

"Was there a man in her life?"

Her voice was quiet when she spoke. Her cousin wasn't going to ever know love or the joy of starting a family, and her throat got tight. She stared back at him, not sure if her voice was going to hold or not. "No, no boyfriend." She loosened her arms and stared down at her hands until she was certain she had her emotions under control, then she looked up at him. Her voice cracked, and she cleared her throat. "Sarah was focused on becoming the best pilot in the navy and has always wanted to become a Blue Angel. She wouldn't have jeopardized that dream for a man, *any* man."

He leaned forward, compassion in the gray depths of his eyes. "That couldn't have been easy for her."

Jenna brushed her chin-length hair over one ear. "Sarah was good, better than some men on the team."

His mouth lifted in a semblance of a smile. "I'm sure that ruffled a few boys' club feathers."

Jenna held his gaze for a moment, then managed

a small smile. "They resented her, and she endured some harassment. I'm not sure if some of it was sexual. Sarah didn't say. She was…so self-possessed. So strong." Stronger than Jenna could ever hope to be. She wished she had half of Sarah's courage.

"Did she happen to mention anyone by name?"

Jenna shook her head. "She was being discreet. She didn't like the way she was being treated, but didn't want to direct attention to herself. In any other situation, she would have made plenty of waves." Jenna swiped at her wet cheeks. "She said she threatened the person responsible with action, but I don't think she was going to follow through. She was just trying to get them to back off. She just wanted to fly with them." They had zipped Sarah into a body bag, and she was being removed from the apartment. She choked up, tears welling and sliding down her cheeks. "She'll never get that chance."

Their relationship had been wonderful right from the beginning. Maybe it was the blood tie and the fact that both of them had no other family in their lives. Getting to know her cousin had been an all-too-brief period, but it warmed Jenna to know that she'd had someone in her life who genuinely cared about her.

He reached out and clasped her hand, his looking big and broad, engulfing hers. His palm and fingers were powerful and warm. He gave her a solemn look, his gray eyes soft now. "I think that's enough for now."

Deep sorrow twisted her up inside. Rising a few feet, he started to release her. Feeling a little lost, she gripped his hand. She didn't want him to leave just yet. When he settled back down, she noted he wasn't wearing a wedding band, but some men didn't. That meant nothing. But she was certain if Austin was married, he'd wear a ring. It had been six years and they were pretty much strangers. She had no right to ask him any personal questions. She wanted to know about his life. About him. But that would only cause her more heartache. She was completely pathetic.

Detective Morton came out of Sarah's room carrying her laptop. "We'll have to take this as evidence, ma'am," he said.

Jenna nodded as she glanced over to where her cousin had been only moments ago, and said, her voice uneven, "Where are they...taking her?"

Austin squeezed her hand, then said gruffly, "She's going to be shipped to Camp Pendleton, where our forensic coroner will examine her."

Experiencing a growing pressure in her throat, she let go of him. "When can...I bury her?"

"I don't know that information yet. It's up to the coroner," he said.

Blinking rapidly to will away the burning in her eyes, she waited for the moment to pass; then she looked back at him. "Would you let me know as soon as possible? I have to make funeral arrangements for her. I have no clue where to begin, but I'll figure it out. I'm her only living relative now. Her mother died of breast cancer and her father from a heart attack."

There was a solemn intensity in his expression, something that made her heart accelerate, and the muscles along his jaw tensed. He stared at her, his gaze darkening, and the muscles in his throat contracted as he leaned forward. For one heart-stopping instant she thought he was going to touch her again, but then he clenched his hand and let it drop. "Of course. As soon as I know, you'll know." He rose. "Do you have someone who can come and stay with you?"

"No. I'm fine. Thank you for everything. Both of you." Detective Morton nodded and handed her a card. "I'll be working this case as needed with Special Agent Beck. Please feel free to call me with any questions."

He headed for the door and Austin said, "I'll be there in just a minute." He turned back to her. "I'm going to get settled into my hotel room, then head out to the base, talk to her CO." He studied her, stepping closer. "Are you sure you'll be all right here…alone?"

His closeness overwhelmed her senses, and she swallowed hard, trying to struggle against the longing that surged through her, making her heart race even faster. She remembered what it had been like to be held by him, to feel the weight of his arms around her. And, scandalously, she wondered what it would be like to lie with him, to feel the full length of his body against hers. It would be heaven to feel his warmth, to experience the comfort of his embrace. To be touched by him again.

"I'll be fine," she assured him.

He nodded. "I'll touch base with you after I've had some time to look into this. Tonight? Would you be free for dinner? We could catch up?"

Her voice was unsteady when she answered. "Yes, I would like that very much." Her insides were in turmoil.

He smiled. "Me, too." He reached for his phone and brought up the display, swiped a few times, tapped the keyboard, then handed it to her. "Enter your cell number, and I'll call you when I know better what time."

She took the phone, warm from his body, and with shaking fingers entered the information under her name. He took it back from her and tucked it into his back pocket. She was so sensitive to him she was conscious of every movement, every breath.

"Bye for now, Jenna," he said, his voice husky.

"Goodbye, Agent Beck," she murmured. Letting her breath go in a rush, Jenna watched him leave, closing the door behind him. She had enough presence of mind to walk over there and lock it.

She turned and pressed her back against the wood, hugging herself again, an awful fullness in her chest, loneliness rising up in her with a desolating force. Sarah had treated her like a sister and it had been so wonderful to visit with her, but they were both aware that Jenna would go home and Sarah would be tied up with the Blue Angels for the rest of the year. Still her affection for her cousin had deepened, chasing some of that hollowness away for a short time. It seemed as if she'd been alone her whole life, except for the brief time she'd had with Sarah. As she mourned her loss, tears sliding down her cheeks, the ache spread.

She wasn't sure what had fueled her interest in Austin six years ago—her need for validation, the fear, his protectiveness, or that she had been coerced into a marriage with a cold man who gave her nothing but condescension, careful lovemaking and a comfortable living.

Maybe this is all in my head.

Realization struck her. It didn't matter one whit. Austin was so off-limits. She'd never cross that line for his and his wife's sake.

Chapter 4

That was one hell of a blast from the past. Seeing her gave him a jolt to the heart, head and other places he didn't want to think about. *Couldn't* think about. Stirred up so much silt at the bottom of his conscience, he was choking on it. He hadn't really wanted to sift through any of this, not six years ago, and not today. But damned if the universe didn't have other plans for him.

Her being here just made it all much worse, all much more unbelievable.

Son of a bitch.

She hadn't changed. She still looked like a wide-eyed, purely innocent waif—wild black hair, cobalt blue eyes, draped in clothes beyond a marine's salary, hell, beyond Midas's, all of it wrapped around a petite bombshell bundle ready to blow his damn mind. That was Jenna Webb, sweet enough to bring a man to his knees, sexy enough to give him night sweats.

Damn, double damn. As a surfer, he believed in karma and at this moment it was being a complete bitch.

This was one vicious ninja punch to the groin.

Experiencing a hot, searing rush in his belly, Austin clenched his jaw. He wasn't going to get sucked back into this...this...sinkhole—he'd spent many years trying to get out of it. Shifting his position, he set his hands on his hips. He could have done without this crap today. He was just too damned tired to keep it in perspective. And besides, it didn't matter anymore. It had been over and done with for a lot of years.

Yeah, that's what you thought.

The past had a way of coming back to haunt him. And she was a big piece of his past. He could see her face, smell her, feel her. And there was no other feeling in his life that ever came close to being there, in her presence. Jarred by the sharpness of that revelation, he swore and wanted to put his fist through a wall, disgust washing through him. Where in the hell was his freaking mind, anyway? The very last thing he needed was to start remembering what it had been like with Jenna Webb.

He needed to focus on Sarah Taylor's murder and give Jenna peace in knowing that her cousin's killer had been found and punished. His heart softened for her and the grief she must be experiencing, especially after having found the body. It took time to recover from that kind of shock.

"Is this going to be a problem?"

Austin looked up and met the deep brown eyes of Detective Morton. Yeah, keen, very keen eyes. He gave the man a tight smile. "What?"

Jack Morton gave him a slow, off-center smile. "Maybe I should rephrase my question," he said, those shrewd eyes studying Austin. "Is she going to be a problem?" When Austin didn't immediately respond, he said, "It doesn't take a detective to realize that you know her, Agent Beck." He braced his shoulder against the wall and crossed his ankles.

Austin exhaled heavily and straightened. He had to work with this guy, so he couldn't exactly say he didn't know Jenna, but he wasn't about to spill his guts to someone who was supposed to supply backup. He didn't march to anyone's drum but his own, and in this case, he would keep his own counsel. "Austin," he said. "Old news, and not something I want to talk about. I got it under control, Detective Morton."

"Jack," he said, pushing off the wall. "If you say so. It's only my business if it's going to be a problem."

"It won't be a problem."

"Okay, copy that." He shifted away from the wall. "Now, down to business. The ME says it looks like she was strangled. Nothing was taken, not so much as a bill from her wallet, so robbery is out. There was no forced entry, which inclines me to say she knew her killer, either by acquaintance or better." Jack held up a cell phone in a plastic bag. Thank God, this conversation was shifting to the investigation. "We found her phone on the counter above her body. The last number she called belongs to the complex's super, Scott Posner. I checked into him. He lives on the premises," Jack said. "According to the property manager, he's been the super here for a few weeks. The previous one died from a heart attack. Let's go pay him a visit. See what he knows."

His apartment was located in the back of the two-story residential complex. They knocked on the door. After a couple of minutes a man jerked it open. He was tall, with wide shoulders and big hands. His hair was dark, cut short, his eyes a dark brown.

"Can I help you?"

Both of them showed him their badges. "El Centro Police Department and NCIS," Jack said. "We'd like to ask you a few questions. Can we come in?"

He opened the door wider and stepped to the side with a wary look. "Sure. What is this about?"

"One of your tenants." Austin rattled off the apartment number and he nodded.

Posner closed the door and led them into the living room, the scent of chicken soup in the air. Looked like they were interrupting his lunch. "Sure, that's Sarah Taylor. She has a guest for a while, Ms. Webb."

"That's correct. You received a call from Ms. Taylor last night. Can you tell me what you talked about?"

He took a moment to answer, looking confused. "Ms. Taylor? Oh…ah…she was having power problems. I told her to check the fuse box and call me back if she couldn't fix it. Never heard from her, so I thought it was handled. I was tied up with a toilet issue across the complex. She complaining to the cops?"

"No, she's dead."

He reared back, blinking a few times at the news. "What? What do you mean?"

"She was murdered last night."

"For real?" He stared at them, but Austin didn't have a different story. Posner's eyes grew wide. "Wow. I gotta contact the property manager."

"She knows," Austin supplied.

"Oh, okay." He didn't say anything else. Just looked at them expectantly.

"How well did you know her?" Jack asked.

He shuffled his feet and ran his hands through his hair. "Not very well. I've only been here a few weeks."

"Seen anyone come and go? Anything suspicious?"

"As a matter of fact, I've seen a guy hanging around out back, but only at night. When I challenged him, he bolted."

"You catch this guy's appearance?"

"No, too dark, but he was lurking in my opinion. I thought he was some Peeping Tom, and if I had gotten my hands on him, I'd have throttled him. I made a couple calls to the cops, but they just said to keep a look out. They checked the footage on the security cameras, but the guy must have known where they were placed. They found nothing, so nothing came of it."

"You have keys to all the apartments."

"Yes, I have a master key."

"Where do you keep the key?"

"On my belt."

Austin held out his card. "If you think of anything else, give me or Jack a call," he said as Jack offered him his card, as well. They exited the apartment and as the door closed, Jack said, "I'm going to canvas the neighbors, head into the station, get her cell dusted for prints and look for any complaints from Ms. Taylor. See if anything pops there."

Austin nodded and handed Jack one of his cards and Jack reciprocated. "Give me a call with an update later. I'm heading to my hotel room, then I'm getting a bite, touching base with the office. I thought I'd head out to the base after that."

"Sounds good. You need me out there with you?"

Austin shook his head. "I've got it covered. I'll update you afterward."

"That's a plan." Jack walked away.

Austin headed for his car, stopped by a burger joint and drove over to the closest hotel. After checking in, he unpacked. Settling into one of the armchairs, he ate some of the fries and called NCIS on his tablet.

Kai's face popped up on the screen. "Beck," his boss said. "Sitrep?"

Sitrep was short for situation report. Austin finished chewing and filled Kai in on what had happened so far. "You got any information for me?"

"Not a whole lot right now. The locals are running prints and other forensics. I've shipped the body, and questioned witnesses. The only information I got so far is that Sarah had no boyfriend, but the super where she lived said there was some guy milling around. Might just be a Peeping Tom. I'm going to be heading to base after this briefing. How about on your end?"

"Yes, quite a bit to share. Let's start with the Blue Angels. There are seventeen officers who volunteer for the honor of representing the navy with three tactical fighter or fighter/attack jet pilots, two support officers and one United States Marine Corps C-130 pilot to re-place outgoing members. Typically, seven members apply for the coveted slots by 'rushing' the team the year before—basically going to air shows and getting to interact with team members," she said. "They leave their home base in Pensacola, Florida, for the desert and winter in El Centro from mid-November through mid-March due to the stable weather. They start train-ing again in January after the holidays."

"So, Sarah rushed them last year and was chosen as one of the new pilots, replacing an outgoing member."

"Correct. I've compiled a profile for the deceased

pilot." The view changed to the widescreen. Jenna's cousin's military photo was up on the big plasma monitor mounted between Derrick's and Austin's desks along with her record. Austin took a bite of his burger. "Lieutenant Sarah Marie Taylor, parents deceased, no other living relative except for Jenna Webb, a distant cousin." Kai looked up at him. "Ambassador's wife. Hmm, didn't you guard embassies when you were in the US Marines?"

"Yes, I did, but we're not talking about my marine career here." Normally, agents weren't permitted to remain on cases of people they knew. There was the problem of bias and being too close emotionally. If he told Kai he knew Jenna, she might pull him off the case. He didn't want that.

Kai returned her attention to the screen. "Exemplary record, not a blemish on it. She's a Naval Air Station Pensacola graduate with twenty-one hundred hours and two-hundred and twenty carrier landings. Decorated with a bunch of medals and various personal and unit awards. Currently stationed at Naval Air Facility El Centro, she rushed them this past year and made the final cut. Becoming a demo pilot is quite an achievement."

Polishing off his meal, he sat back. "I'm going out to the base. Commanding officer?"

"Commander Henry J. Washington. He's been notified and is expecting you. I'll take a look at the rest of the team and the seven candidates who were up for the coveted slot on the Blue Angels but didn't make the cut. I'll get back to you if anything stands out. All of them warrant a look-see."

"Roger that. I'll call when I'm done." He wiped his

mouth and reached to disconnect the call. But Kai's voice stayed his hand.

"Austin, don't lone wolf this." Her brow furrowed, which told him she meant business. "Detective Morton is there to assist."

"Are you handling me, boss lady?"

That only deepened her scowl. "Yes, I am," she said, and Austin tried to keep his jaw from clenching, trying to hold back the first, faint teasing of a headache he felt coming on. Could be nothing but the tension from seeing Jenna, the freaking Santa Anas or the fact that he was omitting important information from his sitrep. "We've been under a lot of pressure and shorthanded. We both need a break, but we're not going to get it. It pays to hire former marines."

After a couple of seconds, he let out his breath in a soft rush and told himself to get a grip. "Ah, Kai, anyone who served knows you don't retire from *Semper Fi*. It's in our blood. Improvise, adapt and overcome. I got this."

She slanted him a dry look. "I know you do—just get it done with help. Copy?"

He didn't answer right away, thinking he should fill Kai in on the fact that he knew Jenna, but what would that do? Just make her worry when there was no need to. They were short-staffed and there was no one to take over this case. It was best to leave the information out and soldier on.

"Beck?"

He conceded her point with a grim smile. "Yes, ma'am. Copy that."

What a freaking mess. He thought about Jenna and he rolled his shoulder where that bullet had slammed into him. Memories flooded his mind, but he pushed them back. He had a job to do—a murder investigation. That was all he needed to focus on now, not how beautiful she looked, not how much her tears had torn him up inside and definitely not how much he wanted to wrap his arms around her.

Naval Air Facility El Centro was located about six miles from the town, smack-dab in the heart of the Imperial Valley and about a fifteen-minute scoot to the Mexican border. There was never any downtime in the military and the Blue Angels were no exception. After their final air show of the season, team members transitioned to their new roles and another season started.

Austin turned onto base, the landscape dotted with palm trees backdropped by a brilliant blue sky, sand everywhere, the distinct cobalt blue and gold aircraft on display.

As he approached, a sign reading NAF El Centro in simple gold letters against a curved facade of granite blocks announced the entrance to the facility. After presenting his badge, he was given a visitor pass and waved through.

Following the directions from security at the gate, he navigated through the base and pulled up to the building housing the commander. He exited the vehicle and was soon shown into his office.

"Hello, Special Agent Beck. It's nice to meet you." Washington reached out his hand and gave Austin a firm handshake. He had close-cropped sandy hair, blue eyes with an underlining sadness in them. "I'm sorry we have to meet under these circumstances." He indicated a seat in front of the desk and then settled behind it. "I expect to lose a pilot to error or miscalculation, not to…murder."

Austin sat, setting his tablet on the end of the desk. "Agreed."

"How was she killed?"

"Strangulation."

His brows rose, heavy sadness in his eyes. "That's pretty personal."

"I'd say. Anything you can tell me about her interactions with the squadron members?"

"Like what?"

"You tell me. I have had a report that she was harassed. The good ol' boys don't like a girl in the clubhouse?"

The commander's lips thinned and he stiffened. "There are always growing pains when there are new members, but if there were such 'reports,' I heard nothing about it."

"Convenient."

"Our executive officer would be in a better position to speak about those issues. But how can we help in getting your questions answered?"

"I'd like to interview each member of the squadron."

"All of them?"

"Yes."

"We have sixteen officers, six support staff and about a hundred enlisted sailors and marines."

"I'll start with the main team and you first as the flight leader and commanding officer."

"Fair enough." Washington turned to a file and reached for a paper. He handed it over to Austin.

He folded it and tucked it into his back pocket.

"Tell me how Sarah got along with everyone during her rush year."

"She was courteous and knowledgeable about a lot of our history. That impressed several of us. It's a dedicated pilot who decides to apply for membership. They have to pay for their own travel to air shows, but get to sit in on team briefs, post-show activities and social events. Sarah was outgoing, personable and a top-notch aviator. I didn't see any altercations or have reports of anything out of the ordinary with the members."

"She got along with everyone?"

The hesitation was very brief, but Austin saw it. "Yes. As far as I knew. Everyone."

Austin narrowed his eyes. That slight hesitation warranted deeper digging. Not that Austin wasn't going to thoroughly delve into every person on the team to suss out what the commander might be hiding. He had been right—Sarah's strangulation was very personal, a crime of passion. Could be hate, and putting hands around someone's neck and squeezing the life out of them took some serious enmity. Or it was love, most likely from a man scorned or unrequited. Whatever the motive, Austin would find out.

"I need one-on-one time with the rest of the team."

"They're training right now and aren't available." He tried to keep his voice even, but Austin heard the clip in it.

"Make them available and let me know when I can talk to them. I'll need a list." Austin rose and handed him his card. "While you're at it, I'd like a list of 'rush' candidates, as well. Thank you for your time, Commander."

"I'll send them right over," he replied, his tone now neutral.

Austin left the base, bracing himself for what he had to do next. He called Jenna and made arrangements with

Jenna to meet her at a Mexican restaurant in downtown El Centro. When he arrived, she hadn't gotten there yet. His tablet dinged and he pulled up the email from the commander, who had sent the lists. The first one was the new members, but it was the second one, titled "Blue Angels Rush Pilot Candidates Who Didn't Make the Cut," he was most interested in.

Austin forwarded the lists to Kai with a note. When he powered off the tablet and looked up, he was knocked for a loop. Jenna was walking toward him as if in slow motion.

Adrenaline pumped and time stood still. Even as he fought it, the memory rushed back and the present melted away.

There was way more to his ending it with Melanie than he'd admitted to himself. He'd been in denial for some time, nothing but lies he'd concocted to make it easier for him to take.

Easier than the true story.

It had taken a long time to get Jenna out of his system, and he didn't want to be reminded of what an impossible situation he'd engineered for himself. Six years ago his world had turned upside down and jerked him sideways. He had fallen for Jenna, her vulnerability, her sweetness, her beauty and that inexplicable connection, both physical and emotional. No amount of denying it to himself would work. He'd wanted her in every way possible. After getting wounded, he'd gotten distance and control of himself. He didn't want to be reminded of what a fool he'd been for a married woman, a woman who was an ambassador's wife. There had been no chance for them under those circumstances. He didn't want to remember how he'd felt during and afterward. And he didn't want to remember the bitterness that fate had thrown him.

But as she approached the table, there was nothing else he could do. She smiled and he couldn't seem to put two coherent thoughts together. But his manners had been ingrained by his mom and he rose.

He pulled out her chair and once she was settled in the seat, she murmured, "Thank you."

He went back to his own seat, wishing he was anywhere but here. After Melanie, he'd dated, but the women never stuck. Jenna Webb didn't fall in the same "easy come, easy go" category. But she'd stolen something those three days he'd been with her and he'd yet to get it back. The memory of the look she'd given him in the helicopter, the same kind of longing and desperation he'd felt, had been mirrored in his own eyes.

"The food is great here, but the portions are huge."

Austin grinned briefly. "Good thing I'm starving."

"So, some things don't change."

He stared at her and she picked up the napkin with nervous fingers and set it across her lap. "You were always starving. I think I slipped you several granola bars during guard duty."

A flush of warmth suffused him. "That's right and, man, did that take the edge off for about…fifteen minutes."

She laughed and the sound of it filled him from stem to stern. "Well, it would have been very difficult to conceal a six-course meal in my bag."

He let out a short laugh, nodding. "You got me there. Someone would have noticed." They sobered and he said, "How you been holding up?"

"It comes and goes," she said as the waiter approached and they placed their orders. Taco salad for her, a burrito platter for him.

"It's not something that's easy to handle."

She nodded. "I went in to work for a bit, even though my boss wanted me to go back home. I told her that I was better off working rather than staring at the spot where Sarah died and thinking about it constantly."

"Oh, you're working here? I thought you were visiting?"

"I am, but since it was an extended stay, I wanted to do something with my time. 'Work' is stretching it. I volunteer at the local library for twenty hours a week. The rest of the time, I've been enjoying myself with some day trips and weekend excursions up and down the coast." She gave a little laugh. "I've been all over the world, but this is the first time I've been to California."

"I'm *from* California, and I've also been all over the world, but have seen very little of this state. When I got a chance to work in my hometown, I grabbed it. I have to admit, I've only seen parts of California and never on vacation. Mostly working the job."

"Everyone needs some down time, Agent Beck. You should make sure to get it before you burn out."

"Too late," he said, then smiled. "Call me Austin. I think I can now safely say there is no protocol here anymore."

She took a sip of her iced tea once the waiter placed it in front of her, as if she needed some kind of fortification for calling him by his first name.

"How goes the investigation?"

"I wish I had more to report, but I'm getting some vibes from Sarah's commanding officer and will be interviewing the main team and the rush candidates that were in competition for the slots."

Their meals came and talk ceased as they ate a few bites. "Your super reported to us that there had been a prowler around your area. Do you have anything to add?" He'd already checked out Jenna's alibi and the cameras at the concert arena confirmed she'd been there. He didn't feel the need to tell her about it and add any more distress to her grief.

"No, we called the police a couple of times, but the super has been keeping an eye out. As far as I know, it hasn't happened for a couple of weeks. He thought it might just be a Peeping Tom out for thrills."

"Most likely, but we'll keep it in mind."

"I heard you got out of the service."

"Three years ago. I was kicking around the idea of going to school for architecture, but after the adventure of serving, it seemed so…"

"Mundane?"

"Yeah. I was working on a navy project. I'm pretty good with computers and fell into NCIS when I met an agent. I thought maybe cybercrime, but after training and being on a team, I found I had the interest and the aptitude for investigations. How about you? What have you been up to these past years?"

"Many posts and a lot of traveling."

"Recently?"

"Ah, no. I've been in DC for the last six months."

"Oh, Ambassador Webb got a cushy Washington post?"

"No, not exactly." She cleared her throat. "Robert and I are no longer married. Our divorce was made final months ago."

Austin choked on his iced tea and started coughing, his eyes watering. She was divorced? Dammit, that changed everything. She was unattached and he was single. That was a recipe for disaster. His interest in her hadn't changed. He should end this now, go back to Pendleton and have Kai assign someone else.

If Kai knew he had a history with Jenna, she wouldn't be happy. But what could he do at this point? The office was already stretched too thin. He would have to put his personal feelings and attraction to her aside. Finding the person who murdered Sarah had to take precedence. He'd have to make it about justice and nothing else. He didn't want to admit that he felt loyal, protective and proprietary, reminding himself with disgust he was no longer a marine guarding her. She wasn't even an ambassador's wife anymore.

"And, you, Austin?"

He so didn't want to talk about his personal life. "I didn't get married," he said softly and her face changed, surprise in her eyes. Those expressive eyes flashed to his ring finger and then away. She bit her lip, and he couldn't help but think she might be...happy.

He wasn't going that route. Not wanting to discuss his failed engagement, he changed the subject. "We should know more about Sarah's death once the body reaches our ME."

She looked back at him. "Right, then I can plan her funeral."

He nodded and grabbed the check. At the register, he paid it and escorted her out into the street. He walked her to her car. She turned before she stepped off the curb to go to the driver's side.

"Thanks for dinner and for catching up," she murmured. Then her shoulders slumped and she brushed at her temple.

"What is it?"

"I have to plan her funeral," she whispered again. "She was so young and so excited about flying with the Blue Angels." Her voice choked off. "I haven't the first clue on how to do that or where to start." She swallowed and when she turned her face to his, tears were filling her eyes and spilling onto her cheeks.

And it tore him up inside. He tracked the first wet streak down her cheek and utter resignation and defeat washed over him. He swore under his breath.

"Aw, Jenna, please. Don't do that."

It was a plea, nothing less. She straightened and tried to hold them back and her courage hit him even harder than her tears. Distance was what he needed, and a little cooling off time, time to absorb that she wasn't married. Her cousin had been murdered, too, and he needed to clear his head and work on figuring it out.

But she sniffed and that's when he did a supremely stupid thing. He pulled her against him, fighting off a little surge of panic. She was warm and her curves fit too perfectly to him. It physically hurt to have her against him. Jenna was so open and nonjudgmental about who he was, where Melanie was always trying to change him, control him. She might have allowed her husband to run roughshod over her in the past, but she was so much more courageous than Melanie. He was proud of her for divorcing him. Another surge of panic sizzled into his veins, and he held her tighter, the memory of that kiss washing over him. The small, distressed sounds she made deep in her throat completely did him in. Made him do something even more foolish and reckless. "Shush, I'll help you. I've been through the process," he murmured into her fragrant hair, so soft against his face.

He would take it easy with her. He didn't want her feeling alone, mourning and bereft all at once. It was more than he could take, so the offer was easy to make.

Then he wanted to kick himself. What was he thinking? Volunteering for things had always gotten him into trouble, especially with her, from the age of twenty-two. He was one badass marine, but she'd broken him with one soft, shuddering sigh, looking up at him with her blue eyes swimming in tears.

Getting tangled up with Jenna Webb was the stupidest thing he'd ever done. He could only chalk it up to the circumstances. The danger and the adrenaline, the way she looked at him like he was her hero.

He had been so wound up in hormones and fantasies that he'd been dumb-blind as far as she was concerned—and she was no longer married…to the ambassador.

What did that mean for them? Had three days of stress led him to thinking they had more together than they really did have? Did she even feel anything for him or was he a port in the storm? Was their past a factor or did he just think it was?

Chapter 5

After leaving Jenna, Austin couldn't seem to shake the giddy knowledge that she was no longer hitched to the ambassador. She was free. He knew that getting involved with her during an active investigation was just as dangerous as it was when he was at the embassy. All the feelings and emotions from the death of her cousin also made her vulnerable. It seemed as if she also had no one in her life that she was close to and he had to wonder why. Why had she isolated herself in the desert where she knew no one and how had her life been in DC?

But he had a job to do and standing around speculating about Jenna and a relationship that he wanted to pursue wasn't going to get that job done.

He video-called into NCIS and Kai answered, looking tired. "Hey, boss lady. I want a rundown of the candidates who didn't make the team, and check out where they were when Sarah was murdered. Do you have their whereabouts?"

"A step ahead of you. I brought in a fledgling agent

to give us a hand. Her name is Andrea Hall and she's fresh out of FLETC, former LAPD undercover cop." She pronounced the center where all NCIS agents went for training as *flet-see*, short for Federal Law Enforcement Training Centers. "She's got some chops and will be working with us until Derrick and Amber are back. So use her."

"I will. Thanks."

"Hello, Agent Beck." A woman's face filled the screen. She had long blond hair, a pretty oval face and gray-blue eyes.

"It's Austin."

"I go by Drea."

"Welcome to the team, Drea." He smiled.

She smiled back, which lit up her face. "At least on a temporary basis. I haven't gotten my final assignment yet, but glad to be of help. Seems I'm a rookie all over again. Anyway, I worked up profiles on those names Agent Talbot gave me. Are you ready for the info?"

"Yes."

She went through each of the six candidates that Sarah had beat out for the job, detailing their records. No red flags in the bunch. "Most of them are on assignment, and on preliminary investigation. I couldn't find any connection to the victim. But Lieutenant Benjamin Torres was on the same carrier as Sarah Taylor." She consulted her notes. "The USS *Bradley Jones*. I could interview them for you and find out where they were the night she was murdered."

"That would be very helpful. Leave Torres to me. Anything on the autopsy yet?"

"No, but I can speak to Dr. Joiner and see when he might have the information."

She laughed softly. "All right. Anything else?"

"Yeah. It's probie, not rookie. Stop lollygagging, *probie*, and get on it."

"Yes, sir. *Semper Fi.*" She saluted with a mischievous grin. He liked this woman, who reminded him of Amber.

"Ah, you do your homework. Smart." He winked at her and she winked back. "Once a marine, always a marine, but the salute was a nice touch." He laughed and disconnected the call.

His email dinged and he checked it to find a message from Commander Washington that the Blue Angel team was assembled for his interviews. He was thankful for the distraction. He didn't want to fill the afternoon chasing his tail over Jenna or spend the rest of his life wondering what would have happened. Now that her cousin was dead, she'd be heading back to DC and he'd finish this investigation then go back to his life at Pendleton. After all, the world didn't revolve around him.

In his car, he caught himself reliving that embrace. It was as electrifying, as strong as the kiss they'd shared in the dark of that embassy office. But he still didn't know if it was the situation that was causing his attraction to her and his doubts only made his resolve not to take advantage of Jenna and the circumstances tighten. He tried to put it out of his mind and focus on finding Sarah Taylor's killer.

Once inside the El Centro base, he was ushered to a conference room. The team was assembled outside, some sitting on a couch, others standing and conversing.

Commander Washington's booming voice filled the open space. "This is Special Agent Austin Beck from NCIS. He is here to investigate the terrible murder of

Lieutenant Taylor. Answer his questions. This team is about honesty and integrity. You all are the best the US Navy and Marine Corps has to offer. See that you live up to the reputation."

Austin entered the conference room and the first team member came in. He asked personal questions he knew the answers to in order to get a baseline on when the men were telling the truth, then he asked the same questions of each of the first three members: *Did you know of anyone who would want to harm Lieutenant Taylor? Where were you the night she died? Did you make any inappropriate advances toward her? How did you feel about her being on the team?*

He made note that three of the members all had alibis he would need to chase down.

The next team member identified himself as the slot pilot, Lieutenant George Houser, and he took the seat across from him as Austin glanced at his notes. "You were stationed on the USS *Bradley Jones*?"

"Yes, I have close to three hundred carrier landings."

"You ran track in school, huh? I was a cross-country guy, as well. Good way to develop the lungs for a pilot." Austin kept his voice even, conversational.

"I always wanted to scream across the skies and protect the country from the air." He smiled, but unlike the first three members, Lieutenant Houser looked a bit nervous. Austin got down his patterns and started on the real questions. "Do you know of anyone who would want to harm Lieutenant Taylor?"

"No, sir. She was a good person and an amazing pilot."

"How did you feel about her being on the team?"

"The vote was unanimous."

"That's not an answer, George. I want to know how you felt about a woman pilot being on the team."

"I voted for her. She was enthusiastic, meshed well personality-wise and she blew us away with her talent. Everyone liked her, as far as I could tell."

"How about you, George? Did you like her?"

"I don't get your meaning, sir. Yes, I liked her."

"A little more than as a colleague?"

He stiffened. "No. I'm involved with someone and I have no interest in ruining that relationship for temporary gratification."

"So you made no inappropriate advances toward her?"

"None." A trickle of sweat slipped down his temple and his eyes darted away.

According to his cues, his answer was correct, but he was fidgety and the sweat was telling Austin he was hiding something. The air conditioner was working quite well in the room.

"Where were you the night she died, at about eleven thirty p.m.?"

"In my rack, getting shut-eye. We have to be alert for our flights and just because we're on winter break doesn't mean we have any time off." His whole body relaxed. So it was the questioning about harassment that was pushing his buttons.

"Can anyone corroborate your statement?"

"Yes, a couple of the guys on the enlisted team. We were playing cards right before I retired."

Austin pushed a pad over to him. "Write down the names."

He complied and pushed the pad back to him.

"So, George. Who was it that was interested in a little 'temporary gratification'?"

His lips tightened and he sat up straighter. "I don't know."

"You don't?" Austin said. "Didn't your commander remind you that this team stands for integrity?" He stayed quiet, and Austin waited a few beats, then filled the gap. "I get it. You don't want to rat out any of your team members. Neither did Sarah. She only mentioned she was being harassed." Still nothing. Austin tried a different tact. "You guys have to fly in precision formation and trust every single member on the team. Isn't that correct?"

George nodded. "It's imperative that we're all as close-knit as possible. One mistake can be catastrophic."

Austin leaned forward. "I can imagine. But Sarah, she's never going to join you in the sky at any air shows. Someone took her life. I'm here to make sure that person doesn't get away with it. Where do you want to be in that equation, George?" George closed his eyes, his jaw clenching. "Will you keep your mouth shut and possibly let a killer go free, or make sure that Sarah gets her justice?"

He swallowed hard and looked away, his face showing not only the distress of losing Sarah, but the truth of Austin's words. He didn't want to be a rat.

He sighed and looked away, clearly fighting with his conscience and his need to be a team player. Finally he faced Austin. "Lieutenant Sims. He was interested in Sarah. I don't believe she was receptive."

"Lieutenant Daniel Sims?"

"Yes. Are we done now?"

"We are. Thank you for your time."

He walked out, wiping at his brow, looking more pensive than relieved. Austin rose and approached

Commander Washington. "I'd like to talk to Lieutenant Sims next."

The commander called the pilot's name and he rose.

When Sims came in, Austin said, "Please identify yourself for the record."

The six-foot, dark-haired guy said stiffly, "Lieutenant Daniel Sims."

"Your position on the team?"

"Lead solo. I've also flown the narrator's slot, the guy who explains what maneuvers the team is performing for the audience at the air shows. I've also flown as opposing solo in formation for the last two years, respectively."

"Have a seat."

He sat down and Austin said, "So you've been on the team for three years. Must be strange to have a woman pilot make it."

"It's a good thing for the Blue Angels squadron and Sarah was amazing in many ways."

"Was she? How?"

"She was personable, would have been an even greater draw for audiences who would want to see her in action and she was also a great pilot."

"She was beautiful, too." He slid Sarah's commercial pilot's photo across the table, then slammed down the crime scene photo on top of it. Sims blanched and looked up at Austin, his face fixed in both regret and distress.

"I know where you're going with this. Okay, I hit on Sarah, a lot. She complained to the commander."

"Maybe you decided if you couldn't have her, no one would, or your fragile ego got all bruised and that made you angry."

"Can we get the executive officer in here?"

"For what reason?"

"He has a valuable perspective that will answer your questions." When Lieutenant Josh Tolbert sat down, Sims turned to him. "Tell him what happened with Sarah."

"I confidentially talked to Sarah about Daniel. She agreed to have a sit-down with him. Their differences were worked out. Daniel stopped asking her out for dates and generally being overtly sexual with her. The matter was handled in-house and was closed."

He looked at both men. "Where were you when Sarah was murdered?"

Josh glanced down at the photographs, compassion in his eyes and his voice. "I was home with my wife."

Daniel said, his voice quiet, "I couldn't sleep, so I took a walk. I don't have an alibi."

Austin dismissed them both. His intention was to keep Lieutenant Sims on the short list.

He left the building and before getting into his car, his cell rang as the sun beat on his unprotected head. The Imperial Valley, even in the winter months, was warm. He answered, "Beck."

"Hey, it's Drea. I talked with Dr. Joiner and his findings are conclusive that the cause of death was manual strangulation."

"Sounds personal."

"Seems so. He said the bruises were deep, as if he bore down on her. He also thinks that it was a slow process because of the extent of the marks. Usually a crime of passion. Normally means the perp wanted to squeeze the life out of his victim." She paused. "Dr. Joiner also said she had a bruise on her chest. It seems he knelt on her to hold her down. Her hands had been bound, so unfortunately, no DNA under the nails. The bruise on her jaw is an indication that he hit her first to incapacitate her. There is a distinctive, round bruise, but Dr. Joiner couldn't figure out what it was. He's working on it now, trying to get a better picture."

"Thanks. Send that report to my email."

"On the crime scene results. One set of unmatched fingerprints. Sarah's, Jenna's and the super's were the only other ones that we found. After running them through the database, there were no hits."

"Okay, so no help there."

"No."

"Do you have any leads?"

"A Blue Angel pilot who was harassing her with no alibi, but with no DNA to place him at the scene, so all I have is a Blue Angel pilot without an alibi. There was a prowler reported—maybe it was him spying on Sarah—but I have to say, I can't see that guy skulking in the dark, hoping for a peep show. He didn't give me that vibe."

"So basically, other than Torres's connection on her carrier, you have zilch."

"Pretty much, probie. But I don't give up that easily. There's her phone ripe for the taking. We'll see what turns up there."

"Okay," she said, her tone brisk. "I messengered Lieutenant Taylor's effects to you to return back to the next of kin. Dr. Joiner said he's not quite done with the body, so the family will have to wait to make arrangements for the funeral."

"All right. Thank you, Drea." He related the information from the interviews to her.

"Sounds like Lieutenant Sims might have had it in for her. She rejected him many times and complained about him to his superiors. Usually joysticks don't like their egos bruised, let alone their careers put in jeopardy."

"Joysticks?"

"That's what I call pilots."

"Uh-huh."

She huffed a breath. "Okay, I have a weakness, but that's all in the past. Pilots are all so egotistical." She paused, but Austin wasn't going to tease her anymore. He had a thing for Jenna and he knew how painful that could be. "Well, back to Sims. He has an impeccable record so far. They could easily have ejected him from the team and that would have made him quite resentful, I'm sure."

"Yeah, I thought the same thing. Gives him motivation. Nice call."

"Thanks. I was a detective, after all."

"Yeah, probie. I bet you were good at it."

She chuckled. "Let me know if anything else pops. I'm still working on the people who were rejected for the open slots. I'll call you with any updates."

"I'll look at her phone when I get back to my room."

"Okay, bye."

He disconnected the call and once he picked up the envelope with Sarah's effects inside, he went to the room and set them beside him as he picked up Sarah's phone. He went through the contacts, and stopped. "Bennie" was all the information listed in the contact detail. Could that be Benjamin Torres? He noticed she had an encrypted messaging app. Could that mean she was talking to someone that she didn't want anyone to know about? Why?

He pulled out his cell. Putting a call through to Jenna he waited. "Hello," she said and her sultry voice washed over him. He closed his eyes. Damn, she'd always had this effect on him.

"Jenna, it's Austin. I was wondering if we could meet this afternoon."

"Sure, I'm at my volunteer job at the library right now, but we could meet after I'm done. I get off about four. I could make dinner."

"Okay, that sounds fine. I'll be there around four."

He disconnected the call and pushed away the sizzle that went down his spine, thinking about being in a homey situation with Jenna. He got down to hacking Sarah's app and her laptop. After further investigation of her phone, he saw that she had a file titled "for my eyes only," but when he tried to access it, he was thwarted with a request for a pin code. This was going to be a bit more involved.

Jenna set her phone back in her purse with an involuntary shiver of anticipation at seeing Austin again and cooking for him. She picked up another stack of books and set them on her reshelving cart. When she looked up, Billy Dyer, a frequent library patron and resident of El Centro, was watching her. He was short, heavyset, with a combover and dark-rimmed glasses. As soon as she made eye contact, she groaned internally. Billy took it as an opportunity to talk to her. She wondered what he did for a living. He often came to the library and asked her for recommendations, which she gave him as a part of her job. He stopped at the desk, his face conciliatory. "That book about Winston Churchill was as fascinating as you said." He sidled closer as she left the front desk and stood next to the trolley.

"I'm glad you enjoyed it. I recommend you read the one about Franklin Roosevelt next, then follow that up with Truman."

"Okay." He didn't make any move to go find either book. She looked at him speculatively. "I heard about Sarah," he said, reaching out and covering her hand. His skin was clammy and moist and she pulled her hand away.

"Thank you, Billy. I really need to shelve these books." She turned away, but he followed her.

"You know, if you need a shoulder to cry on, I'm your man. Maybe we could go out and have dinner and talk." The only shoulder she wanted to cry on was Austin's. But she dismissed that notion. Once the autopsy was over and Jenna could claim Sarah's body, she would bury her cousin and there would be no reason for her to stay in El Centro. She needed to get back to DC, figure out her life and what she wanted to do with it. This brief attempt to run away from her problems was at an end.

"No, thank you, Billy. I can handle it."

She started to go down the aisles, but he followed her again and she reached for a number of books and started to shelve them. She gave him a direct look and frowned. He'd never been this aggressive before, but his attention toward her had been escalating. Maybe she should talk to her supervisor about it.

Austin was here to do a job, nothing else. He'd been nothing but a gentleman, and secretly, she wished it was different. She'd never know what it was like to have him touch her the way she'd fantasized about. The guilt over

that was probably part of the reason her marriage disin-
tegrated once she got back to DC. She wanted to believe
Robert's controlling ways and his inability to see her
as a fully capable woman had caused the rift between
them. She desperately wanted to believe that. It would
make her attraction to Austin just about unhappiness
and loneliness. It would make it easier to go back home.

"C'mon, Jenna, say yes. It'll be good for you," Billy
cajoled, grasping her arm. She was sure it would be
good for him. Billy's attempts to ask her out were now
grating on her nerves.

She was unable to get him to let go of her because
her hands were full of books. Instead, she pulled away
hard, her voice firm with annoyance. "Billy, we talked
about this. I think we're better as friends."

"Right, but this isn't romantic."

"No, no dates. No hanging out. I don't think those are
good ideas. Now, I really need to shelve these books."
He looked downcast as she walked away, but she didn't
want to encourage him in any way. There was no future
between them and zero attraction.

When quitting time rolled around, she headed home,
stopping at the market to pick up some food for dinner.
As she passed the strawberries, automatically reaching
for them, her heart contracted. Sarah had loved strawberries and eaten them by the bushel. Jenna bought
them every time she went to the market. She hadn't
known Sarah well before she came to El Centro, but
they had gotten close, even though her cousin was so
busy with her training. She had been so proud, so jazzed
she was going to fly with the Blue Angels. Jenna felt
a spurt of rage at the person who'd taken that experience away from her. The person who had ended her life.

All the way home she worked at getting her emotions under control, especially knowing that Austin was going to be arriving shortly after she got home. As she went to open her door, Mitch from across the hall was leaving his apartment. "Here, let me help you with those, Jenna," he said kindly.

He took several of the bags, making it easier for her to unlock her door and push it open. They walked inside and he set the bags on the counter, looking sympathetic. "I'm so sorry about Sarah. You must be devastated."

"I am. We only just got to know each other and now she's gone."

"Do they have any leads?"

"Not yet, but they're working on it."

"Let me know if I can be of any help."

When he left, Jenna put the groceries away except for the meal fixings and poured herself a shot of whiskey. She needed the fortification it would bring against her raw emotions.

She then went into her bedroom and stripped off her clothes and got into the shower. She felt tired and couldn't focus after her restless night and full day. The warm water went a long way toward loosening up her muscles and relaxing her. She washed her hair and conditioned it. She'd cut it shortly after she'd divorced from Robert, as he'd always been adamant that she maintain her long hair. It still felt strange when she ran her hands through it. After getting out and drying off, she went to grab her yoga pants and a simple top, then paused. This was dinner with Austin and, although it wasn't a date, she wanted to look her best. It would give her courage. She went to her closet and started to pull out garments, discarding them as she went as either too dressy, too date-y, or too casual. Finally, at the end of her rope, she came across a filmy white blouse. It was ultra-feminine; the stark white, gauzy fabric felt pretty against her skin, not too dressy with a ruffled front and sleeves. She deliberately left the top button undone, showing the skin of her neck and upper chest, and paired it with a pair of skinny jeans.

Then she turned to her hair, pulling it up into a sexy, tousled style that also gave her confidence. Taking another breath to steady her hands, she applied her makeup. When she finished, she stood back and assessed her handiwork. She grinned at herself, a light feeling coming at her in a rush. She really hadn't deliberately set out to mess with Austin's mind, but she wanted him to see her as the woman she was. Not some victim, not a grieving family member. She wanted him to notice her. Even though he'd made it clear he wasn't going to pursue a relationship with her, there was a stubborn need in her to show him who she was, both inside and out. She looked in the mirror. This was a pretty good external.

On a whim, she went into Sarah's room and opened up her jewelry box. Inside were some beautiful pieces, but Jenna went right for the simple necklace with an eagle on it. It was something Sarah always wore when she was off duty and, right now, Jenna wanted to feel close to her. Yet when she looked, it was gone. She must have been wearing it when she'd been killed. Instead, she grabbed a pretty opal that had also been a favorite. She slipped it around her neck and clasped it, touching it briefly to make sure it was centered.

Her throat thick, she stood there for a moment. She startled when the doorbell rang. Walking to the door, she loved the feeling of confidence she got from her girly armor. Expecting Austin, she was surprised to see it was Scott the superintendent.

His eyes went over her in an appreciative slide. Okay, it was working, she thought, but on the wrong man. "How are you, Ms. Webb?"

She gripped the doorknob. Lord, he was a big man, imposing, and his eyes a deep blue, but somehow unsettling in a way that made her guard go up slightly. It could be her imagination. Her cousin had been murdered not more than a few strides from the front door. But Austin had said he'd had an alibi and he'd always been so helpful to them, especially with that prowler situation. "I'm doing as well as can be expected under the circumstances."

He indicated the glass. "You getting yourself a little courage?"

She looked toward the counter and nodded. When she turned back, he was inside. She got a little frisson of unease. She stood there for a moment, and he smiled, giving her a little creepy chill.

"Everything working all right?"

"I think so." She let out a breath. She sure was on edge, so much so that the super seemed menacing and all he was here to do was help her.

"Let me just make sure." He gestured toward the fuse box.

He's just doing his job and you're on edge. Relax. "Okay, that would be good. I don't want any problems with the power."

Jenna went to the closet to check Sarah's pockets for the necklace. When she spied Sarah's flight jacket inside, tears welled. She reached out and stroked the leather as her throat cramped. Sarah had been fearless. She had gone for what she wanted full blast, just like the jets she'd flown. Jenna wished she could be like that, but maybe Robert had been right. Maybe she wasn't able to stand up for herself. Be bold. Her fears and doubts always assailing her. Maybe she did need someone to handle everything?

Sarah's pockets were all empty. Closing the door, she cried out and stepped back. The super was behind the closet door, startling her. As her heart pounded, he took a step toward her.

Chapter 6

The doorbell rang. Scott stopped moving and, for a moment, she could swear he looked annoyed. But it rang again.

"You better get that," he said, his voice neutral. Then he smiled.

She let out a breath, went around him and opened the door. She had to take a breath. Austin was standing there with an envelope in his hands. His hair was a bit disheveled, as if he'd been running his hands through it. He didn't move so much as a muscle, and he stood staring at her, his jaw grimly set; this close, Jenna could feel the rigid tension in him. The flutter was suddenly back. Unable to hold that unwavering stare of his, she looked toward the super.

Scott took the cue. "Well, looks like you have company. I'd better get out of your hair." He opened his hand and revealed a fuse. "Faulty one in there. I replaced it. You have a good rest of the day." He slipped by Austin. "Good evening, Agent Beck," he said as he passed, then he was gone. Jenna dismissed him and stepped back so Austin could enter.

"Hello, Jenna." His eyes roved over her from her tousled curls to the open neck of the shirt, to the tight jeans, then lingered on her bare feet, the bold nail polish a bright hot pink. The doorbell had interrupted her putting on socks. She glanced down. Thank God she'd had her toes done.

When she met his eyes again, she saw the hunger in them. "You look beautiful," he said, his voice filled with a thick gruffness that made her vibrate. Then his expression eased a little. "I mean… Oh hell, can I come in?"

His expression changed again. There was something dark and intense in his eyes, something that was eating away at him, and it made her throat ache and her chest fill up.

She closed the door and said, "Yes, of course. It's good to see you again, Austin. Can I take your coat?" Her voice mirrored the breathless quality in his. His jacket consisted of a stylish black pullover with a pronounced cowl instead of a hood. Unsnapping and unzipping the side, he pulled it off and handed it to her. Austin was dressed in gray pants with a stripe on the back, a tight-fitting, long-sleeved T-shirt in red that hugged the muscles of his chest.

Since Austin had always been in uniform whenever she'd seen him, she'd had no idea he had such a wicked sense of style. It was clear he was influenced by his surfing roots but had moved on to slightly more business casual attire. She liked that a lot, seeing him in this light. He had always been so capable at the embassy. It didn't surprise her that he'd transitioned into another position of authority. It was part of who he was.

He also smelled so good. She wanted to bury her face anywhere on his body and breathe deep. Flustered, her hands trembling, she hung up the jacket. When it slipped off the hanger, Austin caught it, so close behind her she could feel the heat of his body, and that scent— outdoorsy, rain washed and clean-smelling—flowed over her. She closed her eyes to try to ground herself. When she opened them, he'd zipped up the side so it would stay put.

She turned and she was practically in his arms. He hesitated, then took a deliberate step back, and she could breathe again.

He looked subdued, like he'd come to tell her bad news and to add weight to his mood, he ran his hand through his hair again. Why was it that every time she came into close contact with him, she felt sensitized, electrified, as if there was a current running back and forth between them, feeding each other in a sensual two-way connection? But he'd been clear after that kiss they'd shared outside of the restaurant. He was on duty, and he didn't want to muck up the situation between them.

She got that but couldn't shake that buzzing sensation whenever she was in the same room with him, or thinking about him. Maybe it was the danger and heartache that fueled this feeling. She just couldn't be sure. Exactly like the last time they were together. She was going through a terrible personal crisis coupled with a real-world threat.

"You look like you're going to the gallows," she said.

He huffed a short laugh, "Do I? Usually gallows humor helps in a situation where there's so much ugliness, but in this situation, it's not appropriate, as you're not law enforcement. You're also much too close to the victim."

"Sarah," she said. "Please don't call her the victim. I really hate that."

"All right. I'm sorry, Jenna. That was insensitive."

"No, you just aren't used to dealing with someone you know who was close to the deceased. That's all. I can cut you some slack. And, for the record, I've never known you to be insensitive."

He fingered the envelope and sighed. "Let's sit down."

The ominous tone of his voice tightened Jenna's gut. She had to hear what he had to say. She wasn't exactly prepared for it, but then when would she ever be prepared to hear about someone deceased she...loved— yeah, she'd loved Sarah—and what had happened to them? The details of their death.

She moved to the couch and settled on the cushions, and Austin lowered himself down onto the coffee table right across from her, like he'd done when he'd first arrived. It would have made her smile if she wasn't so tense.

Did that indicate he wanted to be close to her while he delivered the news, close enough to comfort her? That made her feel a little less alone.

"First off, I don't really have much to report about the investigation. There is one suspect, but I don't have a thing on him, no DNA, placing him at the scene or hell, even speaking with Sarah outside of work. I'm following up some leads that I got from her phone and email, but I won't detail those until I get more information. But I do have a question."

She took in all the information and her stomach only got tighter. "What is it?"

"Are you sure Sarah didn't have a romantic relationship with anyone?"

"As sure as I can be. She was secretive about her personal life. Maybe that was because she was just getting to know me. We were close, but she was all about the navy and even more gung-ho about the Blue Angels. She breathed, ate and slept it." Jenna's voice broke and she went on softly. "It was her ultimate goal. Why? Is there an indication that she was seeing someone?"

"There are some things that aren't adding up. It could be she put a barrier up with anyone who was interested in her in a romantic way because she was so determined to fulfill her dream of flying with the Angels. But my gut tells me she had something going on. She has an encrypted messaging app on her phone."

"What?"

"It's a chatting tool that has a shelf life. People could send media messages or texts and they would disappear after a specified amount of time."

"It's a clandestine app to keep private stuff private?"

"Exactly. She has a 'for her eyes only' section on her phone that I worked on getting into, but will need to do more work before I can access it."

"Hack it, you mean."

He gave her a slight smile. "Yeah, hack it. Unless you know her pin code?" She opened her mouth and Austin said, "Yes, I tried her birthday already."

"I didn't even know she had something like that. I had no idea what she did when she was alone."

"Of course," Austin said.

"Usually secrets come from a need to protect the person. Why would she feel she needed protection regarding romantic behavior?"

"Scandal, for one, especially if she worried about being in the public eye. The fact that she made the team was huge news. Sarah knew that and anything that she did would become public once it was announced. Besides, Sarah was quite beautiful, and she would become a pin-up girl for male fantasies. A beautiful female sky jockey manhandling a fast jet would fuel plenty," Austin said.

"I see your point. Maybe she also wanted to spare the man she was involved with, as well."

"That's a good point, but it's all speculation until I can access the file." His expression went softer, his eyes filling with compassion. "I'm sorry this is such a painful process and that I have to keep at you with questions, but it's the only way to solve her murder. You understand that, right, Jenna?"

She nodded. He reached out and opened her hands, his fingers warm and stimulating against her sensitive palms, then set the envelope in them. "These belong to you now."

The plain manila envelope felt like a loaded grenade in her hands. Gathering her strength, she opened the flap, her knees weak, her heart fluttering like crazy. Trying to force some calm, Jenna took a deep, stabilizing breath and slid the contents of the package into her hands.

She made a small gasp. These were Sarah's things… oh God, from her body. Her effects. Her watch with the new leather band she'd given Sarah for Christmas. Jenna had snatched Sarah's watch, driving Sarah crazy right before Christmas when she couldn't find it. Jenna had taken it into the jeweler to replace the band, then had them wrap it up; she'd given it to Jenna as a gift. Sarah

had given her a narrowed look and they'd laughed about
how Sarah couldn't imagine where she'd lost the watch,
with Jenna teasing her mercilessly about the worn band.
Then there was a locket, one Sarah's father had given
her. It held the picture of her now-deceased parents.
But it was the eagle earrings that got to her, the ones
that matched the necklace…it wasn't in the envelope.

"Is there something wrong?"

She touched the opal necklace around her neck and
it was too much overload. "There should be an eagle
necklace in here. Sarah always wore it."

"I'm pretty sure that was it, but I'll check back with
headquarters in case it got left out."

Her eyes burning, she rose. "I should get dinner
going." In her haste to get to a task to focus on, to get
her away from another breakdown, she dropped the earrings. "Oh, God," she murmured and immediately knelt,
frantically trying to find them. She found one and let out
a soft gasp when she couldn't find the other, her sense
of loss over Sarah welling up. The knowledge that she
was completely alone now hit her hard, so hard it left
her reeling and disoriented. Her eyes filled with tears
and she bit her lip to keep it from trembling, then she
closed her eyes hard, the tears spilling out.

"Jenna," Austin said, his voice gruff and low. He
placed his hand against her jaw. She opened her eyes,
her heart contracting when she realized Austin was on
one knee beside her, and in his open hand was the other
earring. He picked it up and set it in her palm, closing
her fingers around it tightly.

Her voice husky, clogged with tears, she murmured,
"Thank you."

He made no response, a terrible tension in him as if he was fighting some heavy emotion of his own.

She heard him try to clear his throat as he dragged his thumb across her cheek. His voice was rough and very uneven. "You're welcome."

He shifted his position, sliding his arms around her, gathering her up as he lifted her to her feet. Overwhelmed with a mixture of hunger and unbearable sadness, Jenna wrapped her arms around his neck, hanging on to him for dear life. Locking her jaw to keep her own emotions contained, she pressed her face against his neck, a sob trapped in her chest. He clutched her head against him, his rib cage rising sharply, then he made a ragged sound.

They stood like that until the initial thick wad of emotion passed. When she was strong enough she raised her head. He looked down at her and again, his thumbs swiped just below her eyes.

"You okay?"

She nodded, unable to speak just yet with the huskiness in her voice. "I'll help you make dinner, or better yet, I can make it if you tell me what you had planned." He was trying to distract her, but she saw that he had more to say. She should let him get through all of this before they had their meal. Already feeling as miserable as she could right now, she stepped back and said, "There's more you wanted to say. Might as well get it over with."

"Jenna…"

"It's okay. Really. Tell me."

"The ME has ruled on the cause of death. It was manual strangulation, often seen as a crime of passion or deep hatred. Someone wanted her to suffer." Jenna couldn't imagine anyone in Sarah's life had felt that way about her. She had been liked by everyone who'd met her. "The ME's not quite done with…the body yet, so you'll have to wait a bit to bury her, but there's no reason we can't begin the funeral arrangements. I know it's complicated, and I can help you with that after dinner like I promised yesterday. All right?"

"Yes, I would be so grateful." This whole thing was so awful. Her stomach dropped with each word about her cousin's death.

"You going to be okay?" he said. She stepped back, let go of him with a frisson of heat. "So, what's on the menu?"

"If you don't mind, I would prefer to cook or we can do it together. I really need something to occupy my mind."

"I know the feeling," he said under his breath.

"It's going to be chicken fajitas. How does that sound?"

He smiled. "Sounds good. I'm starving."

She backed away and then turned toward the kitchen. She pulled out the already marinated meat she had been planning for her own meal, then the sweet red peppers, green peppers and onions.

"I'll take the onions," he said.

"My hero," she said. "I hate chopping onions."

She set him up and then began to julienne her peppers. They worked in companionable silence until Austin said, "Have you had a chance to even think about the funeral?"

"I know that she named me as her beneficiary and executor of her will. We talked about that because flying with the Blue Angels, even with all the precautions and training, is still very dangerous. She wanted me to know what to do in case of her death. I have all the important papers in a safe deposit box back in DC. I will need to go back there and get them." She poured some oil into a skillet and dumped all the peppers into a pan, then added the onions. "I know she wants to be buried at Arlington Cemetery in Virginia. She grew up there and her dad and mom are buried there. He was also a navy pilot."

"That's a tough break."

She nodded. "I want to make sure she gets a military burial with all the bells and whistles. She deserves that."

"We'll make sure that happens."

She cooked the vegetables and then removed them from the pan, adding in the chicken after discarding the marinade. The smell made her stomach twist with hunger.

She grabbed the tortillas out of the fridge and popped them in the microwave to heat them. Then she got the shredded cheese, guacamole and sour cream.

"Could you set the table?" she asked. After she showed him where everything was, he got to work while she made six fajitas and set them onto a platter. She grabbed a pitcher of iced tea and went into the dining room. Austin had done a nice job, even lit the candles on the table. She set the platter down and accepted the seat he pulled out for her. Once she was settled, he took his own chair.

They served up their dishes and started to eat. "Did I ever tell you I was in a band in high school?"

"No. We didn't get much time to really get to know each other. All I know about you is you surf, had a pretty blonde girlfriend and you showed stunning bravery the night we were evacuated."

He forked up a bite and chewed. "Well, I was a band geek."

"Don't downplay it. Walking, carrying instruments, sometimes heavy ones, takes a lot of energy. Making music is a gift."

"Yeah, well, I was still a geek, in band, in math and computer club."

She smiled, touched by his wry tone, endeared to him even more.

"Anyway, I played the trumpet. I even considered joining the Marine Corps Band, but decided that I wanted to serve a different way."

"Do you still play?"

"No, not the trumpet. I like the sax and guitar better. Got rusty while I was in the military since it was difficult to carry instruments around in a duffel, but picked it up again when I got out."

"I'd love to hear you play sometime," she said, biting her lip immediately. It was unlikely she'd ever hear him play.

"Maybe I will." He took a sip of his tea. "I'm telling you this information because sometimes live buglers aren't available for funerals. If that's the case, I can play taps for Sarah, instead of that canned crap."

Moved beyond words, Jenna couldn't speak for a moment. She reached out and covered his hand briefly. "Thank you for that offer. I so appreciate it."

They finished their meal and Austin helped her clean up. Once the dishes were done and the leftover food put away, she opened her laptop.

"The first thing you're going to want to do is contact the Military Personnel Records Center in St. Louis, which is part of the National Archives and Records

Administration, or NARA." He typed into the computer and pulled up the website, then clicked through to a form. "This is where you'll get all of Sarah's military records. You'll need those before you can apply for a burial site at Arlington. She will be honorably discharged, even though she's now deceased. It's required before you can access the burial benefits." He slid the laptop over to her and she entered the requested information. "Our ME, Dr. Joiner, will provide you with a death certificate. You'll need to add that to your records."

After she finished typing in everything for her request, he then opened up a Microsoft Word document. "You're going to need a slew of information once you receive the military record and death certificate." He started to type, his fingers flying over the keyboard. She could easily believe he was a hacker with the way he quickly and efficiently made a list for her. "Among some of the things you'll need to know is the cemetery, which we know will be Arlington, and other family members interred there. Here you'll need her father and mother's information, type of burial for Sarah and so on." He finished the list and saved it to a file. "If you have any questions during the process, just let me know."

"Austin, this is so helpful, and I'm so glad I didn't have to do it alone."

"Anything to make the process easier. I know how hard it is to plan this, but it's got to be done." He closed the computer. "You know that you will get taps like I mentioned, a two-person honor guard for a flag-folding ceremony and presentation, and I would suggest you consider a military fly-over for Sarah. She served both on the USS *Bradley Jones* as a carrier pilot and as a

Blue Angel. That seems fitting to me. I added it to your list before I saved."

"I will. That sounds absolutely necessary. Sarah deserved that honor. She loved the navy and flying so much."

"The next thing you should do is contact a funeral director in Arlington so you'll know where we should ship the body. But definitely think about what type of burial you want—casket or urn."

"She didn't have a preference, so I'm going with the simple casket."

"Good. There's a resource online covering funeral directors. It's a good place to start."

He rose. "I should be going. It's getting late."

"Yes, of course." Even to herself she sounded reluctant to let him go.

They reached the closet, and she opened the door and reached for his pullover. The material felt soft against her skin as she pulled it off the hanger and turned to him. He took it and slipped it over his head, leaving the zipper open, the snaps undone. He looked so sexy in the tight red shirt, but the stylish hoodie took that up a whole ten notches.

She pulled her eyes away and made herself go to the door, all the time wishing that he would stay a little longer.

She paused there when she felt his presence behind her. Austin was so close that the heat from his body engulfed her, and it was all she could do not to grab onto him.

She expected him to move away, but he didn't. Instead she felt a light brush against her shoulder, and she swallowed again, that one single touch nearly her undoing. Not knowing what to expect, she looked up at him, her stomach lurching when she saw the dark, somber expression in his eyes. He held her gaze for a long, electric moment, then he drew a deep breath and stepped away. His voice was gruff when he spoke. "Do you want me to stay tonight? On the couch?"

She closed her eyes, the heartfelt inflection in his words touching on the well of emotions inside her, the longing for him only tripling. "Would you mind? Is it breaking some kind of protocol in your job?"

"No. Even super agents need to sleep," he murmured with a smile.

"Then yes, I would love it if you would stay. Let me get you some linens and some towels. I have a spare toothbrush," she said, but she didn't move.

"Thanks." Austin's voice got lower, and she was so grateful for this reprise. So grateful. She wanted to tell him how she felt, but it would only make matters worse for him when he'd already said they should cool it.

"Jenna, time will make things better. I know it's hard right now, but I want to be here for you to support you. It's so damned complicated because we have a past, and I'm on official investigative duty. But I want to do the right thing here. You understand that?"

Jenna caught the back of his head, her fingers tangling in his hair, emotion upon emotion piling up in her. It was as if they were fused together by desperation, by their individual sorrows, by all the things they couldn't say, and it was too much. And it got even worse when she realized how tightly he was holding her.

Clenching her jaw to hold the awful pressure in her chest, Jenna shifted her hold, trying to completely enfold him, trying to tell him without words that she was so grateful to have him be the agent investigating her cousin's death.

Expelling his breath in a violent shudder, Austin roughly turned his head and tightened his hold, nearly crushing her. Jenna cradled his head, absolutely wrecked.

Tightly closing her eyes to try to keep everything contained, she continued to hold him with all her strength, afraid if she loosened her hold just a little, he would disappear like smoke.

She had no idea how long they stood like that, clinging to each other, afraid what would happen if they let go, but Jenna's arms were quivering when Austin finally stirred. His chest rose sharply, pressing against her as he took a deep, uneven breath, then she heard him swallow. "We'd better get some rest," he whispered, his voice rough with strain.

Her insides tied up in knots, she released him. "Let me get those things for you." She went to the linen closet and got fresh sheets, a pillow and comforter. "The couch folds out and the bathroom is down the hall to the left, spare toothbrushes just below the sink."

"Okay. I think I can manage that," he said. She turned to go and he threw the stuff on the couch and caught her by the face, his eyes intent and a stormy gray, his face so handsome, his mouth so tempting. "You are beautiful, Jenna. I meant that and this isn't easy. I wanted you to know that. Give it some thought before we become physical. We both know that's where this is heading, don't we?"

She nodded.

"You could be reacting to the situation. It's not that

I don't want you. I just want you to be sure it's between us and not the situation that's dictating things."

She tried to think of a response, the longing for him now a deep ache. He let her go. "I can help you make up the couch," she offered lamely.

"I got it covered. Get some sleep." His words had a pleading quality to them, as if he was at the end of his control. "I'll see you in the morning."

Stripped of his warmth, Jenna reluctantly headed to her room. Once inside, their closeness, their almost kiss, seemed to have altered things. Granted, he hadn't acted on the impulse she saw so clearly in his eyes. The knowledge that he was watching her to make sure she was okay should have made her feel better, but in some ways, it made her feel worse. She hadn't known this degree of unhappiness even existed—the kind that knotted her up inside and made her heart ache. And there were moments of unmitigated sorrow.

Her separation from Robert hadn't felt this terrible. She bit her lip, quite aware why, and it had everything to do with what was between her and Austin…passion, an attraction so potent, each of them could feel it in the very air, like a thick invisible fog, jacking both of them up. Something had to break, and she shivered at the thought of all his raw power in her hands. Ached to feel his skin, his mouth, his body—to fuse with him until this tension was resolved.

But it was clear there was this huge stretch of no-man's-land between them, a space he refused to cross. And Jenna had had no idea she could feel so awful, so empty, so damned sad.

Feeling completely depleted, she closed her eyes and pulled the comforter off her bed. She knew that sleep was her best ally right now, especially after getting so little last night. She wasn't sure how she was going to make it through the dark hours or the rest of the next day, let alone the rest of her life.

Chapter 7

The chill of morning crawled inside her, and Jenna drew her comforter tighter. Unable to sleep, she was sitting in her comfy chair staring out at the open expanse of the horizon, a hollowness around her heart. She watched the sky, still dark with predawn, and she faced another reality she had been skirting for a long, long time. She had always cared about Austin, from the moment she met him. Somewhere along the line, she had gotten in deeper than she'd realized.

What she'd felt for Austin was so very different from what she'd felt for Robert. She thought she was in love with Robert, but it was a need for security and comfort that had driven her to marry him. The prodding of her father was firm and strong, but ultimately, it had been her decision. She'd chosen the easiest course. Admitting that to herself made her tremble with an odd kind of alarm. Had she been lying to herself all these years? That she was forced into a loveless marriage? She'd wanted to believe it was Robert's fault, or her father's, but in the end, wasn't it really her own?

She had never taken responsibility for her choices.

She made a soft sound of distress, her throat thick. She'd gone along with the flow for so many reasons: fear of getting hurt, fear of hurting her father, fear of making a stand, causing the serene boat she was on to rock, fear of betraying her beloved dad. In the end, she had cut off her own feelings, and that kiss six years ago had woken her up. But the circumstances and her inability to stop blaming everything and everyone around her had lasted for another six years until she couldn't live the lie anymore. She wanted love, a passionate, can't-live-without-him love.

Austin, all those years ago, had opened her eyes to what real awareness, a real relationship could be. But she'd ignored it, chalked it up to his gorgeous looks and his humorous but intense personality. She'd thought she'd been reacting to her fears and her unhappiness at the prospect of no children, feeling inadequate in getting to what she'd thought she'd wanted: a family with a secure, decent man.

But Robert had never been, nor would he ever be, that man. He never saw her, just his own selfish needs. Austin considered her in everything he did. Her attraction to Austin went way beyond just being unhappy with Robert. There was so much *more* with him.

Austin had blown that out of the water when he'd shown his interest in her. As dawn filtered into the room, she knew what she wanted. She rose and opened her bedroom door, the apartment silent and shadowed with the imminent dawn. A new day, and a new revelation for her.

She approached the couch, the sheets gray in the predawn light. Austin was on his back, the sheets and comforter covering him up to his waist, with the smooth expanse of his chest exposed. She just stood there, looking her fill at the definition of the lean muscles across the broad expanse of his chest, the curve delineating his biceps, the hollow of his throat and the strong column of his neck, his big hands slightly curved in sleep. Everything inside her went liquid. She was tired of waiting and wanting. She was tired of thinking over the six years since she'd last seen him and now. Tired and done with it.

Never in her life had she acted on impulse, except with Austin. Her eyes burning, she undressed, a weird kind of anger setting her resolve. She took off every stitch of clothing she had on and stood in the chill of the room, her stomach fluttering, her body aching, aching. Regardless of where this was going, regardless of how it would end or what their future held, she wanted to know passion. She wanted to know Austin body and soul.

She didn't have a plan, she hadn't thought it out, but just when her nerve faltered, she thought about taking responsibility for what she wanted.

She lifted the covers and slipped inside, the tips of her breasts tingling, hard and aching, the place between her legs moist and throbbing. The smooth slide of Austin's skin against hers only jerked her heart into stuttering, and the relief of skin-to-skin contact was almost more than she could bear. She pressed her whole body against his as his even breathing ceased, and she waited in an agony of anticipation for him to wake up. He stirred, and she knew when he was fully cognizant of her against him, *naked* against him. He froze, then turned his head. He just stared at her with a stunned, heated look in his eyes.

Austin rolled, his breathing suddenly ragged. He stared at her face, then closed his eyes. No, no control. She simply reacted. Her voice barely above a whisper, she spoke his name. She covered his mouth with a soft moan. He went still. She could swear she could feel the tension arcing between them.

Another sound was wrenched from her as Austin's arms came around her, crushing her in a hard, fierce embrace, his hand cupping and holding her jaw.

The onslaught of need ratcheted up and Jenna clung to him, certain she would simply cease to exist if he let her go. She had never experienced anything like it—the heavy surging feeling of two halves coming together, the awesome power of two universes colliding, the stunning rush of wanting. It had been too long and she wasn't waiting another minute. So much need, unsatisfied hunger, raw emotion. But not nearly enough of anything.

Her breathing out of control, she locked her arms around him, pressing her body against his heated, smooth skin, needing him, needing more.

Hoarsely whispering her name, Austin pressed her back into the mattress, then sent his hand over her body, and he groaned when he encountered her bare, throbbing, tingling flesh, everything on fire, waiting for this moment when he would touch her like this.

His heart pounding in tandem with hers, he brushed his mouth against hers as he held her even tighter. Body to body, heat to heat, he took her mouth, and Jenna yielded everything to him, her need fired by his.

Everything she had ever believed about herself—about the kind of woman she was, about her libido, which had seemed lackluster at best—was simply incinerated by that hot, wet, plundering kiss. Making a low sound of restraint, he tried to tear his mouth away, but she grasped his face, holding him to her, unable to bear a separation. She knew if they didn't finish this, if they didn't take this to completion, she would simply break into a million wild bits.

His breathing labored, Austin ripped his mouth away and threw the covers back, his eyes roving over her as if he couldn't quite believe she was here next to him, offering everything she had to him.

Terrified he might stop, that he might do the honorable thing, Jenna locked her arms around his neck, her breath catching. But he clearly had no thought of stopping. He covered her with his body in one powerful move and roughly used his knee to push her legs apart. Pelvis against pelvis, he held her fast as he claimed her mouth again, his thick hardness fused against her.

Jenna had never known this fever of need, this raw, urgent hunger, and she gave herself up to the frenzied sensations, knowing that Austin would never let her down.

Roughly changing the angle of his mouth, Austin thrust against her, and the throbbing heaviness in her groin intensified. Desperate for more, Jenna sobbed and locked her legs around him, transfixed by the unbelievable sensations he'd set off inside her. He moved again and she clutched him, her senses disintegrating, desperate for more, much more.

Tearing her mouth away, she lifted her hips against his, her voice barely coherent. "Please, Austin. Please," she begged hoarsely, rubbing against him again. The unsatisfied pulse thickened and she found his mouth, desperate for the taste of him, wanting to center her pulsating need.

On a jagged intake of air, Austin caught her jaw and dragged his mouth away. His breathing ragged and labored, he tried to gentle his hold. He stroked her head, his voice so rough, it was as if he was speaking through some unmanageable pain. "Jenna," he whispered brokenly, his breath hot against her ear. "I'm not going to risk you in that way."

But Jenna was too far gone to stop. The hunger was centered in her and getting stronger. She rocked her pelvis, her breathing as labored as his. "It's okay," she pleaded with him, her voice breaking. "It's okay. I want you, Austin, please. I'm still on the Pill."

Desperate to persuade him, she moved against the hard ridge beneath his underwear, and he clutched her and stiffened, his body rigid with tension. She moved again, and he clutched her tighter, then abruptly he turned and covered her with his body. Bracing his weight, he fumbled with his shorts, and Jenna cried out when she felt him free and hard. Blinded by sensation, she arched her back, wanting him to thrust deeply into her, but he teased her with his hard-on and his fingers, building, building, dragging her to the edge. Then with a groan he thrust into her, sending her over. He choked out her name and thrust again, his body grinding into hers. Every thrust sent her higher and higher until her whole body focused into one white-hot light; then everything exploded, and pulses of relief ripped through her, a million lights going off in her head. And on a tortured groan, Austin twisted his hips, pumping his own release.

Incoherent and shattered, she hung on to him for dear life—on to her lifeline, her rock, her still center.

It seemed like an eternity passed before flashes of consciousness sifted down, like softly falling snow. Trembling, weak and feeling as if every bone in her body had been liquefied, she folded herself around him, aware of how tightly he was holding her, aware of how badly he was trembling.

She wrapped both arms around him and tightened her legs, an unbearable tenderness welling up in her as she cradled him against her.

She was so shattered, she was incapable of speech. But she was filled to the brim with feelings for him, and she gently combed her fingers through his hair, wishing she could wrap up every inch of him. He was so extremely special. So precious.

Austin turned his face against her neck, his hand wedged under her head. Then, as if too spent to move, he tightened his hold. His voice muffled, he spoke, his tone very gruff, saying, "Jenna, I've wanted you for so long. You took all the control I had, and I was helpless."

Moved beyond words by his admission, and overcome with the need to comfort him, she pressed her mouth against his cheek. Her own voice was very uneven as she whispered, "I was the same. I just couldn't wait, couldn't deny this anymore." She rubbed her hand through his hair, then hugged him close. "I think this may be what heaven feels like."

His chest rose on a deep intake of air, then he tightened his grip on her head. He didn't say anything but she felt him smile. And she hugged him again.

"What about your job?"

She was relaxing into him, so tired now that she'd

seen this through. "Didn't sleep last night," she said drowsily. "Staying right here, but I don't have to work until later."

He chuckled softly and she drifted off as he said, "What am I going to do with you?" The last thing she felt was him covering her with the sheet and comforter.

The next thing she was aware of was the tantalizing smell of coffee, and the sound of someone in the kitchen. She opened one bleary eye and sighed. The pillow smelled like him. There was a crackle of electricity in the air, a heated smell like there was a fire burning somewhere, awareness sizzling along her nerve endings.

Then she heard it, the wind howling outside. The Santa Anas always left her buzzing, but now added to the mix was the scent of Austin, the imprint of his body deep into hers, and she never wanted to shake that feeling.

It took her a moment to raise herself up, clutching the sheet to her breasts. She looked toward the kitchen, and Austin was in there in nothing but those sexy gray pants, his hair tousled. He was pouring coffee into two mugs, situating them on one of her decorative trays, and he added what looked like…pastries.

Her stomach grumbled. But Austin was what looked good enough to eat.

His expression softened into an intimate half smile when he saw her. "Hello there, sleepyhead."

She pulled up her knees and wrapped her arms around them. Wishing he would come close enough for her to touch him, she smiled at him.

"Why are you way over there? I can't reach anything I want."

He stared at her a moment, then shook his head and chuckled, coming across the room. "You're incorrigible."

"No. I'm hungry."

"I went out and grabbed some Danish." He got to the bed and knelt on it, careful not to spill the coffee. He had set a little creamer on the tray, too. Warmed that he remembered how she liked her coffee, she reached for him first. Caught the back of his head and kissed him. He sighed into her mouth and pressed his forehead against hers.

"Incorrigible, I like that."

He sighed again. "I like that, too."

Experiencing a strange, quivery feeling, she stared into his eyes. Reality checked in, and she thought about what had happened between her and Austin, how up in the air everything was, but she couldn't regret one moment of this morning. But she wasn't sure where that left them.

Closing her eyes, she tightened her grip on him, feeling as if she was caught in the current of a rushing river, struggling to keep from going under. Part of her was so damned uncertain. And the other part of her didn't want to think about it—it was just too important to start dissecting. But after what had happened in this bed, she couldn't exactly ignore it, either. Only the thought of getting real with Austin scared her to death. What could she say without diminishing it? Because she knew it wasn't just casual sex for either one of them.

It was real, and it was honest. And it had so many complications tied to it, she couldn't even think about them. But the straightforward, direct person in her could not leave their involvement unexplored. As much as she dreaded it, they were going to have to talk about it.

But Austin didn't seem inclined to right now, and she let her breath go in a rush. He fixed her coffee, handed it to her and reclined next to her, pulling her into his arms. They ate Danish and listened to the wind howl outside.

"How long have you been divorced from the ambassador?"

This was a volatile subject and not just because if things hadn't gone so wrong at the embassy, she might have gone much further with Austin, broken her vows, something she would never have even thought about before she'd met him. She constantly wondered if it had been the situation that had kept her from cheating. She wasn't proud of that, but guiltily she couldn't regret it.

"Nine months. I was separated for six months and have been divorced for three. It was a hard transition going from a houseful of people and activity to being alone. I think that's why I jumped at the chance to come here and get to know Sarah better. We had a nice time of it. I still can't believe she's gone."

He tightened his arm around her briefly, stroking down her arm. "I know about that loneliness." His voice was soft. "I know I crossed the line back then and, for my part, I should be sorry, but I can't seem to be. What happened to make you so unhappy? I had half a mind to throttle him, thinking he was abusing you. I would probably have been court-martialed, but it would have been worth it."

"He was, I guess. It just didn't leave bruises on the outside." He turned to look at her with an expression that told her he was sorry he hadn't kicked her ex-husband's ass. "He refused to have children with me." She took a bite of her pastry, then a few sips of coffee. "As soon as we were married, he took control of my life and I let him. It was a gradual thing until I had lost all my power. When I tried to fight back, he would punish me. I wouldn't put it past him to refuse me a child because I had become unruly."

"I'm sorry, Jenna. You got out, though. You had the courage to divorce him."

She nodded. "You never got married?"

"No, got engaged to Melanie, but then I joined NCIS, and she wasn't on board with that. Was livid, in fact. She didn't want me to live for my job—wanted me to make her the priority."

"Sounds like she was selfish to me. Anyone who even knew you for half a second would know that when you invest in a relationship, it is important to you." He stared at her. "Am I wrong? Do I have Danish on my face?"

He shrugged. "You're not wrong. That's just the thing." He shifted so he could look her in the eyes. "It was that she was so close-minded about it, and I really wanted the job. I had to accept then that I must not be as invested in our relationship as I thought I was. In fact, I think I asked her to marry me just because it seemed like the next step. But she wanted me to be an architect, and I wanted to continue to serve. It was then I realized I was royally pissed at her for giving me such a hard time about being in the marines. I wanted to make a career out of it. After some distance, I realized I'd made a mistake. I should have stayed in."

"Why didn't you just reenlist?"

He shrugged. "It seemed like the time had passed for that path, and I was being called to duty by NCIS. I haven't regretted a moment of it. I've made a difference, and I feel good about that."

"Are you married to your job, then?"

"Not exactly. It's a give-and-take, but if I had some-one to come home to, I might be more inclined not to burn the midnight oil."

The sound of his voice and her desire for the same thing dropped on her like a ton of bricks. She glanced at him, but he was polishing off his Danish and didn't look at her. She couldn't read too much into those words. He was just talking.

"Jenna, I think we need to talk about this thing be-tween us."

She set her empty cup on the tray with a thump. She stared at him for a moment. "I know. But I don't want to pick it apart, Austin. I feel something for you and you feel something for me."

"It's not that simple. I'm working on a case that di-rectly involves your family member, we have a past and if my boss finds out I'm sleeping with you... Jesus." He ran his hand through his hair.

"We won't tell her, Austin. It's our business. Sure, we have a past, and we have some things we need to work through and figure out, but I want to do that. You have a life in San Diego and I have one in DC. We have limited time together—do we have to be rational and serious?"

His expression changing again, he reached down and cupped her jaw, running his thumb along her bottom lip. His eyes were dark and shadowed, but she could see the hunger in them. "I'm a realist," he said, his voice gruff. He caressed her mouth again. "I understand what you want to do, but we'll have to face whatever comes. I just don't want to be blindsided, and I don't want to freaking take advantage of you."

She couldn't help but smile through this serious conversation. "Were you there this morning when I seduced you?"

He released a breath on a half laugh. "Right, and lady, you did a thorough job of it." He caressed her cheek with his thumb. "I'm serious about this. I don't want to hurt you, and I'm not keen on getting hurt, either."

"I don't want that, either. But can't we just enjoy this for as long as we can? Save the big decisions for later?"

He closed his eyes and pulled her close. She slid her arm around his waist, and her eyes burned as he caught her up in a fierce hold, his face turned against hers. "All right. I'm apparently weak when it comes to you. I can't resist this...or you," he whispered.

She wanted time with him to discover exactly what had driven them six years ago. But a little voice whispered in her head, *You're afraid*, as the wind whipped up into a frenzy and blew hard and hot against the complex. She shivered and he drew the covers up over her shoulders.

Or maybe it was because she might discover something she couldn't live without, like falling in love with Austin.

Chapter 8

When Austin opened his eyes again, it was midmorning. His cell phone buzzed, and he carefully reached for it so as not to disturb Jenna's soft warm body against him. He could die right now a happy man. "Beck," he said.

"Hey there, Austin," Drea said. "I have secured transport to the USS *Bradley Jones*, part of the ninth carrier wing that's currently docked in the San Diego Bay. They have a small window to refuel and restock as well as some shore leave for their sailors. The chopper will be there at fifteen hundred hours to fly you over and back for your interview with Lieutenant Benjamin Torres. Torres and Captain Noah Dahl are expecting you."

"Got it."

"The chopper will pick you up from the base, so just show your badge at the gate for entrance. Someone will be there to drive you to the runway."

"Did anyone tell you that you make a passable probie, Agent Hall?"

"With all due respect, Agent Beck, stuff it."

He chuckled, and she hung up. He really liked that girl and looked forward to meeting her in person. The smile died on his face when he looked down at Jenna again. Jesus, what a freaking mess he was in, right up to his eyeballs. There was such a crap storm of issues between him and this beautiful, seductive and determined woman. All he could do right now was just stare at her. The sheets were pushed off her upper body and her creamy skin glowed, her breasts rounded and tipped with blush-pink nipples.

Just looking at her made him hard. Who was he kidding? The thought of her made him hard.

There was a time just after the embassy takeover, when he was recovering at Walter Reed, when if he even smelled the scent of jasmine, he'd be transported back to that night in the helicopter when she'd pressed her hands on his wound. She'd looked into his eyes as if she was trying to transport her thoughts into his brain. He remembered he'd wanted to hold on to that moment but it had slipped away and had left him feeling hollow and guilty.

But then she shifted and the past disappeared into nothing but smoky streamers. Rehashing what happened only made him want to understand what was happening here. They were caught up in this temporary situation. He would eventually solve this murder; his determination to find Sarah's killer settled in him with purpose. He wanted that for her justice, for his duty and Jenna's peace of mind. He wasn't sure what else he could give her, but he was sure that solving Sarah's murder was a forgone conclusion.

As he stared down at her, mesmerized by a face that had haunted his dreams, the craving for her grew beyond his control. He slid down, getting closer to her face, leaned over and brushed a light kiss against her temple. She stirred and he watched her face change from indicating a peaceful sleep to a sated expression.

Learning Jenna's morning faces could become one of his most favorite pastimes. He leaned over again, this time honing in on her mouth. She sighed heavily and kissed him back, her mouth languorous and sweet.

"You taste good," she said, mirroring his thoughts.

"I bet you taste better," he murmured against her mouth, then bit her jaw, trailing his tongue down her neck to the soft hollow of her throat. He pressed several kisses there, then moved down to the tip of one breast.

She made a soft sound when he sucked and her eyes opened, sleepy and dazed with desire. She clasped his head and tangled her fingers in his hair. Before he knew it, she was straddling him, leaning over him, giving him access to more of her skin.

He looked up, something painful happening around his heart as he took all of her in. Sliding his hand down to her waist then in between them, she cried out when he found her wet and soft. "Austin," she whispered.

He took her nipple deep in an openmouthed kiss that made her buck against his fingers; he was tormenting her with the tip of his tongue, back and forth until she was gasping. When she came with a soft cry, her hips rocking, he grabbed her waist, and before she was even finished with the pulsing sensations of her orgasm, he entered her to the hilt.

She moaned and her hips surged against his groin. Closing his eyes against the onslaught of sensation, Austin turned his face against her and wrapped his arm around her lower back, pumping into her without pausing, the sound of their flesh slapping echoing in the room, mixing with the whine of the wind.

He grasped a handful of her hair, clenching his jaw against the raw and chaotic need breaking loose inside him. Inhaling raggedly, he clutched at her. She collapsed her upper body on top of his, still moving with a wild abandon. She left a trail of hot, wet kisses on his face down to his throat. Another tremor shredded through her, and she rose up, taking him deep inside her. He was naked, unprotected and deeply lost.

His skin slick, Austin's face contorted in an agony of pleasure. The Santa Anas blew as hot as the inside of the room, as hot as their slick bodies moving in harmony, the electrifying surge of sensation tingling along his skin causing a frenzy in his chest, his pulse thick and heavy. He threaded his fingers through hers in a white-knuckled grip, turning his head against the pillow. Bending over him, her breasts grazing his chest, she whispered, "Austin... *Austin*." Another shudder coursed through her, and she tightened her hold on his hands, her breath catching as she flexed her hips, her hot, wet tightness gripping him, stroking him, drawing him closer and closer.

An agony of sensation shot through him, and he rolled his head again, the cords of his neck tightening, and he sucked in a breath through clenched teeth. She moved and it sent a shock wave of heat through him, as if the Santa Anas were now locked in every cell of his body and he was as insubstantial against them, the sensation sizzling like a thousand caresses against his skin.

Unable to control the urge, he rose, flipping her onto her back, giving in to the need to be in control, to take her, to growl like he was savage. Her mouth, hot and urgent against his, sent a bolt of pure, raw sensation and made the vortex of need tighten like a vise. Austin shuddered, and widened his mouth against her, feeding on the desperation that poured back and forth between them. She made another wild sound and clutched at him, the movement welding their bodies together like two halves of a whole, and he lost himself completely in her.

The heat of her, the feel of her, the weight of her. He needed her like this, craved her losing it, along with him. Grasping her buttocks, he thrust again and again, a low groan wrenched from him as she moved with him, riding him.

Making incoherent sounds against his mouth, Jenna sobbed out his name and locked her legs around him, her movements urging him on, and Austin crushed her against him, white-hot desire rolling over him. Angling his arm under her back, he drove into her again and again, pressure building and building. A low guttural sound was torn from him, and his release came in a blinding rush that went on and on, so powerful he felt as if he was being remade.

Instead of letting it roll over him and take him beyond the moment, he fought against the pleasure to keep moving, to give her what she needed, and his fight wasn't in vain. She cried out and clutched at his back, then went rigid in his arms, convulsing around him.

His heart hammering, his breathing so labored he felt almost dizzy, he weakly rested his head against hers, his whole body quivering.

Bathed in sweat, their bodies slick and moist against each other, Austin held himself above her, still deep inside her. When he opened his eyes, she was staring up at him, her eyes open and intimately warm. Her hand came up and rubbed against the stubble on his face.

"Austin." She breathed his name in a voice that reflected the look on her face. "That hasn't happened to me before, ever."

He closed his eyes and rolled, bringing her with him. "First for me, too. Jenna, I think you've ruined me."

"I could say the same thing about you." She turned and draped herself limply across his chest. "When can we do it again?"

He threw his head back, his spine arching as he burst into laughter. "Can I get five minutes?"

"What," she whined, her breathing still rough, "that long?"

He hugged her hard, and she kissed him just as hard. "You look like a desperado with that shadowed jaw," she said, running her forefinger over his stubble.

"You look thoroughly and completely done, lady."

She smiled in such a sated way, he kissed her again. Then she sobered. "You've got to go?"

"Yeah. I've got an interview on the USS *Bradley Jones* with Lieutenant Benjamin Torres, a pilot who's in Sarah's contacts, and I think she might have been involved with him."

"You do?" She frowned. "Sarah mentioned him a few times. Said he was a friend and that she flew with him on carrier missions. She also said he'd rushed the Blue Angels but didn't get a slot. If she was involved with him, she didn't give it away."

"When do you have to be at the library?"

"Not until one thirty. I'm closing tonight."

"When do you get off?"

"Other than just a few moments ago?"

He chuckled. "From your job, babe."

"Oh, that."

He kissed her on the end of her nose. "Yeah, that."

"Seven, but I have to clean up and shut off all the equipment and lights, so I'll be ready about seven fifteen."

"How about I drop you off on my way out to the base and pick you up for dinner tonight? I'll fill you in on how it went and we can talk some more about this… thing that's going on."

She folded her arms across her chest and smiled. "If that will make you feel more comfortable. Okay."

"Jenna, I want us to both feel comfortable."

She caressed his face. "I know you do, and I appreciate that. So how about a shower? Oh, wait, you need a change of clothes."

"I got a change when I went out for the Danish. So, let's go clean up and we'll get some lunch before you have to go to work."

She lifted away from him and looked out the window. "Ugh. I hate days like this when the winds blow. I always feel…on edge and gritty by the end of the day."

"I know exactly what you're talking about…damn Santa Anas."

After a shower where there was more kissing and fondling than there was washing, he stood in front of her mirror and shaved. She was doing her thing behind him.

"I like your hair," he said, rinsing his razor in the sink as she combed out her hair.

"I cut it after my divorce."

"It's curlier."

"That's all natural."

"You kept it so straight in Ja'arbah."

"It's the way Robert liked it. He said it looked perfect straight and long. When I saw him to finalize our divorce settlement, he was very disapproving. I told him that it was my hair and my life and for him to mind his own business. That felt really good."

He scraped off the last of his whiskers. "Good for you. Sounds like he had a heavy hand in your marriage. No kids, how to wear your hair? Geez. Did he dress you, too?"

He looked up and the look on her face made him realize that Robert Webb had had control of every aspect of Jenna's life. Pulling his gaze away from her reflection in the mirror, he turned around at her stricken and ashamed expression.

"I'm sorry. I just blundered into it like a bull in a china shop."

"No, it's true. He ruled like a king. I had no say, no voice, and I usually went along with it. He put me on a pedestal, said I had to be protected and cherished." She looked up at him with sad eyes. "But that was the problem. He didn't cherish me—he had the vision of a perfect woman in his head and that's what he wanted me to be. I wasn't perfect and after Ja'arbah, I couldn't really pretend anymore."

"Because of me?"

"Yes, Austin, that was part of it. I realized that if I could have those kind of feelings for you, then what foundation was my marriage based on? Simply vows. It seemed as if nothing was real, but it took me six years to get where I am now. I wasn't ever in love with Robert. I was in love with what I thought my life would be like with him. I still have doubts and am struggling with my own voice and what I want out of life. I'm wandering a little aimlessly right now."

"Sometimes wandering leads you right to the place you need to be."

She nodded and rested her forearms on his shoulders. "I think I like the desperado look better than the clean-shaven special agent."

"Oh, yeah? Well, I like you just the way you are, Jenna, curls and all."

It was true, even back then. With her smooth, styled hair, big, cobalt blue eyes and an air of sophistication about her, she had been dressed to the nines, looking cool, composed and aloof—until she smiled.

That's what had knocked his socks off. The first time she smiled at him, even behind that bullet- and blast-proof glass, he'd felt as if he'd just been sniped right in the heart. He reached up and ran his hands through her hair and her eyes searched his. "We'll be okay, Austin, whatever happens," she said quietly. "Just one day at a time is about all I can manage."

He nodded and just for the hell of it, ran his hand through her hair again. He couldn't shake the sense that he was taking advantage of this situation, but had to remind himself it had been her who had ambushed him with her deliciously naked body this morning. He hadn't been able to take a breath since.

Because if he was being honest with himself, she wasn't the only vulnerable one here and it wasn't only her heart that was involved. It was his, too.

She leaned in, her eyes on his until the moment her mouth connected with his. She gave him a gentle, searching kiss and his arms came around her and dragged her against him as he deepened it.

* * *

Later, as the chopper lifted off from NAF, his laptop open while he worked at Sarah's encryption app, the sun blazed in the bright blue, cloudless sky and beat down on the tan, dusty, scrubby desert below him, causing shimmering waves of heat to rise. The hills and gullies lay like enormous, heaving wrinkles in the earth's surface, the folds held in place by the sharply defined Chocolate Mountains rising in the northwest. The relentless Santa Anas sent dust swirling and a vast cloud hung in the air, forming a golden aura that cloaked the landscape and distorted the horizon. To his left, two red-tailed hawks circled, watching for unwary prey. He tried to focus on what he was doing, but the erotic memories of his morning with Jenna kept intruding. He sat back as the pilot said over the headset, "Five minutes, sir."

"Roger," Austin replied over the rotor noise, frustration making him shut the laptop with force. He looked out over the expanse of San Diego, the traffic moving below him like ants on an anthill, the ocean stretching out as far as the eye could see. Winds buffeted them as the pilot navigated the helicopter to the huge, rolling and pitching carrier, his target a large round circle on the deck. As they set down, the whine of the rotor charging down, Austin slipped his laptop into the backpack. He and most agents carried them as their ready bag.

As soon as the pilot gave him the all-clear, he opened the door and saw two men waiting for him. Ducking his head, he shrugged into the backpack and walked briskly across the pitching deck.

"Good afternoon, Special Agent Beck. Welcome aboard," the man closest to him shouted. He held out his hand and Austin shook it. "I'm Captain David Weaver,

XO, and this is the CAG, Captain Gill Everson." Austin knew that the XO, or executive officer, pretty much ran the ship, leaving the captain free to work on the tactical and logistical planning. CAG stood for carrier aviation group commander, who handled the carrier wing.

"I'm going to escort you to the bridge to have a few words with Captain Dahl, then CAG will take you to meet with Lieutenant Torres."

"Sounds good."

"This way," the XO said as they headed toward the main command center, then up a set of metal ladders until they reached the interior of the ship and entered the bridge.

The captain was looking over a map in the center of the bridge. He looked up when they entered. "Agent Beck, welcome aboard."

"Thank you, sir." He shook Captain Dahl's hand.

"Is it true? Lieutenant Taylor has been murdered?"

"Yes, two days ago."

"I'm so sorry to hear that news. She was a fine pilot and sailor, one of my best. We were so proud to have her rush for the Blue Angels. It's a terrible shame she'll never get to fly with them."

"Yes, it is, but I'm here to hopefully find her killer."

"Lieutenant Torres? I'm afraid you're barking up the wrong tree there. He's been on this ship doing maneuvers for the last two weeks. We haven't had anyone leave this ship between our deployment and redocking."

"Do you know the nature of their relationship?"

"Same strike fighter wing as Lieutenant Taylor and as far as I know, they worked well together, no complaints and no problems."

"How about Lieutenant Taylor? Did she have any enemies aboard ship?"

"No. None. She was an exemplary pilot. CAG, if you will take Agent Beck to the Ready Room."

"Aye, sir. This way, Agent Beck."

The CAG led him through the ship until they reached the room where pilots got prepared to fly missions. They entered a small room and the man at the table stood to attention.

"At ease." Torres relaxed but remained standing. "This is Special Agent Beck," he said to Torres. Then he faced Austin. "Just let me know when you're finished."

"Aye," Austin said. As soon as the door closed, he indicated the chair and said, "Why don't you have a seat?" The man gave him a wary look and sat. "Do you know why I'm here?" Austin asked.

Torres shook his head. "I have no idea. I was told there would be an NCIS agent on board who had questions for me, but not why."

"How well do you know Lieutenant Sarah Taylor?"

He blinked a couple of times and frowned. "Sarah and I are wingmen in the same squadron…at least we were, until she rushed the Blue Angels." His eyes lit with pride. "She's going to be flying with them. That's Sarah for you."

Austin realized two things—this kid was in love with her and he didn't know she was dead. Suddenly this was about delivering terrible news instead of discovering information about her killer. Worst part of the damn job, and these dead ends were beginning to make him rethink this whole investigation.

Austin leaned back and composed himself. "When was the last time you talked to Sarah?"

"What makes you think I talk to her?"

"Lieutenant, she has an encryption app on her phone. I think it's there so that the two of you can keep your relationship quiet and under wraps because you're in the same squadron and there could be repercussions if the brass knew."

He swallowed and his eyes shuttered. "I'm not saying anything about that. Are you here to bust us? It's a moot point because she's flying with the Blue Angels now."

"We both know that doesn't matter and your previous behavior still stands. It's an offense against the UCMJ."

He looked away. Torres knew they had both violated the Uniform Code of Military Justice. "You'd have to prove it, and Sarah and I aren't going to talk."

"I can hack the app, Lieutenant. I just haven't had success at it just yet. But it's only a matter of time." The lieutenant's mouth tightened and he looked away. "Were you and Sarah involved?"

He huffed a breath and said, "Do I need a lawyer?"

"No, because I'm not here about your violation of the UCMJ."

"You're not?"

"No."

"Why are you here?"

Austin took a breath and leaned forward. "Two days ago someone murdered Sarah."

Torres just stared at him, then his eyes began to well up. "What? That's not possible." Tears spilled over and ran down his cheeks. His voice was thick and broken. "Are you sure it was Sarah?" Devastation and shock in his eyes, he bowed his head. Austin was now certain this guy had nothing to do with Sarah's death.

* * *

Jenna hummed as she checked in the books in the return box, unable to stop smiling. *So, this is happiness.* She simply couldn't wait until her shift was over and to get back to Austin. Just being with him made her happy.

Sarah's death had brought them together and Jenna had to wonder if it was fate. Although she hadn't really thought much about destiny, it was a cruel way to bring him back into her life. He was here and regardless of what was going on, it was a chance to see what happened between them.

A little boy walked up to the counter; he must have been about eight. "Could you help me find a book?"

"Did you have anything specific in mind?"

"One with words in it," he said decisively.

Jenna smiled and came around the desk. "I meant more along the idea of a subject."

"No. I just need one with words so I can learn better."

"To read?"

"Yeah."

"All right, come with me." She walked into the children's stacks and pulled out a book. "Have a seat…"

"Dustin."

"Dustin. Very nice. I'm Jenna." He reached out his hand, and she shook it with a chuckle. She pulled out a chair and he sat down. Settling into the small chair next to him, she set the book in front of him. It was a story about a bunch of birds who lived in a manor. They got loose and the owner had to go throughout the house to find them. Jenna loved this one and recommended it often.

She sat with him as he opened the book and looked at the first page. For the next ten minutes she read with him, helped him with the words he didn't know. Her resentment toward Robert was now tempered after six years and so much distance between them along with the divorce. He had been completely…unemotional about the whole thing and it only made her realize how much power she'd given him in their marriage. Looking at this little boy made her only want kids even more. She was determined that would be her future.

The more he stumbled, the more frustrated he got, but she soothed him and sounded out the words with him until he had the first page down pat.

Pam, the manager and a full-time employee, called her name and Jenna looked over her shoulder toward the front desk. "I've got to go, Dustin, but you can come in anytime, and I'll help you with any book you want."

"Thanks, Jenna. May I take this one home?"

"Sure. Let's get you checked out."

She took care of Dustin's borrow, then said to Pam as she watched him walk out of the library, "Do you think there is a possibility that I could suggest a function each week where kids would be invited to read and there could be people on hand to help them?"

Pam sighed. "I think that's a great idea, but with the tight budget we have, it's probably unlikely."

Jenna thought about Dustin and kids like him who could benefit from this type of programming and so much more, but she got it that small libraries needed funding. "How about fund-raising?"

"Believe it or not, that costs money, too. Thanks for thinking about it, Jenna. It's really appreciated. I wish you weren't going back to DC."

"Me, too. But with Sarah gone…"

"I understand."

"Pam, let me donate enough funds to get you through the first year. Then we can talk after that about continuing the program. Would you be all right with that?"

"Would I! Thank you, Jenna. That is so generous of you." Pam reached out and squeezed Jenna's arm, and they got back to work. The day dwindled down and Pam left. Jenna did some cleanup and got ready to shut down the equipment, shelved her last book and headed toward the front desk. Just then, the lights went out.

Chapter 9

Jenna froze in the pitch black. The only light to guide her was coming from the front bank of windows and the glass doors. Must be a power outage. Wait, if it was a power outage, the streetlights would be out, as well. Jenna looked around; where was the emergency lighting that always came on when the power went out?

She heard someone at the front doors, then the rasp of something metallic. She turned back to the front and saw a big man's silhouette. Fear washed through her, telling her to be quiet. He turned to the darkened area where she was standing. Nerves trilled at the base of her neck. Panic climbed up the back of her throat. She immediately ducked down. For a moment, her breathing harsh, she thought about what to do. Without any light, she was almost blind. Almost.

She knew this library like the back of her hand. She'd head to the rear emergency door. Not only was it a way out of here, but it would set off an alarm. She cursed. Her purse was locked in a drawer at the front desk with her phone. When she peeked up to track the progress of the man, he was already at the front desk, and she swallowed hard, her mouth dry; he had a flashlight. His search for her was menacing, without eyes or face. As her skin crawled and pebbled with goose bumps, the light flowed around the front desk, checkering the space. That route was cut off.

Her only choice was the back door.

She turned and started to crawl toward the exit, navigating the tables, chairs, stacks until she reached it. She pushed on the handle, but the door wouldn't budge.

"Oh, God," she whispered, her throat nearly closing on the words. "He's locked me inside."

The knowledge hit her like a sledgehammer, literally knocking her back into the wall. This door should have opened easily, but someone had disabled it. There was no doubt in her mind he was here to do her harm. What the hell was this about?

The sense of dread and shock seeped deep into her bones as she considered what to do next. Getting to her purse or the front door was her only hope. If he caught her… Her thoughts trailed off. He would harm her, or worse…kill her.

Like Sarah in the dark.

A flash of light appeared in the dark space near the door. He'd heard her attempt to open the door, of course, and was now headed this way, his progress slow.

Jenna slid along the wall, disappearing behind a large bookcase. At least she had the light to tell her where he might be.

She took off her shoe and with all her might threw it over the stacks, as far as she possibly could. It hit with an audible smack and the light turned away from her.

Jenna let out a soft, imperceptible breath, scared even her breathing could be heard in the silent dark.

Had this been the same man who had killed Sarah? Why? What was this all about?

As she stood there, panting for breath in the cool shadows, the sounds of traffic rumbled in the background like the murmur of the waves of a distant ocean. Cold sweat trickled between her shoulder blades and tracked down her temples.

She mustered the courage to move. She couldn't stand here like a frozen ninny. He would find her and then it would be over. But even as she started to move, she was determined that she would put up the fight of her life.

She clamped a hand over her mouth as her stomach heaved. She bent over, putting her head between her knees, and gagged as terrible images flashed behind her eyes. The memory of Sarah's dead, cold face, her fixed, terrified gaze looking as if she'd pleaded with her murderer. Her heart thumping at the base of her throat, Jenna hardened her resolve.

She crouched down on all fours and wound her way through the stacks, always keeping her eyes on the light that was now on the other side of the library. She looked toward the front doors, illuminated by the streetlights. He would see her the moment she made a beeline for them. She would have to hope she got out and found help before he caught her. It was her only chance.

She took off her other shoe and again, with everything she had in her, she threw it to the back of the library. Her muscles bunched, waiting. The light froze then, after a soft curse in the darkness, bobbed at a pace that caused the man holding it to hit tables and chairs in his haste to find her. That gave her a great amount of satisfaction, but also sent a chill skittering along her taut nerves. He was pissed.

Jenna exploded off the floor and ran full-out to the front of the library. She hit the front doors and pushed frantically to get them open, but a sob caught in her throat when it opened partially and then a metallic clang reverberated in the open foyer.

That was the sound she'd heard when he'd come in. He'd chained the doors closed. She looked frantically over her shoulder, well aware the she was now visible, illuminated by the light. Something flashed red in her peripheral vision. Her heart leaped, and she pelted toward that brief glimpse of color.

But before she could get to her destination, a hand clamped over her mouth from behind. An arm banded around her middle, as strong as steel, and hauled her back against a body that was lean, rock-solid and indisputably male.

Panic exploded in Jenna, shooting adrenaline through her veins, pumping strength into her arms and legs. She tried to bolt, tried to kick, tried to jab back with her elbows all at once, twisting violently in her captor's grasp. He grunted as her heel connected with his shin, but her satisfaction was small and short-lived as he tightened his hold around her middle.

Reaching out frantically, her hand caught on something solid: a pen. Without hesitation, she stabbed down and hit the man's forearm. He howled and let her go. She stumbled forward, right into a table, and knocked it over, books toppling. Grabbing for anything else as a weapon, she clutched at the first book she touched, rose and with all her might swung it at the man's shadowed face. It connected and he reeled backward.

Her target in sight, she jumped for it. It was her only hope.

Austin rubbed his temples on the ride back to El Centro. It was dark now and he sat in the interior of the chopper, his mind going over everything. The poor guy had broken down, asked questions, which Austin had answered. Even though Torres didn't seem to care, Austin made sure he knew the brass wouldn't hear about any violations from him. All Torres had done was grab his arm and growl, *Find the bastard who did this to my Sarah.*

Austin intended to do that, no matter the setbacks.

When he landed with a heavy heart, he was frustrated and annoyed that every lead he'd had was now dry as a bone or a dead end.

He drove to the El Centro Library and parked outside. He had some time to kill before the beautiful Jenna was free.

His stomach grumbled, but he ignored it. He lifted the cover of his laptop and sent a video call to NCIS in Pendleton.

Drea's face popped up on the screen with a hopeful look, but then drooped when she saw Austin's face. "Doesn't look like it went as well as you planned," she said.

"No. It was another dead end. I ended up telling him the worst news of his life. Turns out they were romantically involved. He gave me the access code to her app and sure enough it's filled with lovey-dovey chats and naughty pictures. Nothing there."

"Dammit." She sighed. "I'm afraid I don't have any

good news, either. I checked out the rest of the candidates. My God, I've never seen such a squeaky-clean bunch of people in my life. All of them were on deployment when the murder happened. So I don't have any leads for you. All of them loved Sarah."

Austin rubbed his hand over his face. "What are we missing? It seems that everyone loved her. We have no DNA, no suspects and no leads."

"Seems that way."

"I'd go back to the prowler report if there was at least some kind of sexual assault or something taken. But there was no forced entry, nothing disturbed, no indication of robbery."

"Yeah, it's like he was just there to kill her."

"Yeah, he turned the power off. Did he want her to die alone in the dark? Or was that just a way to conceal himself?"

He mentally reviewed everything in the apartment, stopping when he thought about what was on the counter…an envelope, a ticket sticking out. To the concert that Jenna had attended? If Jenna hadn't gone, she would have been the one alone in the apartment… Then a terrible thought came to him, his breath catching, his eyes widening. "Drea, the crime scene report. There was an envelope on the counter."

"Just a minute." She disappeared from the screen, then came back, opening a file folder and scanning the contents. "A concert ticket for Nora Anderson in San Diego."

Austin swore softly under his breath. "Whose name was on the envelope?"

"Sarah's." Her head jerked up as she understood

where his thoughts were going. "Oh, God, Austin, that means—"

"In the dark, he *mistook* Sarah for Jenna. He killed the wrong woman! Jenna was the target!"

Just then the fire alarm in the library went off.

"What was that?" Drea's voice followed him out of the car as he opened the door and pelted for the entrance. When he got there, the lights were out and it was pitch black inside. When he tried the door, it wouldn't open all the way. With horror, his heart in his throat, he realized that it was chained from the inside.

"Jenna!" he yelled.

Sirens wailed as fire trucks pulled up outside. As the firefighters ran toward the building, Austin turned toward them. The first guy on the scene was carrying an ax. "Federal agent. I need this," Austin said and snatched it out of his hand. Without another word, he drew back and hit the window glass and it shattered into pieces. Austin kicked the shards out of the frame and ducked under the chain, drawing his weapon.

"Jenna!" He moved forward until he saw a prone body. Then, keeping his vigilance, he surged forward again.

It was Jenna. She was slumped against the wall just below the fire alarm, her eyes closed. "God, please, no," he murmured. He pressed his fingers to her neck and then with a hard exhale, he was able to breathe again. She was alive.

More sirens sounded in the distance as he checked all the exits. They were also chained, except for the last one in the back. The emergency exit door was open. With his weapon at the ready, he stepped out, his body tense, searching the parking lot. He rose and holstered his gun. There was no one in sight.

Rushing back into the building, he saw an EMT bending over Jenna and that she was now conscious. Firefighters were milling around and then the El Centro police came through the door.

When Jenna saw him, she rose shakily and rushed to him, throwing her arms around him. He clasped her to him and hung on just as tight. He had been right outside while she was being terrorized. He'd just found her, but he could have lost her. That ripped him up inside.

Guilt and remorse welling up in his chest, he realized that she was now the one in danger and that he wasn't going to let her out of his sight. Not for a moment. Not for one goddamned moment.

Austin first stopped at the hotel and checked out, then he'd taken her home. The EMTs had looked her over and with Jenna's assurance she was all right and rest was the best thing for her. Once they were inside and the door was locked, he'd gathered her against him on the couch, and that's how they were currently, wrapped around each other. She was still trembling and he was still sick inside with how close he'd come to losing her.

He'd explained everything to the police and the fire chief, Detective Morton backing him up. Currently, the NCIS crime scene team was collecting data, but Austin had a feeling that once again, they wouldn't find a thing.

Jenna had been barefoot, so he'd picked her up in his arms and carried her inside the apartment.

After about half an hour, she stirred and looked up into his face. "I'm going to take a shower."

"You going to be okay?"

"Yes," she murmured and disappeared into the bathroom. He paced and let the truth wash over him again. Someone was trying to kill Jenna and he'd been chasing his tail. This had nothing whatsoever to do with Lieutenant Sarah Taylor.

Receiving a notification that there was an incoming video call, he sat down, his whole body buzzing with energy. He opened his laptop and immediately Kai materialized on the screen.

"Austin, what is going on?"

He filled her in. She rubbed at her temple and folded her arms across her chest. "So, what are you suggesting?"

"She has to be protected."

"She's a civilian."

"Who's being threatened by the person who murdered a navy pilot. The same guy I'm chasing. I'm not leaving her alone, Kai."

"Can't the police—"

"No!" He slammed his hand down on the coffee table, and Kai raised her brow.

"Austin, you need to calm down."

He rose and started to pace, his agitation spurred on by the memory of Jenna slumped against the wall, when he thought he might have been too late. "I missed this. This is on me that she was attacked and almost killed. Let me question her again, this time with it in mind that she was the target."

"Going totally by your reaction, is there something about this woman you're not telling me?"

He looked away, setting his hands on his hips. He wasn't about to outright lie to his boss, not about something that was so important.

When he looked back at the screen, Kai was pensive and wary. She was much too intuitive and too smart for her britches. "I knew her in my past when I was guarding the US Embassy in Ja'arbah." He ground out. "We were…friends."

Her mouth pinched, she said wearily, "You should have mentioned that to me before this investigation went any further. You're too close to this."

"And who's going to take over? Drea? You? We're shorthanded, and I'm already here. I can see this through."

Kai looked away and Austin realized that if she told him no, he wasn't going to walk away. He had to protect Jenna and nothing was going to stop him from keeping her safe. With his argument forming, he said, "She's key in this, Kai. If we lose her—" he swallowed hard "—we could lose any advantage we have here. Our responsibility is to Sarah Taylor. But her cousin is in danger now, the actual target. We have a responsibility to keep her safe and to follow the leads to discover who wants her dead, because it will also solve Sarah's murder. That path is clear to me. It's our duty and our oath to give Sarah justice. Tell me I'm wrong and give me a good argument why protecting Jenna shouldn't be our top priority here."

Kai rubbed her temple again, her eyes closed. She often did that when she was making a major decision. She opened her eyes and gave him a direct look. "You really are good with your words." She sighed. "There isn't anyone who I believe is better suited to solving this murder than you, Austin. I have faith in you. You wouldn't be on my team if I didn't. Do what you need to do. Protect her, and get me that killer. I'll clear it with the director, but keep yourself professional and your mind on the job."

He nodded, the movement curt. He had planned to do exactly that.

"And Austin—watch yourself and stay safe."

"Yes, ma'am."

"I mean it. Get back to me after you question her. I want to know everything you find out and what your next step is." She disconnected the call, and Austin sat back against the couch, his head aching. Kai was always fair and she always gave him the benefit of the doubt. Austin could say with confidence that, to date, he'd never failed his boss. It would kill him to let her down because she was the freaking best he'd ever worked with.

He didn't want to jeopardize his job. He loved it. But with Jenna's life hanging in the balance, going rogue seemed like a great idea. He now fully understood his team member Derrick's descent into madness. He'd gone after a drug lord to rescue Emma's kidnapped nephew. He took a breath. Going off the grid wouldn't be necessary, unless the director nixed him protecting Jenna. If that was the case, could he turn her over to the local cops? He took a breath. His logic was sound. She was the key to finding the person who had murdered a navy pilot; that was his job and Jenna was tied to it.

"I guess she knows now," Jenna said.

He looked over to see her standing close to the couch. She was dressed in nothing but a pretty blue robe with lace on it that hit her at midthigh, leaving all that creamy skin bare. Her chest was rising and falling, her hands twining together, the bruise on her forehead starting to discolor. He reached out his hand and she came to him. She was trembling and he enfolded her in his arms because he couldn't stop himself. She needed comfort from not only the attack, but the news he was about to break. "Have a seat. I have to ask questions."

"What was this all about, Austin?"

"I think that whoever killed Sarah thought she was you," he said quietly.

Jenna's face froze in horror, and she stared at him as her eyes filled. "No. Oh, God. She died because of me?" Her voice thick and uneven, she said, "Why would anyone want to kill me?"

He ran his hand up and down her arm. "I don't know. Tell me everything from the beginning."

She did, explaining how Sarah hadn't been feeling well, how she had gotten these free tickets through a phone giveaway and she'd been heartbroken that she was getting a cold and had decided she needed rest instead of seeing the concert. She'd offered them to Jenna, and Jenna had gone alone. That was it.

Austin sat back, ran his hand through his hair and genuinely felt like he was completely clueless about this case. He had to back up his train of thought, had to reassess everything and think about it all from the beginning.

The Blue Angels angle had been all wrong—that's why he hadn't come up with a single lead that'd panned out. There'd been nothing to find. Sarah had been murdered in error. In the dark, the killer had mistaken her for…Jenna.

He caught his breath on that, the thought that he could have lost her before he'd ever found her again. The shock of discovering her dead instead of her cousin. That would have done some irreparable damage to him.

He closed his eyes, realized how much he'd been into Jenna at the embassy, how much he'd swept it all aside and buried it deep, tried to make it work with Melanie. The time he'd known her had accelerated their relationship because the circumstances had been so forbidden and so dangerous—both professionally and emotionally.

He was sure neither of them suspected how much of an impact it had made on them and now they were right back in the same boat. Forbidden and dangerous.

"You said it was a phone offer. Do you remember when she got that call?"

"Yes, it was several days before she was murdered. I don't know the details. She didn't say. The tickets came in the mail a couple days later."

He nodded, making a mental note to check with Drea about the envelope and to examine Sarah's call log for the incoming number. They had only looked at frequent calls and ones she'd made that day. The number hadn't been relevant during the first pass of Sarah's log.

"Let's talk about the attack."

She closed her eyes for a moment, then opened them. "He cut the power, searched for me in the dark with a flashlight. I threw my shoe to distract him, but the emergency door was locked. He must have gotten the key from the front desk when I was tidying up. I thought my best bet was to go for the front door. I distracted him again, but when I got to the front door, they were locked, as well. I couldn't get out. I went for the fire alarm and he caught me, but I fought him off, stabbed him with a pen—"

"You stabbed him?"

"Yes, he let me go and I pulled it. He shoved me hard into the wall and I hit my head. That's all I remember."

"That means there should be some blood."

"Then you'll know who he is?"

"Maybe. If he's in the system."

She nodded.

"Did you recognize anything about him?"

"No. It was too dark. He didn't speak. It was terrifying."

"I know." He squeezed her arm. "Anything else you can remember?"

She shook her head.

"Do you know of anyone who would want to hurt you?"

"Hurt me?" She thought for a moment. "No, no one that I can think of."

"I can think of one person who isn't too happy with you right now."

"Who?"

"Robert. How amicable was your divorce?"

"Very. He didn't protest a thing. He just signed the papers and let me go."

"Hmm, he did? He could have been hiding his anger and resentment, Jenna. He could have planned to kill you as retribution."

"That's hard to believe. I don't think Robert would get his hands dirty at all. He didn't care enough about me. I was just a trophy wife to him."

"Are you sure about that?"

"Yes. He wouldn't even consider having children, didn't care about my wishes." Bitterness colored her words.

"You took a substantial amount of money with you?"

"Yes. Half the marital assets and all my daddy's money. I even got our town house in DC."

"Maybe he resents that he had to give that up?"

"It's not like he can get it back, Austin. We're divorced. It's final and he wouldn't get a cent if I died. Besides, Robert is still quite wealthy."

"Maybe it's not money-related. Maybe it's just plain old revenge."

"That's hard for me, to believe he even cares."

"I say we cover all the bases." He rubbed her arm again and she moved closer, snuggling against him. "Are you hungry?"

"Yes, believe it or not. I think I could eat something."

"All right, let's get some food, then you should get some sleep."

"Are you...staying with me, Austin?"

"Yes," he said, then tilted her head up. "I'm here to protect you, so we'll have to cool off our relationship until this is over."

"But...I don't want to do that."

"I get that, Jenna. I have to be responsible here. Jumping in with both feet at this point could distract me." Who was he kidding? She distracted him without any provocation.

"This really sucks."

"Yeah," he whispered against her hair, Kai's urging him to be professional clashing against what he felt for Jenna. How much he wanted to be with her. "It does."

Later on that night, after they had eaten, and Jenna had reluctantly gone to bed without him, Austin contacted Drea.

"I can't believe you're still there," he said. "Was that a temporary job or indentured servitude?"

"I'm just trying to squeeze every last minute out of these clues. I'm mad I missed something."

"Yeah, join the club. Talk to me about the crime scene."

"We analyzed the blood," she said wearily. "But unfortunately, no hits in any databases. No fingerprints. No other DNA."

"Damn."

"Yeah, but when we catch him, we'll have him dead to rights."

"I like your thinking. What about the envelope the tickets came in?"

"There's no post office mark on them. They were deposited directly into the mailbox. The sender tried to cover up with a stamp, but it's clear it was hand-delivered. Also, there's no return address. No finger-prints either, and it's ordinary envelope stock."

"The tickets—"

"Ahead of you. They were purchased with cash, no way to trace who bought them."

"How about camera footage?"

"A dead end. The camera was busted, so no foot-age. Maybe it was the killer who tampered with it. We don't know. It's impossible to find out who made the transaction and what window they were bought at, but someone went to a lot of trouble to get Sarah out of the house. Why?"

"Both time the lights were turned off. He wanted to kill her in the dark."

"Yeah, I thought about the fact that he could have killed her in the library, but didn't. Made me think there were parameters to the murder. Like darkness and—"

"Strangulation."

"Yeah," she said quietly. "Jenna doing all right?"

"She's spooked and grieving about the fact that she feels responsible for her cousin's death."

"That's understandable, but you tell her for me that

he's the asshole. He's the one that killed Sarah, not Jenna. Tell her we're going to get him." She sighed.

Austin smiled and nodded. "Good night, Drea. Get some sleep."

"Okay, if I come up with anything, I'll call you. And Austin?"

"Yeah?"

"You get some sleep, too. Getting overtired isn't the best way to protect her."

"Roger that."

After he hung up with Drea, he called Kai's cell. Her voice was drowsy when she answered.

He filled her in on all the details Drea had uncovered, and he was relieved that the director agreed that Jenna was a priority for NCIS. She was a direct link to discovering the murderer.

"What's your next step?" Kai asked.

"I want to go to DC and interview her ex-husband, Robert Webb."

"All right, I'll contact the Navy Yard and get you some backup. Keep me posted."

After checking all the windows and doors, Austin made up Jenna's pullout sofa bed, his thoughts going around and around and over the clues. He agreed with Drea—getting sleep was important. He closed his eyes and just as he drifted off, Jenna's cry brought him fully awake.

His gun, already locked and loaded on the side table, was in his hand when he burst through her door. But she was in the throes of a nightmare. He set the weapon on her nightstand and sat on the edge of the bed. "Jenna," he said softly, clasping her flailing hands in his. She fought him, then her eyes popped open. "You're having a nightmare," he whispered.

"Austin," she breathed and went limp with relief. Then she wrapped her arms around his neck. She wouldn't let him go, and protested when he tried to release her. Giving up, he folded down onto the bed and pulled her against him. He gritted his teeth.

Damn, this was going to be so freaking hard.

Chapter 10

When Jenna woke up the next morning, the sound of the shower going in her room made her gaze go directly to the open bathroom door and the frosted glass where Austin's gorgeous, muscled body made a tantalizing silhouette.

She watched him reach up and wash his hair, the breadth of his shoulders taking up most of the available space, his biceps rounded and fuzzy through the glass. When he rinsed, the outline of his wide chest tapering down to his lean waist and tight butt made her sigh. The man was put *to-get-her*.

The water turned off and the glass door opened. Austin stepped out and Jenna watched him grab for a towel and start to dry off. About halfway through the process, he froze when he met her gaze. His eyes narrowed slightly, then when she just stared at him boldly, a small smile curved the corner of his mouth.

His gaze intent, he wrapped the towel around his waist. His eyes were a steady gunmetal gray, and the flutter of reaction climbed into her throat. It had been so much easier when she had taken the brazen move and slipped into bed with him. But, now that he was guarding her, she wasn't sure how to proceed from here, how to handle the awkward silence and her own uncertainty—or his stillness. She gripped the covers, unable to think of a thing to say that wasn't either *Come here* or *I want you.*

"You know the way you're looking at me doesn't help, Jenna."

"Then you shouldn't be so darn beautiful, Austin."

He snorted and turned to the sink. "You make cooling it seem like a very distant concept, babe."

She sat up in bed as he lathered his face and started to shave. She couldn't remember one moment in her marriage where she'd been enthralled with Robert enough to just watch him shave.

She shrugged. "You're the one who wants to cool it, Austin. I want to see where this could go."

He rinsed, dipping his gaze down to the sink, then he gave her a sidelong glance. "Afterward, when I'm not responsible for your life. When this is resolved and we can move forward without a threat hanging over your head. I was told to be professional, and Kai is right."

"Kai?"

"My very perceptive and awesome boss."

"Oh."

He bent down and rinsed off his face, then came into the room. "I know this isn't optimal. Do you want someone else to handle this instead of me?"

She stiffened and her head jerked up. "No!"

The tension left his face as he walked over and slid his finger under her chin, his thumb caressing her jaw. "Then cut me some slack, Jenna. I'm dying here, too."

She curled her hand around his wrist and smiled softly. "Good. At least this isn't one-sided."

He crouched down and said, his face now serious, "No, this isn't one-sided in the least."

He smelled like citrus and spice, a heady combination that she was now associating with Austin. She reached out and ran her hands through his damp hair. "You are so noble. Why do you have to have so much integrity?"

He chuckled and rose. "You'll need to call your boss at the library. Let her know that you'll be out of town for a few days."

"Why? Where are we going?"

"To DC. I'm going to interview your ex-husband."

That froze her insides into an ice block. The thought that Robert could have been involved in murdering her cousin, wanting her dead, it was so surreal. He'd seemed so milquetoast about their relationship, at least as long as he'd been in control of it. She had to admit that she'd seen the flare of anger in his eyes more than once before he masked it. God forbid Robert should raise his voice.

"You should get going and get packed. We're leaving in two hours."

Austin went back into the bathroom and closed the door. She was apprehensive as she pushed the covers back, got out and started to make the bed. She'd really fled DC in desperation, the unhappiness of her failed marriage and her empty life making her long for more. It had all seemed so overwhelming and moving here, even temporarily, had been good for her. She'd found family and a job that she loved.

But she wasn't going back to hiding her head in the sand. She'd have to face whatever came, regardless of Robert's possible involvement or how she felt about Austin. She couldn't say it wasn't ironic that the man she had considered having an affair with all those years ago was now confronting her ex-husband about whether he'd made a premeditated decision to end her life. She bit her lip. That did sound like a man who considered her his property, no matter how their marriage had ended.

When Austin came out, he helped her make up the rest of the bed. "How many days are we going to be there?"

"Two, one to talk to him and the next day for me to do any follow-up. While you're there, you can get Sarah's will and maybe we can go out to Arlington Cemetery and you can see the plot they have available, and lock that in so you can bring Sarah home when the time comes."

She folded her arms across her chest and nodded. "It's a practical trip."

He looked delectable in a pair of charcoal-gray pants tucked into black, flat-soled, military-inspired lace-up boots and a simple cranberry pullover that looked like it was as soft as cashmere. The leather gun harness was buckled around his chest. He reached for his weapon on the bedside table and tucked it into his holster with the ease of a man used to handling something dangerous. "It is. I want you safe, Jenna. I'm going to make sure that happens."

She came around the bed and threw her arms around him. "You are so thoughtful and sweet, Austin."

He held her close, the feel of his hard body and firm grasp making her feel safe. He always made her feel so safe. "But I'm really glad you're armed and mean."

He chuckled. "Get going, sweetheart. I'll make us something to eat while you're showering."

Jenna headed toward the bathroom and took her shower.

Before long they were at the airport and Austin took the extra step to get his gun through security, but it was a very smooth process, with him showing his badge and presenting a special code.

Once they were on board, the flight took off on time. After landing in DC and hailing a cab, Jenna gave the driver her town house address. They were soon inside. Austin set down their baggage and said, "I'm going to get the lay of the land both inside and out. Then I have an appointment with your ex in about an hour."

There was a knock at the door and Austin walked over and looked out the side glass panel. Satisfied, he opened the door and a tall, very good-looking man stepped through. "Hello, I'm Special Agent Beau Jerrott from the Navy Yard. Your boss, Agent Talbot, requested backup."

Austin reached out and shook Beau's hand. "I'm Agent Beck." He turned to her and she clasped his warm hand. "Jenna Webb," Austin said.

"Pleased to meet you, but sorry for the circumstances."

He had a sexy Southern drawl to go with his stunning features. She noticed there was a ring on his finger and wasn't surprised this hunk was taken.

"So, you're Amber's former teammate?"

"Yes. How is Amber?"

"She's doing great, happily married, and one of the best people I've ever met."

"I know about the marriage. I was at her wedding. I thought you looked familiar."

Austin nodded. "I was just about to check out the area and the house. Want to come along?"

"Sounds like a plan." Beau turned to her. "Lock the door after we leave."

She complied as they started going over the property. She took their luggage upstairs and settled Austin's in the spare room, even though she wished he was sleeping with her—and more. Much more.

As she looked around the room, she felt strange, like she didn't belong anymore. Like the woman who had lived here had somehow passed on. She closed her eyes, thinking that was more true than not. She had moved on. Being with Sarah had given her confidence to look for a job, then she'd excelled at it. Sarah gave her the courage to continue.

She thought about Dustin again and how enthusiastic he was about reading, then she thought about the fact that the library couldn't afford any events because of the budget.

Maybe she could do something about that. Robert had known a lot of movers and shakers in DC. While she was here, she might look into how she could do something to help raise funds. She'd never thought of herself as someone who was bold enough to run around asking people for money, but after being an ambassador's wife, she sure had the connections and the determination.

The more she thought about it, the more she was hooked. She picked up her cell phone and looked through her contacts. Elise Sonnet. She was definitely a go-to personality. She was involved in DC high society, would have some ideas on who to talk to and how to get this going. She would have planned a visit with her while Jenna was here. Elise and Tom were such good friends of her father.

She pressed Elise's number and got her voice mail. "Elise, this is Jenna Webb. I'm back in town for a couple of days and was hoping to have a chance to meet with you. Call me back when you get a chance. Thanks and hope you're doing well."

When she came back downstairs, she pulled her laptop out of its case and went into the office located off the living room. She settled behind the mahogany desk, opened up the lid of the computer and started typing.

"Jenna?"

"In here," she called out and soon the two men materialized in the door frame.

"I'm heading out for the appointment. Beau will stay with you."

"Okay, thanks. I'll talk to you when you get back."

He nodded, then left.

Beau sat down in one of the leather chairs and said, "What's got you so interested with that fire in your eyes?"

"I'm thinking about fund-raising."

"Oh, that's worthwhile. What kind of fund-raising?"

"For libraries and literacy."

"Really worthwhile. Hey, you might talk to Piper Kaczewski. She used to be a senator here, but moved out to San Diego to be with Dexter, a Navy SEAL. You should ask Austin about her. She does fund-raising. I bet she could help."

"A former senator? I'd say. Thank you for that information."

"Sure. Amber keeps me up to date about all the goings-on in San Diego. She loves it there."

"It's a beautiful city." She smiled at him, and he smiled back. "All right, I'm going to check out the house and take another turn around the grounds." He paused in the doorway. "Austin mentioned that you had some errands to run, too."

"Yes, I do. Thanks for *babysitting* me."

He nodded. "You bet. NCIS is here for you, ma'am. I'll be back in a bit."

Her cell rang as soon as the front door closed. She saw it was Elise.

"Jenna, darling! It's so good to hear from you. I missed you bunches when you went out to California. I would love to get together. How about dinner?"

"That would be wonderful."

"I have a dinner party tonight, so that will be wonderful to have you attend. How many should I expect?"

"Three."

"Wonderful. Tom will be thrilled to see you, as well. I'll see you at six sharp."

"We'll be there and thank you so much, Elise."

She was going back to DC, back home, but it wasn't pleasant, nor any kind of homecoming. They were going back to see if her ex-husband—the man, whom she'd been with for twelve years, had tried to murder her.

Chapter 11

Austin parked at the curb, and turned off his engine. He thought briefly of Jenna alone with Beau, but Amber trusted him, so Austin would trust him, too. He stepped out of the car and faced Jenna's ex-husband's estate. The thought that she had lived here twisted through him. For six years, while he was finding his way after the marines and pissing his fiancée off by choosing NCIS over her, Jenna had been living in a loveless marriage as a trophy wife.

Georgetown, a neighborhood populated by the upper stratum in DC society, was quiet. The ambassador lived in a cold, narrow, three-story, modern-looking white house. The lawn was manicured but with very few plants and white stones on either side of the walk.

Tall hedges lined the backyard and when he looked at the upper floor, a curtain flicked. He pocketed his keys and walked the concrete path to the front door, which was also white.

When he got to Webb's front door, he lifted the brass knocker with a lion's head and let it drop. Compared to this sterile, almost vacant place, Jenna's home reflected her warm and generous personality. What did this home say about her ex-husband's nature?

After a few moments, the door opened and a woman said, "May I help you?" She was as austere as the residence.

He flashed his badge and said, "Yes, I'm here to meet with Ambassador Webb."

Her smile was tight. "He prefers to be addressed as Mr. Webb now that he's retired."

Austin nodded, and she stepped aside to allow him into the house. The foyer was as grand as the entrance, with a grandfather clock that chimed three times. The smell of lemon polish hung in the air; the surfaces, including the wood floor, gleamed.

The maid held out her hand for his coat; he shrugged out of it and she walked to a hall closet and tucked it inside. "This way," she said.

He followed her down the hall, passing the posh, furnished living room, and Austin stopped dead. Over the fireplace was a portrait of a much younger Jenna, looking exquisite in a beautiful blue dress that brought out her eyes, and long, dark hair, a stunning combination. The woman cleared her throat and Austin turned to find her frowning. They continued on, passing an elegant dining room and stylish powder room. She turned toward a set of wooden doors and slipped through, halting him with her hand up.

She disappeared. Moments later, the doors opened. Bookcases covered the walls from the twelve-foot-high ceiling to the polished pine floor. Here the scent of the ambassador's expensive tobacco was strongest, the furniture polish an undertone to leather chairs and the faint, musty-sweet aroma of books. An ornate mahogany desk dominated the floor space. Behind it, an entertainment center held shelves of sophisticated stereo equipment. But what caught Austin's attention were the number of photos of Jenna displayed in frames dotted here and there in the bookcases, with one on the desk next to the humidor, a tray of correspondence and an immaculate blotter.

Behind the desk sat Robert Webb, his features weathered and his eyes shuttered. Webb was now in his sixties, but still looked fit and healthy. "Special Agent Austin Beck. My, you've come up in the world, haven't you, boy?"

Austin tried not to let the condescending tone of Webb's voice taunt him into responding. He was a professional, and it was clear he didn't like being questioned, especially by someone who had once been under his command.

"With all due respect, Mr. Webb, I didn't come here for small talk."

He extended his hand toward one of the leather wing chairs in a cherry red. "Right down to business, eh? Let's get on with it then."

Austin settled in the chair as the woman who had let him in backed toward the door and closed it behind her.

"What can I do for you, Agent Beck?"

"I'm not sure if you're aware, but Lieutenant Sarah Taylor was murdered a few days ago in her apartment in El Centro, California. She was part of the Blue Angels team and a navy pilot, which makes that NCIS's responsibility."

He didn't say anything or react in any way, did not

seem surprised, puzzled or sympathetic. He just stared at Austin as if he hadn't spoken.

"She was Jenna's cousin. The only family she had left."

He blinked a couple of times and sat forward, setting his hands on the meticulous blotter. "What exactly does that have to do with me?"

"It seems that Sarah's killer made a blunder and murdered the wrong woman. Jenna was the target."

This time his brows rose and concern filled his eyes. "Jenna is in danger? Surely you're doing something to keep her safe."

"She's in good hands," Austin said.

"I'm sure she is. You were adept at handling her at the embassy, if I'm not mistaken." This time his eyes narrowed and something potent slipped through before it was immediately squelched. Had Webb suspected that he and Jenna had a thing for each other? Did he realize that embassy assignment had been the first step in Jenna leaving him? Webb had always struck him as an austere cold fish. One who did what was necessary and expected of him, but didn't go out of his way to do more. He had been a good ambassador, as evidenced by his many posts. But Austin had never liked him or respected him, which was colored by his attraction to Jenna, no doubt. Still, his dislike of Webb was more than his jealous feelings for the man who'd had the woman he'd wanted.

"I did my duty and followed your orders to the letter. It's a pity that when we left the embassy that day, you didn't even spare a glance backward for your beautiful wife."

Webb's face tightened, his eyes finally showing some emotion—anger. "It was a distracting time, and I put her in your hands. You even got a medal for your *duty* if I recall correctly. Risked your life to save wounded employees. You even got to meet the President."

Not about to go off on a tangent and get distracted, Austin stuck to the point. "Now you and Jenna are divorced. How do you feel about that?"

Webb reclined back into his chair. "It was amicable, and I gave her what she wanted. I've always striven to give Jenna what she wanted, except a few things that didn't fit with my lifestyle."

Like children, Austin thought, but didn't say out loud. "Not exactly answering the question. I want to know how you feel about the divorce. That would be an emotion, Mr. Webb. Mad? Glad? Sad? Any of those would be an appropriate response."

His eyes flashed and narrowed. "I was surprised and disappointed that she'd made such a rash decision, but I couldn't change her mind. Sometimes you just have to know when to let go," he said flatly.

Austin wasn't sure he had let go at all. He had to wonder if Webb had kept tabs on Jenna—whether he was so consumed with his bruised ego that he wanted Jenna dead.

Austin picked up the framed photograph on the desk. He studied it, got lost in the beauty of Jenna's smile. Webb reached forward and snatched the photo, then set it precisely back in its spot. He hadn't let go, not in a pig's eye. The portrait and these photos said he was still hung up on his ex-wife.

"So, it stands to reason that if Jenna was the target as you have deduced," the man said disdainfully, making it clear he didn't think Austin could investigate himself out of a brown paper bag, "you'd head for the most obvious suspect."

"You," Austin said, leaning forward, his voice ringing with accusation.

"Me. Exactly. I'm sure you'll want to know where I was when poor Sarah died." He said it without a speck of remorse or empathy.

"That would be a good start," Austin said.

"When was she murdered?" he said as if he was completely bored by the conversation.

He named the time and date.

Webb sat there for a moment, then leaned forward and tapped the spacebar of his computer. He consulted the screen for a moment, then said, "I was at a fundraiser that evening, here in DC. So, you see, I couldn't have killed her."

Maybe not with his bare hands, but Webb had resources and the motive to kill Jenna. Spurned ex-husband with a bad case of narcissism. The perfect setup for murder. Narcissists usually talked mostly about themselves, believed they were superior to everyone and tended to view women as playthings. They had an inflated sense of self-importance and a noted lack of empathy.

"Can you think of anyone who would want to harm Jenna?"

"Not of my acquaintance. I have no idea who she's been consorting with since she left me. But Jenna is a lamb, gentle and caring. She needs someone to help her navigate life, a guiding hand. I regret I can't help you any further than that."

"She is quite capable, Mr. Webb. At least from what I could see."

"I'm sure you've seen…a lot of her," he bit out, then

smoothed his hand down his shirt as if he was upset he'd shown any kind of jealousy.

Male narcissists directed their anger mostly toward women because they held the rejection keys. For Webb, that rejection must have hit so hard, he'd been completely enraged. But his sense of decorum helped him to effectively hide it from Jenna and the people around him. Austin was convinced that Webb might not have put his hands around Sarah's neck and squeezed the life out of her, but he would have hired someone and given them strict orders.

Webb didn't have a problem with everyone. He had a problem with people who rejected him. Jenna's husband was a patriarch. There was no surprise he took an innocent, pampered and sheltered woman as his wife, a beauty that would make him look good.

Even now, with the divorce final, he still had pictures of Jenna to remind him that he'd once had her under his thumb.

Webb rose. "I'm sorry that you wasted your time coming all the way here to talk to me. Marta will show you out." On cue, the door opened and the stern-faced woman stood there.

"I'm not quite finished. I'll need names of people who saw you at the fund-raiser." Austin reached into his back pocket, pulled out a pad and threw it down on Webb's desk.

Webb looked toward the door and with a wave of his hand sent Marta away. He settled back into his chair and started writing on the pad.

Finally Webb shoved it back at him. "I'm going to follow every lead, talk to every person, pull your phone and financial records. If you had anything to do with this, there won't be a rock you can hide under."

"This sounds like intimidation to me. Perhaps I need to contact the Secretary of the Navy."

Austin smiled at the threat, snatched up the pad and rose, tucking his card into the corner of Jenna's picture frame. "If you think of anyone who would want to harm Jenna, you give me a call. Have a good day, Ambassador. I'll show myself out."

Webb didn't even look down, his stony gaze telling Austin that he was jealous of him. He was aware Austin had a thing for Jenna back in Ja'arbah. He deliberately threw them together. Had he been spying on them? Had he seen the kiss?

At this point it didn't matter. Jenna's safety was all he cared about now.

Austin paused at the door. "Give SECNAV my regards."

Austin got back to the town house and entered using his key, but he suspected Beau and Jenna were doing errands since Beau's car was gone from the driveway. He settled down at her kitchen table and opened his laptop and got to work.

"Let's see if you're hiding anything, Ambassador."

Jenna chose a purple cocktail dress with black-and-purple lace at the shoulders, a chiffon bodice and skirt with a sumptuous charmeuse belt. The back had a plunging lace V and a silky bow. She paired them with black patent leather heels. She wanted to look good, mostly because she wanted to garner Elise's help. She'd be going with Austin and Beau in tow, and she felt nervous to have her bodyguards subjected to the DC high society party. But she couldn't go without them; that would make her much too nervous. Austin wouldn't have agreed anyway.

As she pinned up her hair, she was determined not to allow her current predicament to stop her from living her life. She wasn't going to hide anymore. She grabbed her black velvet swing coat and her purse. Exiting her bedroom, she went to Austin's door and knocked. It opened quickly and she caught her breath.

She expected some variation of his surfer chic look, but instead he was wearing a suit jacket over a black T-shirt and black pants, black dress boots on his feet. He looked…devastating, the chocolate stubble on his face just showing and only accentuating his strong jaw. She just stared at him like she'd never seen him before.

"What? Did you think I was going to embarrass you?"

She jerked out of her sensuous haze. "No. Not at all. You just look so…good."

With a twinkle in those sultry gray eyes, he smiled, his gaze going over her in slow motion. "Wow. You look stunning." The hint of amusement instantly faded, replaced by a glint that was more heated, far more potent, far more intent. Far more male.

"Thank you." Austin looked away, the muscles in his jaw clenching, annoyance flaring in his eyes, his mouth compressing into a hard line as he took the coat off her arm and helped her into it, his warm hands lingering on her shoulders while the fabric settled against her body. She stood there for a moment, so conscious of him as a man. Experiencing a head rush from his hot touch, Jenna closed her eyes, her pulse going wild. And she remembered that first instant when he'd entered her, when she'd felt the full thrust of him, and she tightened her grip on her small, glittering purse, her breath jamming up in her chest.

Without consciously thinking, she leaned back into him, and he buried his face into her hair with a soft sound. She closed her eyes as he breathed deep, as if this was the last breath of a drowning man and he was going under.

"Jenna," he whispered into her curls and she wanted to turn in his arms and kiss that tantalizing mouth, feel the burn of that stubble against her cheeks, her lips, her neck, breasts, anywhere and everywhere.

His hands squeezed her shoulders, and he let her go. She found her footing and took a breath as she headed toward the stairs. Grabbing the handrail to support her trembling body, she started down. Beau was waiting and he had already shown up this morning in a very nice suit with a gray tie.

He stared at her as she came down, but didn't say a thing. His admiring gaze said what he was thinking. She set the alarm and he held the door for her as she and Austin went through.

She gave him directions to Elise's Bethesda home, where they pulled up and parked at the curb across the street. The white-and-gray showpiece of a house was lit from within, the lower level a gray, tan and white fieldstone, surrounded by wrought-iron railing up to the porch with peaked gables. Austin slipped his arm under her elbow as they climbed to the wide, nine-pane-windowed mahogany door.

It opened before they could knock and as they entered the foyer, she heard, "Jenna!" Her dark-haired friend, wearing a smile that was crinkling the corners of her handsome face, rushed forward out of a crowd of three women, who had all turned to look at them as they arrived. Elise's eyes were on her, but the three women were more interested in her escorts.

Elise threw her arms around Jenna and hugged her tight, her winsome body feeling solid and warm.

"It's so good to see you." Then she whispered in a rush against Jenna's ear, "I'm so, so sorry. Robert's here. He came with some people we invited without my knowledge. I would have warned you."

Jenna froze inside at the thought of seeing Robert after all this time and with the threat of death hanging over her head. Austin was convinced her ex-husband was behind Sarah's murder.

She turned to Austin and he didn't miss the paleness of her face. He gave her a quizzical look and she shook her head slightly. "This is Austin Beck and his friend Beau Jerrott." They had already agreed there was no need to alarm Elise and her guests by introducing them as her bodyguards.

When they parted, Elise gave her an apologetic look, and her husband, Tom, looked agitated as he hugged her tight. He was tall and fit with a bald pate. What hair he had was shaved close to his head. He looked more like a hard-charging general than a politician. "Sorry, kitten," he whispered. Tom and Elise were her father's oldest friends and she'd spent more time here with them and their rambunctious and totally cool sons than with anyone else. Their sons were grown now; one was an attorney and the other was pursuing a military career. Tom was one of the high muckety-mucks on the Hill.

As Jenna mingled with the people at the party, some she knew and others who were strangers, she noticed Robert talking to a man near the hors d'oeuvres table.

He glanced in her direction, his cold look only making her palms sweat. She didn't want to be intimidated by him, so she squared her chin and turned away. She ignored him all through dinner and conversed with Elise and Tom mostly. Once dinner was done, Jenna said, "Could I have a private word with you, Elise?"

"Of course," she said. "Let's go into Tom's study." Austin followed at a safe distance, watching her as Jenna deliberately left the door open. She sat down in one of the stylish wing chairs, and Elise took the sofa. "What did you want to talk about?"

"Fund-raising."

Elise's brows rose and she smiled. "A subject near and dear to my heart. What did you have in mind?"

"I wanted to raise money for libraries and literacy. I'm just figuring this all out and it's new and intriguing. I know I have a lot to learn and consider. I was wondering if you could help me get started."

"I sure can. I know the director of the Institute of Museum and Library Services. She's a valuable resource. Also, you should contact the National Library Association."

"That's a good start. Would you be willing to call her or give me her number?"

"Sure. This is exciting. You're going to get involved with raising money for very worthy causes. I'm proud of you."

"It's time I find something I enjoy, and since I don't have to make a living, I can put my efforts into something that I'm passionate about." Elise nodded, sipping at her tea. "Do you know Piper Kaczewski? She's married now to a Navy SEAL, Dexter Kaczewski."

"Yes, I know Piper well—she used to be married to Senator Brad Jones."

"The one who was murdered? I read about that in the news."

"Yes, she took over his seat to serve out his term. I've met that hunky, new husband of hers. Yowza. You know he saved her life?" She explained briefly and Jenna was wowed by the story. "She's opened an non-profit office in San Diego as a fund-raiser. You should definitely look her up. She would be a great asset to help you get started or maybe even take you on board. She's always looking for good people."

"That sounds pretty perfect. I'll definitely contact her. Thank you so much. I knew you would have good contacts and advice."

"Anytime. Now spill about your two hunky escorts. Which one is yours?"

Jenna laughed and said, "Neither."

"Now I know you're fibbing. The way that young man with the beautiful gray eyes looks at you, it's clear something is going on."

"It's complicated right now, so, yes, I'm interested in Austin and he's interested in me."

"Well, I wouldn't wait too long to sail that boat if you get my drift."

Jenna flushed, her face hot.

"Oh." Elise leaned forward and patted her arm. "You already have. Good for you, and I say full steam ahead." She winked.

When Elise rose, she gave Jenna a soft smile. "I'll call Piper for you tomorrow and tell her your plans, pave the way for you," she said as she left the room. Jenna remained preoccupied with her thoughts about how to go about fund-raising, the calls she needed to make and her determination to see it through, and after a few minutes, Austin walked in and said, "How did it go?"

Jenna stood and turned toward him, getting hit again by how amazing he looked tonight. "She was the right person to talk to. Thanks for bringing me here and being so supportive, Austin."

The instant he moved, Jenna's senses went wild, and she closed her eyes and drew a shaky breath, trying to curb the feelings inside her. Opening her eyes, she looked at him, almost afraid to move for fear of doing something to break the spell. His expression compressed into hard lines, he stared at her, his eyes giving nothing away. Then he held out his hand, and Jenna let out a tremulous sigh and took it, her grip urgent and tense, almost desperate. He held her gaze for an instant, his hair shining in the soft glow of the desk lamp, lending a hushed, romantic aura to the room.

He looked dark, foreboding and unapproachable, but the look in his eyes made her heart pound and her knees go weak, and she swallowed hard. There was a flare of emotion in his eyes, and he tightened his grip on her hand and slowly, so slowly, stroked her palm with his thumb. It was too much. That one slow, sensual touch put her in such sensory overload that the glow from the light made her skin feel too tight. Lacing his fingers through hers, he drew her toward him.

"I promised myself I would behave," he whispered. "But Jenna…" He trailed off, his voice thick with strain. He went still, then released an unsteady sigh and slid his hand against the nape of her neck, spanning the base of her head.

He walked her back behind the door until she was

pressed up against the wall. His chest expanding, he turned her head and covered her mouth with his hot, soft lips. He cupped her breast, kneading slowly, his thumb rubbing rhythmically over one hard, aching nipple. With a honeyed gasp, she opened to him, the thrust of his tongue sending hot, weakening need through her.

Moaning softly against his mouth, desperate for the feel of him, she reached for his waistband, an avalanche of wanting compressing her lungs as she ran her hand over the bulge in his pants. He shuddered and crushed her against him, grasping her wrists and trapping them against the wall above her head.

Jenna was lost. Lost to the hunger. Lost to the sensations pumping through her. Lost to the urgency of his questing hand, slipping beneath her skirt to cup her butt as he pressed his heated groin against her. His mouth and teeth scored her neck.

He let go of her wrists as he thrust against her, sliding his hand into the waistband of her panties, to the wet core of her. She cried out, the sound muffled against his mouth as he found her center and brushed his fingers against her, over and over again.

The sting of pleasure coasted through her as she kissed him, his mouth hot and hard against her lips, her breath ragged. Her climax rocked through her as his thumb played her like an instrument, masterful and knowing how to get the best music out of her. She came so hard, her knees buckled, but he had her around the waist as if he knew she would collapse.

"Jenna," he whispered over and over again. He waited a beat, then his fingers were back, making her come again.

He took her hand as the stars faded and molded it

over his erection straining behind his fly. She pulled at his pants, got the zipper down so she could delve inside and find him hard, hot and smooth. She worked him against her palm. His breathing harsh and labored, his body rigid with tension, he twisted her head back and trailed hot, openmouthed kisses down the arch of her neck. "Please, Jenna," he groaned and rocked his hips against her hand. "Please."

She choked out his name as he moved her panties out of the way, his hand sliding over her butt, then to her knee as he lifted her leg.

She guided him to her and a violent tremor shuddered through him, a low groan breaking from him as she directed him into her. He was so rigid and thick and even as he wanted her, she could tell he was trying to hold back, but she didn't want his restraint. She needed him hard, deep and out of control. Feeling her whole body collect and tighten, she arched her head back and lifted her hips to meet him, choking out his name. He shuddered again, then clutched her against him and drove into her again and again and again, finally sending her over the edge of a high, splintering chasm. He thrust into her once more, grinding against her, then stiffened, an agonized groan wrenched from him as he climaxed deep inside her.

After a few minutes, Austin took a breath and said, "Jenna." He let her go. She adjusted her clothes, and he tucked and zipped up. "I can't seem to keep my hands off you." He frowned and brushed at the wisps of hair at her temple, then bracketed her face. "At a party? People in the next room and…your ex. That has got to be a first for me. Not very professional."

"Austin, we're obviously very attracted to each other.

There's nothing wrong with what we did." She closed her eyes and sighed. "Not a darn thing."

He chuckled, but when she opened her eyes, his expression was still pensive. "Come on. Don't beat yourself up over it. It's bigger than both of us."

"That's what worries me."

She reached up to her hair. "How do I look?" she said.

His features softened. "Beautiful."

Her brows rose, and she smiled. "Disheveled, mussed up, a mess?"

His chest heaved and he rubbed her bottom lip with his thumb. "All those things, but still freaking beautiful."

"Do you think people will know what we were doing?"

"I should care about that, but I don't."

"You are incorrigible."

"Come on. I'll shield you into the bathroom."

He clasped her hand and steered her out of the study right to the powder room. The conversations continued to flow and no one seemed to notice them at all. She ducked inside and laughed at her reflection in the mirror. She positively glowed with happiness, her cheeks rosy, her eyes bright, but she definitely had to do something with her hair and reapply her lipstick.

Emerging with her exterior looking together and proper and her insides anything but, she was a mess of tingling awareness, her thoughts dirty and unkempt as she wanted more of Austin, and not just the physical.

The party was breaking up, several people in the foyer saying their goodbyes to Elise and Tom. She passed the bar, and a hand snaked out and grabbed ahold of her upper arm. Robert's hard eyes and pinched face thrust into hers. "I want to talk to you."

Austin and Beau were a few steps from her. When she gasped, they turned to look and started forward, but she held up her hand. It was time she dealt with Robert. Once and for all.

"You're hurting me," she said, yanking her arm away, but he only squeezed it tighter. His eyes narrowed as if that had been his intention. "What do you want?" she snapped, keeping her voice low. She could see Tom watching them with a protective and militant look on his face, but Elise grabbed his arm, her eyes very concerned. Jenna gave her a reassuring look and a quick shake of her head to Tom. He relaxed but kept his eyes on her.

"You cheated on me in Ja'arbah. Didn't you?" His eyes, filled with hatred, cut to Austin. "With him," he hissed.

She lifted her chin, well aware of Robert's machinations. "And you threw me in his path. Was that some kind of test?"

"Yes! You failed."

"I will admit that I kissed him, and I thought about sleeping with him. But that's all. Your twisted games make me sick. I realized over the years that if I was that attracted to Austin, then I couldn't be in love with you. I was too young when I got married. You knew I wanted children, and you never said one word about it." He opened his mouth, but she cut him off. "Don't say that you did. You're controlling, self-centered and cold. You had no faith in me, and I was nothing to you but a pretty trophy wife. Now let me go before I allow Austin to do his job."

He didn't just let her go, he shoved her hard away from him, and she hit the bar, using it to keep herself from falling. He then pierced Austin with a look full of disdain and strode away, then out the door. She closed her eyes and rubbed at her upper arm. Austin, Beau, Tom and Elise all converged on her. Thank God most of the guests had already left.

"Are you all right?" Austin said. She took a breath and nodded.

She accepted all their concerned words, and Tom's angry declaration that Robert Webb was no longer welcome in his house.

She realized that Robert had masked quite a bit of his anger and frustration at her rejection. Their divorce might have been amicable, but that had been a smoke screen. She wondered with a shiver down her spine what that smoke screen was obscuring.

And if Sarah had paid the ultimate price for Jenna's sins.

Chapter 12

When they got home, Beau said, "I'll be down here until midnight, then Agent Vin Fitzgerald will relieve me, so don't be alarmed if you hear voices and the front door."

Austin nodded. He hadn't left her side since Robert's outburst. Her arm throbbed where he'd held her and where it had cracked against the bar.

He walked her to her room, and that's where he stopped. "Austin, please. I don't want to sleep alone. I want to be with you." His face was tight with strain and his eyes tormented as he fought against his duty and his desire. "I respect your position, but this isn't a normal situation, and we are involved. I don't care about protocol anymore."

"I just don't want this to get any more complicated than it is, Jenna. I shouldn't have touched you in the first place, especially with circumstances being so unsettled for you. It makes me remember the embassy and how jacked up we were on fear, adrenaline and lust."

"This isn't the embassy and we're different people.

We have a fully capable NCIS agent downstairs watching out for us."

"For you. I'm watching, too."

"Of course you are. Vigilant and intense as usual."

He looked away, and she consoled herself that his eyes gave away the battle going on inside his head. "We can just snuggle and talk."

He let out a short laugh. "Yeah, right, Jenna. We both know what will happen if we're in the same bed together." Resting his jaw against her temple, he gathered her close. "A houseful of people, and I couldn't keep my erection to myself."

"Erection. You had an erection during the party before you came into the study?" She reached back and opened the door. "Tell me what brought that on."

He gave her a look that told her he knew exactly what she was doing. "You in the dress. The moment I saw you I got hard."

She reached down and slid her hand over his groin. "Like you are now?"

He groaned softly. "You're still wearing the dress. I guess it hasn't worn off yet."

She pushed the suit jacket off his wonderful shoulders, molding her hands over the muscles on the sides of his chest, bypassing his shoulder holster and weapon, deliberately brushing over his nipple. "You came at the party, didn't you?"

He made a soft male sound of pleasure that she knew she could never get enough of. The jacket dropped to the floor and Austin, breathing raggedly, caught the door with the heel of his boot and nudged it closed. Jenna smiled. Seduction was new to her. She'd never had her way with a man before Austin. She liked the feeling of being in control.

"I came deep inside you." He shrugged out of the holster and set it on the dresser. "I liked putting my scent on you. Maybe that was male domination, to show your ex-husband that you're mine now. I wanted to kill him when he treated you like that." He rubbed at her arm lightly. "That's going to bruise."

Anger and resentment curled in her as she murmured, "He meant for it to hurt."

"What did he say to you?"

"I'll tell you what he said, but not now. I'm busy."

She couldn't get enough of looking at him. She reached for the hem of the T-shirt and pushed it up over his hard, washboard stomach, her breath catching at the beauty of Austin's body. The shirt hadn't even cleared his ribs before her mouth was on him, her tongue trailing over each ridge. His hands went to her head, and tightened when she scored her nails over his lower abdomen. She moved her mouth up, pushing the shirt as she went and again, she stopped. She breathed in the scent of his skin, placing small kisses against that wall of heated muscle, then she covered the flat disk of his nipple. His chest heaved when she sucked, then used her tongue against the now rigid tip. Gripping her arm, he gazed down at her, his eyes hazed with sensation as she continued with her slow, soft exploration.

"Take it off," he whispered and she slid her hands over his warm flesh and pulled the T-shirt over his head. "Strip me bare, Jenna. I'm naked with you. I have no armor left. No reason, no will."

She reached for his waistband, cupping him firmly but gently through the fabric. He stiffened and groaned, twisting his head, but he didn't try to make her hurry. She unbuckled, undid and unzipped him as the garment fell to his ankles. He toed out of his boots and then she was eagerly pushing him back on the bed. Stripping off her panties, she climbed on top of him and took him inside.

Nothing mattered. Nothing but him. Nothing but her. Nothing but them.

Later, after the passion had played out, she rested against his chest, moving her fingertips over and over his satiny skin. The night was hushed, but she heard voices downstairs and the opening and closing of the front door. Vin had arrived. They were protected, and she loved every minute of being with Austin.

She curled her leg over the top of his, flattening her palm and mapping the contours of his chest. Too spent to move, not wanting to speak, she savored the heady sensation of contentment, loving the feel of his smooth skin beneath her touch. She found a ridge of scar tissue on his shoulder and lightly traced it. Dredging up energy from somewhere, she said, her voice husky, "This where you got shot?"

Stirring heavily, Austin reached up and cupped her hand, rubbing the back with his palm. Then he lifted it to his mouth and placed a kiss there. "Yes. It bled so much because it hit a good-sized vein. Lost too much blood too fast and passed out." His voice was gruff. "Not the way I wanted to say goodbye to you."

She rose up and bent down and kissed the area, sighing. "I was torn up about you getting hurt. Robert gave me reports about your condition. I was glad to have them."

"I was surprised you didn't come to Walter Reed to see me. Webb did. Thanked me for my service."

"What?" She sat up a little straighter. "You were in DC? Robert didn't tell me. All he said was that you were treated overseas, then sent home to recover. Damn him," she bit out. "I would have come to Walter Reed to see you." She bit her lip, her insides twisting at the thought of what would have happened if she had gone there so shortly after the embassy takeover. "I wonder how it would have changed the course of our lives if I had. I'm not sure I would have wanted to say goodbye to you a second time. I was frankly afraid."

"I understand why you would have been afraid, Jenna. This thing between us was intense."

She nodded, her throat thick. "I was so lost after the embassy takeover. I was raw about not having children and thinking about a bleak future being nothing but arm candy. It took me a long time to get over that... and over...you."

He turned his head and opened his eyes, blinking a few times. "You got over me?"

She dropped her head. Then shook it. "No. I only thought I had. You were between us after that. Your courage fueled mine and as the years passed, I got more vocal and unhappy until finally we were living separate lives. I think Robert was okay with that."

"Foolish jackass."

He pushed up on his elbow and rubbed the now black and blue fingermarks on her arm. He frowned. "I think it's him, Jenna. My gut tells me it's him. Except I have to prove it. Tomorrow, I'm digging into his life."

She nodded, rose up and kissed his jaw. "I know you are," she whispered. His mouth was moist, warm and slightly swollen. She drew her thumb along his bottom lip, thinking about the care he'd taken with her. "He accused me of cheating on him with you."

His eyes narrowed. "What did you say?"

"First off, he threw me at you on purpose. He said it was a test, and I failed. I told him he was wrong. Only that I kissed you and thought about sleeping with you." She closed her eyes and leaned her head against his jaw. "I think he knew he was starting to lose control and it had something to do with you."

This time his eyes widened. "You thought about sleeping with me?" He looked away. "Damn, I was so close after that kiss to taking you right there in full battle dress, the embassy under attack. Damn, my duty…" His voice was pitched low when he said, "I'm glad I didn't compromise you, Jenna. Part of me wished I had, but you were married, and I was with someone. It would have been wrong."

She nodded. "Maybe, but we don't have those constraints now. We can explore as much as we want."

He grabbed her chin and looked deeply into her eyes, and she got just as lost in the gray fog of his. He dragged her mouth close, adjusting the angle of her head as he kissed her. Releasing a long sigh, he kissed her again. There was a solemn tone to his voice as he responded, "This case will be over eventually, Jenna. I go back to Pendleton and your life is here in DC. You've got to bring Sarah home. Lay her to rest. Figure out what you want to do. I don't want to get in the way of that or muddle your thinking. This has been…exciting, satisfying and forbidden. Right back to that—the forbidden. I can't help thinking everything is fueled by that."

"I don't think so," she said, placing a string of kisses down his neck, shifting her naked hips closer to his, her breasts pressing against his chest. "But I see your point. It's smart to have a clear head when making final decisions. I can't thank you enough for helping me navigate the funeral arrangements. Sarah deserves fanfare—and justice. If Robert is behind this…he definitely should pay." Anger creeped into her voice and settled like a hard knot in her belly.

He brushed back the hair at her temple, then lowered his head and kissed her. Neither of them spoke for several moments, content with gentle stroking and even gentler kisses. Making room for her knee between his, he nestled her head on his shoulder, his touch caressing as he stroked her hip, his hand so warm and big. After a comfortable silence, he tucked in his chin and brushed a kiss against her forehead. "Did you get her will yesterday?"

Drowsy with contentment, she sleepily watched the shadow of the moonlight fall across the bed, comfortable in the cradle of his arms. "Yes, Beau took me to the bank, and I got it out of the safe deposit box. It made me so sad. I truly thought when I put it in there, I wouldn't need to even look at it for a long time. Barring an accident, Sarah was so competent in the air." He had been quiet and stoic while helping her, it had to have brought up memories about his dad. "I'm sorry if this stirs up emotions about your dad's death. That must have been very hard for you."

He didn't answer right away. Finally he shifted and settled back against the pillows, his arm curling around her and dragging her close. "It was. My dad was career military. He was sorry about the time he had missed with us, my sisters and me. But we had some good times after he retired and was home more. My mom loved it."

"Sounds like you had an idyllic life."

He hesitated, then said, his voice quiet, "It was, for the most part. My mom had a firm hand, but she's the one who taught me to surf. We lived on the ocean, but my mom couldn't bear the memories of the house and she sold it and moved to a town house a year ago. She still does the holidays up and loves to cook, so home-made meals are always waiting for me."

"I think I would like your mom very much."

"She'd love you."

Avoiding his gaze, he carefully tucked her hair behind her ear. He finally spoke again, his tone gruff. "The worry about him not coming home was written on my mom's face every day. When she lost him, she was devastated, and it made me glad that I wasn't in the marines anymore. Her worry transferred to me when I was serving. She was really scared after the embassy takeover, but I was determined to be career. But as you know, that all got waylaid."

Cupping his jaw, she stroked the curve of his cheekbone with her thumb. "You're still in a dangerous profession. Does she worry about you being an NCIS agent?"

"Some, but not as much. At least I'm not a world away with a whole country trying to kill me." He smiled and she smiled back at him. "My sisters are there and have been since my dad died. It's one of the biggest reasons I wanted to come back to California. I was lucky to get the San Diego posting, but had to spend a couple of years in Minnesota. Brr."

She nodded and shivered. "Brr, indeed."

"I'm sorry about you losing your family, Jenna. Talk about hard."

"Yes, terribly. My dad was wonderful, but overprotective. My mom died while she was overseas working on an architectural project. She owned her own firm, but my dad sold it outright when she died. He was devastated. I was the spitting image of her, and I think sometimes he'd look at me and think if he wrapped me up in cotton wool, I'd be safe. He'd be livid to know that Robert became an ambassador and took me all over the place. But Ja'arbah was by far the most dangerous of his posts."

Covering her mouth in a drugging kiss, his fingers snagging in her hair, Austin caught her by the hips, drawing her fully on top of him, then settled her between his thighs, running his hands along her rib cage until he reached her breasts. His touch sent spirals of sensation through her, and Jenna closed her eyes. "I never want to be controlled like that again. Ever," she whispered, yielding to his mouth.

Afterward, Austin had drifted off, but she was unable to sleep for the fluttering of anxiety churning in her gut. This was a fantasy come true, but at some point she was going to be forced to deal with her life. She couldn't stay in El Centro—there was nothing for her there anymore—and this trip had been temporary. She had finally figured out the path she wanted to take in her life. Working to give the gift of reading to anyone who wanted it filled her with joy and purpose. Kids like Dustin would be able to reap the benefits.

But this time with Austin was a gift, and she wanted to hold on to that for as long as she could. She was realistic enough to know that there would be countless hazards along the way, and any one of them could destroy something so fragile and new. That realization filled her with such cold hard dread that it sat like a rock in the pit of her stomach.

And there was Austin. He was worried about both of them falling victim to the adrenaline and heat they had generated under dire circumstances, concerned that after things evened out, so would the passion.

The only thing that was for certain was the here and now. She had made up her mind that she was going to celebrate the gift she had been given for as long as it was hers to hold. She would make the most of what she had today and worry about tomorrow tomorrow.

She dozed fitfully, woke up from a nightmare to the warmth of Austin's body. He snuggled her close, murmuring something that she couldn't make out. It comforted her to have him beside her. As soon as he dozed off again, she slipped out of bed. It was early—about six—and she figured the man downstairs guarding them was probably hungry.

She showered and then dressed. When she came out of the bathroom, Austin was on his back, snoring slightly, his hair mussed, his golden lashes thick on his cheeks. She walked around the bed and pulled the covers over his naked chest, then bent down and kissed him on his slack mouth.

Exiting the room, she went downstairs. At the sound of her footsteps, a tall, dark man came into the foyer. Geez, NCIS was a handsome-man magnet. His face smoothed out when he saw her. "Ms. Webb, good morning."

"Agent Fitzgerald?"

"Vin. It's nice to meet you. Where's Austin?"

"Still sleeping."

He chuckled. "That California boy slacker."

She smiled. "He's actually a hardworking guy."

"I'm sure." He grinned. "I was just kidding."

She nodded. "I thought you could use some breakfast. How would you like your eggs?"

She needed to stay busy to keep her mind off Sarah's murder, Robert's possible involvement in it and the very delectable Austin.

Chapter 13

Austin woke up to an empty bed—a bad start to his day. He was already used to having her warm body against him, and he wanted it to stay that way. Dammit. He pushed away the memories of his loneliness and sat up.

He had more pressing matters to deal with. Like what a complete idiot he was. He'd acted like a love-starved teenager last night, but that dress… Damn that dress and her delectable body in it. The minute he saw her, he'd wanted to do her up against the wall.

Her ex-husband had been fuel for that fire, like he'd said last night. He wanted to mark her with his scent. Make Webb understand that she was his. Austin shook his head and ran his hand through his hair.

She was his—for now. Who knew what would happen after she went back to DC? She might decide that everything had been out of control and their relationship was based on nothing but hormones, the need to feel safe and adrenaline.

Throwing back the covers and snatching up his

clothes, his anger at himself already enough to make him jerky, he slipped out of her room to his and threw his clothes on the floor. He should hang up the jacket, but he instead went to his laptop and opened it. He was about to dial NCIS when he realized he was stark naked. Wouldn't that surprise the hell out of Drea.

He went to his suitcase and donned a loose pair of charcoal sweatpants and grabbed the black tee he'd worn last night. Smoothing down his hair, he sent the call through.

Drea's face appeared as soon as the screen showed the office.

"Hey, how's DC?"

"Cold and rainy. Did you finish looking into Webb's financials?"

With a disappointed look, she nodded. "There's no large withdrawals, Austin. Nothing. I also checked with the airlines and he didn't leave DC."

"Great," Austin muttered, anger churning. "Phone records?"

"Nothing suspicious."

He swore loud and long. Drea turned to look over her shoulder while she was cuing the volume control on her remote to Low. Austin rubbed his hands over his face and sat back against the headboard.

"This case has no damn leads. None. I'm positive he's behind it. If he didn't leave DC, he hired someone to kill Jenna. If nothing on his phone is suspicious, then he's using a burner. He's behind her getting trapped at work, hunted like an animal. I want him!"

Drea stepped closer to the screen and said, her voice hard, "Then this isn't the way to go about it, Austin. You need to keep your emotions under control. I know from experience that losing it doesn't help anyone. Not you, not the victim, not the family members. Get a grip, and get it now. Kai is not happy about any of this. She's ready to pull you out. So calm down."

He took a breath and had to admit that he'd needed that stern talking-to. She was right. He was letting his frustration and anger get in the way of solid investigation and reasoning. He took a breath, then let it out. Looking away from the screen he wrestled with his annoyance. When he looked back to the screen, Drea relaxed her frown. "Thank you, probie, for that. I needed a dose of cold water."

She nodded. "Look, if you're sure about him, I will keep digging. But right now, there's nothing to charge him with. When are you coming back to California?"

"Tomorrow. We have a morning flight."

"Okay. Hopefully I'll find something between then and now, but do the interviews for his alibi. Stick to process."

"Yes, ma'am."

One corner of her mouth quirked. "I'm not going to address you as 'sir,' so you can forget it."

He laughed half-heartedly, still peeved.

"In the meantime, don't go over to Webb's house with rubber hoses or brass knuckles to get a confession."

He rolled his eyes. "I won't, and I don't need rubber hoses and brass knuckles. A good, old-fashioned fist to the face would make me feel a whole lot better."

"Curb that."

"I'll talk to you tomorrow. Have some good news for me." He slammed the laptop lid closed and gathered up clean clothes. Frustration eating him up, he undressed and tossed the clothes out the open door near his suitcase. He turned the water on full blast, then stepped in. He roughly soaped himself, then closed his eyes and let the water beat down on him, using the stinging spray to ease the tension left over from his conversation with Drea. Bracing both hands on the wall of the shower stall, he bent his head and made himself let go of the tension, focusing on the hammering spray and the heat. He was on borrowed time here. If he didn't come up with a solid lead, Kai was going to pull him off this case. It could go cold or even worse, Jenna could—

He cut off that thought. That wasn't going to happen.

He'd make damn sure of it.

The hot water was starting to fade when he finally got out, and the room was full of steam. He made a cursory effort to dry himself, then pulled on a clean pair of pants, not bothering to do up the snap. Avoiding his reflection in the fogged mirror, he reached for the can of shaving cream, his mood no better.

There was a knock at the bedroom door and he said, "Come in."

Jenna poked her head in and smiled at him. "I heard the shower. How would you like your eggs?"

"Over easy."

She eyed him. "Talk about easy on the eyes."

He draped a towel around his neck, then smiled, absently rubbing a drop of water off his bare chest. "Why don't you come over here and say that?" His voice was husky.

She gave him a soft chuckle and shook her head. "Do I look like I was born yesterday? You'll have me tied up and there won't be any eggs to eat."

"Mmm-hmm. Tied up. I like the sound of that. I do have my handcuffs." His voice was even huskier.

"You are a very bad man."

Amusement tugged at his mouth, his frustration and anger were pushed away. He couldn't seem to hold on to them when she was near. A flood of sensual memories poured over him.

His eyes must have broadcast what he was thinking. She blushed. "I'm going to make you breakfast now. You're getting bacon," she called over her shoulder before she closed the door.

"I love bacon," he yelled back.

The flight back to San Diego was behind them and they pulled up to Jenna's apartment. Austin got their luggage inside and took her hand. "Let's sit down for a minute." He was still irritated, still sure it was her ex-husband, but Kai would get testy soon enough if he wasn't following other leads. He'd go through the motions if it got him more time with Jenna to protect her from a threat he was sure was very real. Technically, they were walking a thin line here. She was a civilian and the actual target. No one at NCIS would bat an eye if the agency wanted to turn over the protection of Jenna to the local cops. But Austin couldn't leave her knowing that a killer, a hired gun, was actively stalking her.

She took off her coat and hung it up. Settling on the sofa, she started to smile when he sat on the coffee table across from her. But he gave her a stern look.

"We couldn't find a thing on Robert, Jenna. No suspicious withdrawals or phone calls. His alibi is airtight. All four of the people I talked to remembered he was there at the fund-raiser. Drea is going to keep looking, but we're going to have to move on to different suspects."

"How do we do that?"

"That's where you come in. I want to know about

anyone who you feel might want to do you harm. Anyone come to mind?"

"No. No one has threatened me."

"Anyone paying you overt attention?"

She bit her lip, and he leaned forward. She looked pensive, then said, "There's a customer at the library. He's harmless, though. He's been pestering me for a date. I tried to be nice at first, but he got angry when I wouldn't say yes."

"What is his name?"

"Billy Dyer." He rose, reaching for his cell phone. Jenna rose with him. "I don't think he could hurt a fly, Austin."

"We're checking it out, Jenna. Have a seat."

Her eyes emitted blue flames, but he wasn't going to leave one thing to chance when it came to her life.

She sat down with a plop, and he sent a call to Drea. It only took her a moment to get the address. He then dialed Detective Morton. Two uniforms showed up about fifteen minutes later. Jenna's face was a stony mask, but Austin and Detective Morton left even with Jenna's protest, telling him again that Billy was not the guy. He realized he was being high-handed, but he was in charge of protecting her life. It was in his hands and he wasn't going to fumble this. With the conviction that he was buying time and sure that the real suspect was back in DC, he followed up on the lead. It was routine police work. Check out everyone and everything.

When they arrived at Billy's house, Austin knocked. He noticed a pretty nice blue-and-black Charger in the driveway. It was vintage and tricked out. A guy with glasses and a bad comb-over answered the door. He was shorter than Austin's six feet and he blinked at them as if he hadn't seen the light of day for some time. The house behind him was a mess, especially the computer station, where Austin could see a popular game up on the screen.

"Billy Dyer?"

"Yes. I'm in the middle of a raid. What do you want? I ain't interested in what you're selling." He went to close the door, but Austin stopped it with his boot. When he flashed his badge and Detective Morton did as well, Billy swallowed hard. "What is this about?"

"Jenna Webb."

He looked excited for a minute. "What about her?"

"Have you been harassing her? Making unwanted advances?"

His eyes went wary and his voice dropped. "No. I asked her out a few times. I didn't do anything illegal."

"We need you to come down to the station with us, Mr. Dyer."

"What?" His small eyes popped, his mouth agape. "Are you arresting me?"

"No, we just have some questions for you."

Billy protested all the way to the precinct, demanding to be read his rights, saying they couldn't arrest him without reading him his rights. That was the law he said, and he knew that because he said he saw it on *Law & Order*. Once they were in the interrogation room, Billy sat there as if he was on death row. He was fidgety and nervous. "Do I need a lawyer?"

"I don't know, Mr. Dyer, do you?" Detective Morton said. He was standing near Billy, an intimidation tactic, while Austin reclined in a chair across from him.

"Why are you asking me? I've never been arrested before."

Detective Morton gave Austin a pained expression

and sighed. In a weary voice, he said, "For the last time, Mr. Dyer, you're not under arrest."

Billy hunched over the small table. He ran his hands over his thinning hair; even with his eyes wide and nervous, they were too small for his face. His yellow-and-orange-checked shirt had stains on the front, the short sleeves revealing his pasty white, flabby arms. "Feels like it, and that navy guy is giving me the evil eye. I don't like him."

Austin was feeling exhausted and mean. "I'm not navy. NCIS is a civilian agency. You can address me as Agent Beck," Austin bit out.

Dyer just gave him a hostile look. "I missed my raid because of this," he muttered.

"Ms. Webb's cousin, Sarah Taylor. Did you know her?" Austin set down Sarah's navy photo and Billy looked at it.

He pushed it back. "She came to the library a couple of times, but I didn't say anything to her. She was talking to Jenna. She was a pilot, huh? That's cool. But I didn't kill her."

Austin got a text message. He looked down to see it was from Drea. She told him to check his tablet; she'd found something on Dyer's car. Opening the tablet and pulling up the email, he saw Billy's Charger parked on the curb across from Jenna's apartment building with a direct line of sight to Sarah and Jenna's apartment and Billy behind the wheel. Drea had been going through surveillance footage from the bank across the street ever since the murder. She'd remembered the car.

Austin turned his pad around. "Is that you, Billy, sitting outside of Ms. Webb's apartment?"

"Yeah, so? It's not against the law to park in the street. I was getting doughnuts."

"My associate found more footage of you. You were there in that spot. A lot. There are stalking laws in California, in case you were unaware. It states that if you willfully and repeatedly follow or harass another person with intent to do bodily harm, that's stalking."

"I wasn't stalking her." He pushed up his black-framed glasses. "I didn't do anything to her," Billy whispered. "I wouldn't hurt her. I like looking at her."

"And that's not creepy," Detective Morton muttered.

"It's not. She's beautiful and sh-sh-she's nice to me. I like her."

There was another picture that had popped up on his tablet. The time and date were highlighted. "Look at this, Billy. You were there the night Sarah was murdered. This is your car, but you're not behind the wheel."

"I got hungry and went to get doughnuts. I told you, I like the doughnuts there."

"There were reports of a prowler at the windows of their apartment. Was that you, Billy?"

He looked away and Austin knew that was a tell. He couldn't meet Austin's eyes. Austin slammed his hand down on the table and Billy jumped.

"Were you there? Did you look in the windows!"

"Yes! I was looking in. I just wanted to see her."

Detective Morton said, "Billy, that is also against the law. Delaying, lingering, prowling or wandering on someone else's inhabited private property when you don't have a lawful reason for being there and you peeked inside is a violation."

"I didn't see anything. They kept the blinds closed," he groused. "Besides, the night I was there, the lights were out. I thought I saw someone, but I couldn't make out who it was. I know it wasn't Jenna because the shadow was too big."

Austin sat up straighter. "You saw someone. The night Sarah was murdered?"

"What? You mean it happened when I was watching?" He twisted his hands together. "Oh, man. I coulda helped her?" He looked completely distressed.

"Do you remember anything about this guy? Anything would help, Billy."

He dropped his head into his hands. "I'm in a lot of trouble. You going to arrest me now?"

"We'll talk about that later. The guy?" Austin said.

"I was sad that Jenna wasn't there. She said she was going to a concert, but I was hoping to wait until she got home, but since she wasn't there, I left."

"Billy, focus on the man you saw."

"Okay, he was tall."

"Any details? Hair color, clothes?"

Billy thought for a few minutes. "No, it was too dark. I just could tell he was big." Billy's face lit up. "Wait. I saw a flash of light. Then it was gone."

"A flash of light?"

"Yeah, like a screen. Then it was gone."

"Anything else?"

"No. I'm sorry. I wished I could have seen more."

Austin slid his card over to Billy. "If you remember anything, call me right away."

Detective Morton followed Austin out of the room. "Not much to go on."

"No. Not much help at all, but we know it was a man and he was big. You going to charge him?"

"Yeah, he broke the stalking and Peeping Tom laws.

I don't know if we can make the charges stick, but that's up to the DA, not me."

"All right. Let's get him booked, and I need your help in guarding Jenna for a bit. I want to talk to the super and see what else he might remember and if he's seen Billy around the place."

"You bet."

Austin and Detective Morton returned to Jenna's apartment and relieved the uniforms. She was talking on the phone and Austin paced while Jack sat down on the couch. *A tall, big man.* Just the thought of the killer in the library with Jenna made his blood run cold. Then a thought occurred to him: Why didn't he kill Jenna when he had the chance? He'd obviously gone through a lot to trap her in the library. Why just knock her out instead of finishing the job? This was the most puzzling case he'd ever been on and much harder than chasing Dexter Kaczewski, a navy SEAL; and Piper Jones, a senator, through the desert and DC. They were very happily married now.

She finished the phone call and came into the living room. "What happened?"

"Billy was here the night Sarah was murdered. He saw the guy, but it was too dark to make out anything that was helpful. He was camping out across the street a lot. He was also your prowler, trying to catch a glimpse of you."

She folded her arms and shivered, rubbing at them. "Could he be lying about the man he saw to cover his tracks?"

"No, I'm sure he's telling the truth. He's not too bright for one thing, and for another, I don't think he would hurt you. He…uh…liked looking at you." *Join the freaking club*, Austin thought, his eyes going over her. He liked looking at her, too.

"He was persistent, and I had a hard time shaking his advances. I didn't want to hurt his feelings, but he just wouldn't stop asking me out. So what happened with him?"

"We had to arrest him, Ms. Webb," Jack said. "He broke the law."

"Oh, I see. He didn't seem dangerous to me, but I guess you never know."

"No, you don't. He'll probably get out on bail if he gets himself a good lawyer. They have to make the charges stick and right now all we have is his confession and the surveillance video from the bank across the street."

"He didn't threaten me in any way," she said. And Jack shifted at her unhappy tone.

Austin met Jack's eyes, and he cleared his throat. "I need to get something from the car. I'll be right back," Jack said.

He left and Austin turned to Jenna. "We have to run down every lead."

"I know you're frustrated and angry, worried about me. There's no need to be distant. We're in this together."

"I'm doing my job. I'm trying to keep you safe."

"I understand that." She stepped toward him, but he stepped back.

"We have to be smart about this. Now that we're back in El Centro, where I think the killer is just waiting for another chance at you, I can't be distracted."

She folded her arms across her chest, the hurt on her face scoring his insides. He had to be strong here, draw the line with her.

"This is a murder investigation. Your life is in danger. If I'm pushing, it's because I'm trying to keep you safe, eliminate this threat. I need you to work with me."

She raised her chin, her mouth tightening. It was clear he was pushing some of her buttons, but he couldn't help that now.

"Who else?"

She gave him a blank stare.

"Jenna, who else hit on you?"

"It was just a couple of times."

"Who?"

"Lieutenant Sims."

"Why didn't you mention this when I was interviewing the squadron?"

"He wasn't pushy or hostile. He just asked me for drinks, and I thought, at the time, it had to do with Sarah. It slipped my mind. I was thinking about other things."

Him. She meant she'd been thinking about him and this was why he shouldn't have gotten involved with her. "He doesn't have an alibi and he's big and tall."

"He was much more interested in Sarah, not me. I think it might have been a ploy to get to her. If she's not the target, then he has no motive, Austin."

He sat back. It was a sound argument, but he'd already decided to go at Sims again. His gut told him Billy hadn't killed Sarah.

Jack came back into the apartment and Jenna gave Austin one more bruised look and retreated to her room, closing the door.

"You're doing the right thing, kid," Jack said. "But just remember—she's scared, too."

He gave Jack a harried look, and Jack shrugged. Austin turned to go, realizing Jack was right. Jenna was scared, and she had every right to be. Austin wasn't so quick to acknowledge his fear. It was one of those situations where you just had to man up and soldier on, as his dad would say. He was the only thing that stood between her and the person who wanted her dead. If he faltered, made a mistake or dropped his vigilance— He couldn't even finish that thought. Now that he'd found her, been with her, he was losing himself all over again, just like at the embassy, but this time it was even worse. There might be a chance for them in the future once this danger was past, but if he lost her… He wasn't sure he could come back from that kind of loss. The word *fear* didn't even cover it.

A few minutes later he knocked on the super's door and Posner invited him inside. The man's place was immaculate, but kind of barren. It looked as if the furniture had come with the apartment and there didn't seem as if there was anything personal in this place. No pictures, no art, no books and no music. Everything was beige with this guy, even his clothing. Seemed like a bland way to live.

"What can I do for you, Agent Beck? Is Ms. Webb okay?"

"Yes, she's fine. I wanted to ask you if you saw this man around."

Austin brought up Billy's photo on his tablet. Posner studied it and nodded. "Yeah, I ran him off a couple of times. He said he was looking for an apartment, but I told him there weren't any vacant. The second time, he didn't have an excuse. Who is he?"

"Billy Dyer. He was Jenna and Sarah's prowler."

"Ah, the little weasel. The two times I caught him, he was in a general area, not anywhere near their apartment."

"He had a car across the street. He was watching their place. Do you recognize it?"

"Yeah, I remember that sweet muscle car. What happened with him?"

"We arrested him. He was here the night Sarah was murdered. Did you see him then?"

"No, I didn't. So he was peeping at the time Lieutenant Taylor was murdered?"

"Yeah, he's given us a description of the man who killed her. I was hoping you might have more information."

"I'm sorry. Like I said, Lieutenant Taylor called me right before she was murdered. I wasn't home. I was at the other side of the complex fixing a toilet that was overflowing. It was an emergency, and I couldn't get away right then. I'm sorry that I didn't."

"I'm sorry that you didn't, either." Austin's shoulders, already tense, tightened even more, the frustration building. "Thank you for your time." In the back of his mind, he noted that Posner was a big, tall man, but he had an alibi. He couldn't have been on the phone with Sarah across the complex at the same time she was being murdered. The phone records had exonerated him. But it could be possible that he played the system. There was no way Austin could prove that but Posner didn't have a motive. He didn't really know Sarah. The strangulation was very personal and seemed like it would be carried out by someone Sarah knew.

Austin left Posner's apartment and headed for his car. He'd go at Sims again, then check in with Drea. Sims could be one of those guys who couldn't handle

rejection from anyone. *Let's see if he has an alibi for
the night Jenna was attacked in the library.*

He didn't want to think about how he would handle
Jenna tonight when they were alone. She was angry
at him about Billy, sure he didn't have anything to do
with Sarah's murder. But he had to cover all the bases.

Chapter 14

By the time Austin left the base, his frustration had settled into a lump in the pit of his stomach and set off one hell of a headache. He couldn't remember his head ever hurting this much. The freaking devil winds started to blow and it only made his jaw tighten. There was an uneasiness in the air, the stirring of something hot and buzzing down his spine, and a hot, dry heat that lingered in his lungs, as if an inferno was trapped in his chest. A feeling of being crowded, of being boxed in, moved in on Austin. He wasn't used to being stymied like this. Feeling ineffectual, he hit the wheel several times, sweat slipping down his temples as he realized how close to the edge he was. How much Jenna mattered to him, and because of that, his emotions were heightened. He needed a cool head and he could feel nothing but fever.

By the time he got back to Jenna's apartment, it was bad. He knocked at the door and Jack answered, his hand on his gun.

When he saw it was Austin, he relaxed. "Boy, you look roughed up. You okay?"

"Headache and another dead end. Sims has an alibi for the night Jenna was attacked. It's not him, either."

"Well, damn," Jack said with disappointment.

"Hitting a dead end has never happened to me before."

"Well, then, you're one of the lucky ones."

Austin leaned against the door frame. "I got it from here."

"Don't look like it. How about I stay for a while until you feel better?"

"What's wrong?" Jenna said, coming out of her room.

"He's got a doozy of a headache."

Austin looked at her and she came immediately forward. "Come with me."

"I'll be fine."

"You will be once we get some pills into you and you get some rest."

Gritting his teeth against the sickening jolt of pressure in his skull, he let her lead him. He closed his eyes, fighting the pain, and when she stopped him, she undid the snaps on his pullover and slipped it off over his head. She reached behind him and unclipped his holster in the middle of his back, setting it on the bedside table. Before he knew it, a mattress was against the back of his knees and he was on his back. He wrestled with the pain, feeling the need to be there for Jenna, but it wouldn't abate. It was the tension, the pressure of knowing that time was running out, and he wasn't any closer to stopping the man who was here to kill her. Trying to release the grinding tension in his jaw, he took a deep breath, then exhaled.

Unable to let go of his duty, he reached over, pulled

his Glock from the holster and checked the gun, removing the safety and chambering a round. Headache or no
headache, he'd be ready for anything threatening her.

Then he settled back against the pillow, the weapon
on his chest.

There was soundless movement beside him and
Jenna very gently slid her hand under his head. "Here,"
she said softly. "Take this." Carefully cradling his head
against her hand, she pressed two tablets against his
mouth. He opened his mouth and took them as a glass to
his lips followed. She lowered him back down and fixed
the pillow under his head so it was supporting his neck.

After a few moments, the excruciating pressure in
his head eased, and he was finally able to unclench his
teeth. Letting go of that grating, brittle tension left him
feeling cold and shaky. As if tuned in to his every need,
Jenna drew a blanket over him, her touch so gentle as
she tucked the fabric around his shoulders. His throat
closed up, and he had to shut his eyes against the sudden surge of emotion. He needed this in his life.

He needed her in his life. He had to save her. Had
to protect her.

She gently brushed his hair from his forehead, her voice
husky with concern when she asked, "Would ice help?"

He opened his eyes and looked at her, her profile
blurred in the semidarkness of the room. Warmed by the
pressure of her body against his, he caught her hand and
pressed it against his chest. "I'm sorry," he murmured.

She laced her fingers through his, and Austin tightened his hold, then closed his eyes and began stroking
her palm with his thumb. The frustration was banked,
the anger cooled, replaced by a haunting ache that
sat squarely in the middle of his chest. He wondered

how many more chances he was going to get with this woman before it was too late. The timing with them seemed to really suck.

The heaviness in his chest expanded, and he clenched his jaw against it, then reached up and caught Jenna by the back of the neck, pulling her down beside him. Her hair was like silk beneath his fingers as he cradled her head against his shoulder, then began stroking her upper arm. In spite of the shape he was in, he couldn't get the unsettled feeling in his gut to go away. He wished like hell he could stop feeling as if they were living on borrowed time.

The next thing he knew, his cell phone woke him up, and Jenna was gone. For a moment he panicked, but then remembered that Jack was here. He sat up, and a washcloth slipped off his forehead and dropped into his lap. He picked it up. The headache was just a buzz at the front of his head, most of the blinding pain gone. His weapon was once again on the bedside table. He grabbed for his phone.

"Agent Beck, this is Billy. Am I calling at a bad time?"

Austin hesitated, then said, clearing his voice of the gravel from sleep, "No, now's fine."

"I know it isn't much. But I noticed things since I hung around Jenna's place so much. Her neighbor across the hall watches Jenna a lot, like when she gets in her car or on her shopping days. He always seems to be there when she needs a hand with her groceries."

"Mitch Campbell," Austin said, swinging his legs to the floor, trying to clear his head of cotton wool. The neighbor? Austin had already talked to him, and he said he had been with his girlfriend that night and couldn't help. Morton had talked to the girlfriend—

Tina Guthrie—and she had corroborated his story, but now Austin wondered. Tina's apartment wasn't that far away. Could Campbell have come back and killed Sarah, thinking she was Jenna? This development put a crimp in his supposition that Robert Webb was behind it, but Austin couldn't discount any clue.

"Yeah, that's the guy," Billy said with a sullen voice. "I considered him a rival for her affections. I got out on bail, and I have to talk to the DA. My lawyer thinks he can get me off with community service. I'm sure sorry if I scared Jenna. I didn't mean to. Would you tell her for me? I'm not supposed to be anywhere near her."

Austin pushed off the bed. "Sure, Billy. Just be careful in the future and make sure you accept no for an answer."

"Yes, sir. So long."

Austin pushed off the mattress, reaching for his gun. Slipping his cell into his back pocket, he tucked the gun into the holster and clipped it to his pants. He dropped the washcloth into the sink as he passed. He could smell something delicious in the air and his stomach rumbled.

When he walked out, Jack was watching the news, and Jenna was in the kitchen at the stove. Jack shut the TV off and turned to look at him. "You look like you're feeling better."

"Much. Thank you for staying."

Jenna turned from the stove with an uncertain expression in her eyes, indicating that she had picked up on his edginess. He felt like a complete jerk.

"It's no hardship to watch a pretty lady and get out of those thrice-cursed winds."

Austin rubbed the back of his neck—the pressure of the winds was relentless—and Austin shifted to look out the window. The moaning increased in volume, howling as it shook the trees, dust and debris swirling and shuddering, caught fast in its grip. A force of nature that everyone from LA to San Diego endured this time of year.

Austin glanced at Jenna and he didn't realize he was staring until Jack cleared his throat. Her back looked rigid, her shoulders stiff. "Won't you stay for dinner, Detective Morton?"

He rose from the couch and adjusted his gun. "No, my wife is holding dinner, and I need to skedaddle, but you've got my home number. You need anything, just call. I have a uniform coming by this address every half an hour."

Austin nodded, and Jack headed for the door. "Step into the hall for a second," Austin said. Austin closed the door behind him. "I got a tip from Creepy Billy that Jenna's neighbor has been overly interested in her."

"I checked him out. He had an alibi."

"Yeah, I know, but his girlfriend's apartment isn't far from here."

"I got you. He could have snuck out and killed Taylor. I guess that's possible. I'll be back tomorrow, and we'll talk about this some more."

"All right."

Jack eyed him, and Austin met his eyes, his attention sharpening when he saw the concerned expression on the cop's face. Austin stared at him for a moment, then leaned his back against the door. "Something on your mind?" he said quietly.

Jack frowned and glanced down, his expression solemn as he adjusted his belt. "You tell me, Austin. I asked if the lady was going to be a problem. Seems like you're on edge here. Normally, it wouldn't be any of my business in these personal circumstances, but I have a fondness for her and for you."

Austin looked away. "It's complicated."

"I got that. Look, this case is a bitch. There are absolutely no leads, nothing to go on. In this instance, look at everything again. Maybe we missed something. I'll do the same. We're not going to give up on her."

"You might not, but NCIS isn't going to let me stay here indefinitely. In fact, guarding her at my request didn't go over all that well. I'm on borrowed time here, Jack. I can't let her down, and I can't leave her exposed to danger."

Jack exhaled heavily and gave a terse nod. "Yeah, I get that. Rest assured if you are pulled off and have to go back to San Diego, I'll keep an eye on her."

"Until she goes back to DC. Then who's going to watch out for her?"

Jack's expression went grim and he stuck his hands into his pockets. "Ah, I see your point."

"I think her ex-husband hired someone to kill her. I think there's a specific way he wants her murdered. I know that coldhearted bastard. I worked for him when I was a marine."

Comprehension dawned in Jack's mud-brown eyes. "That's the way of it, then? She was married when you first met her."

"Yeah." Austin's mouth tightened, the memories fresh and strong. "We got close and then the embassy was overrun. I haven't seen her since."

Jack shook his head. "Unfinished business in the midst of all this turmoil and danger makes for a volatile situation."

"I know, hence the edge."

Jack heaved another heavy sigh. "The winds don't help, but keep it together, boy. We'll work this case until something pops. I'm with you. This ain't over. I feel it in my gut. You make sure to call me if you need help. Don't be a hero."

Austin huffed out a laugh, and Jack slapped him on the back. His gaze somber, he leaned his head back against the door and stared after Jack as he went out into the wind, a whirl of dust and heat sweeping in before he closed the door. Austin stood there for a moment, then he turned and swore, slamming his hand into the door frame. Damn it! Why in hell did life have to be so freaking complicated?

With the heel of his hand throbbing, he opened the door and went back inside, securely locking it.

She was at the counter, cutting up garlic bread and setting the slices into a basket. Looked like dinner was almost ready. He walked toward her, and she went to the stove, turned the heat down under the sauce and dumped spaghetti into the boiling water. Setting the timer, she headed past him and disappeared into the laundry room, reemerging with a basket full of clothes she settled on the sofa.

He folded his arms, watching as she pulled a shirt out of the bundle and started to fold it. With a little shock of surprise, he realized it was his. She'd done his laundry?

Her short haircut, the curls so dark against her creamy skin, clung to her damp cheeks. He closed his eyes as he suddenly remembered what it felt like to have the soft strands tickling his chest and abdomen. He clenched his jaw against the heated rush of physical response, knowing that after the way he'd been acting, she deserved more than a quick tumble. But with Jenna it was hard to go slow. She always made him feel...urgent.

He wasn't sure how to fix things, but he knew it wasn't going to be by asking her about her day. He watched her as she untangled their clothes more easily than he could untangle how he felt about her. She set the neatly folded article on the pile that was growing on the coffee table, aware she was wary about meeting his gaze. If he'd learned one thing in the marines and then in NCIS, it was the importance of hitting any problem head on. And by the stark look in her eyes, he knew this wasn't the time to hedge. "Dinner smells good," he started off and cringed. That was a lame way to start this conversation.

Her gaze swung sharply to meet his, the lamplight washing her skin in a golden hue. She stared at him for a moment, then looked away, suddenly intent on separating two sweaters and folding them.

Hooking his thumbs in the front pockets of his pants, Austin watched her, his expression solemn. He didn't say anything for a moment, then he said, his tone slightly husky, "Come here, Jenna."

He saw her swallow hard, then she met his gaze, her eyes dark and haunted. He shifted, widening his stance, then reached out his hand. "Come on," he urged gruffly.

She set the sweaters aside, and drawing a deep, unsteady breath, she crossed the room, her body stiff with tension when she slipped her arms around his waist and turned her face against his neck. Drawing her hips against his, Austin exhaled heavily and drew her fully against him, resting his jaw against her head as he began slowly massaging the small of her back. Jenna tightened her arms around him, and Austin felt her shivering, as though she had expected pain. Shifting his hold, he cradled her head firmly against him and brushed a gentling kiss against her temple, feeling disquieted. He didn't know what in hell was going to happen to them. And if he'd realized anything during the past few days, it was that resolving his personal relationship with Jenna hinged on getting her out of danger and safe from the bastard who had set all this into motion.

Time was running out for her. That had fueled his edginess because he was no closer to resolving this case and freeing her from the terror of living under the shadow of death.

He gave her a reassuring hug and pressed his mouth against her hair. Shifting his hold, he turned slightly, keeping her against him as he checked to make sure the spaghetti wasn't one big lump of starch, then rubbed her shoulders. "Looks like we're almost ready to eat," he said gruffly. "I was thinking of taking a shower real quick. I feel like I'm coated in dust and sweat."

Jenna exhaled heavily and reluctantly eased back in his embrace. Avoiding his gaze, she nodded. "It's hard enough without those damn winds stirring everything up."

Hooking his knuckles under her chin, Austin lifted her face and made her look at him, the heavy feeling in his gut intensifying when he saw the bleak expression in her eyes. He held her gaze for a moment, then tightened his hold on her jaw and brushed a soft kiss against her mouth. "This has been a bitch of a case," he whispered huskily.

She gave him a shaky laugh and looked up at him, her eyes not quite so stark. "That's an understatement. Our timing sucks big-time, too."

He held her gaze, the corner of his mouth lifting a little. "Yeah, I got that. We're out of sync."

She stared at his mouth, the humor in her eyes lightening her expression. "The world can go to hell," she answered, her tone fierce. "We're going to do our own thing."

When he grinned, she gave him another quick kiss, then turned him around and gave him a push toward the bathroom. "You've got ten minutes, Agent Beck, then I'm eating."

"Ho, there. I really think that you could use a shower, too. You look hot and sweaty."

She gave him such a pure feminine look of exasperation, he laughed. "I've been slaving over a hot stove," she said matter-of-factly.

"I don't want to let you out of my sight, Jenna. Humor me."

Expecting some sort of smart comeback, Austin was caught completely off guard when Jenna buried her face into the crook of his neck. Swearing to himself, he stared down at her dark, bent head, trying to ignore the tight feeling in his chest. Why couldn't they just be a freaking normal couple? He heard her take a ragged breath—a breath that sounded too much like a sob for him to ignore—and with his resolve evaporating like smoke, he caught the back of her head and tightened his arm around her waist. "Jenna, babe," he whispered gruffly. "We're going to be okay. And I think you still smell really good."

Drawing a hard breath as if she was impatient with herself, she slipped her arms under his shirt and around his back. She laughed. "Is that what you're using for an excuse to get me naked?" she whispered, her face wet against his neck, her voice breaking.

Tucking her head tighter against him, he savored the silky disorder of her hair, a flicker of amusement surfacing. Sweeping her hair back, he cupped the side of her face and brushed a light kiss against her cheek. "Naw, I just need someone to wash my back."

He got an unsteady laugh, and he hugged her tighter. Jenna's voice was a little stronger when she responded. "I think I have a wire brush around here somewhere."

"Ouch. Good thing I only asked you to wash my back."

He waited until he felt her begin to relax; then he eased his hold and lifted her face so he could see her eyes, his expression sobering. "Now that we've settled that, even though you smell good while being hot and sweaty, you'll take a shower with me...sans wire brush."

Her black lashes matted, her mouth not quite steady, she looked at him, her eyes so dilated there was hardly any color. She stared at him a moment, then said, her voice husky, "You're no fun, Austin."

He squeezed her and the timer on the stove went off. "Let me get this handled, and I'll meet you in there."

He nodded and backed away from her as she went to the boiling pot and grabbed it off the stove, draining the spaghetti and dumping in the sauce. He went through the doorway as she was stirring in the meat. He started the water heating in the shower and stripped off his clothes, glad for the release of the heavy cloth. The cool air of the bathroom felt good against his heated skin. This whole thing was hard for her. Not because she would evade the truth, but because Jenna had spent most of her life acquiescing to others, letting them drive. She didn't know how to ask for something she wanted. Everything between them was uncertain and that made for a messed-up mind. He should know.

She came abruptly into the room while he was standing there, musing. She stopped dead and stared at him. She released a pent-up puff of air in a slow breath. Her eyes traveled over him. "God, Austin, if I ever needed a distraction, you'd really fit the bill."

Realizing that she was really struggling, he pulled her into a tight embrace and rested his head against hers. Not sure what they were getting themselves into, or how they would come out of it, he let his breath go. "I'm glad I can do something constructive here."

He felt her catch an uneven breath, and he tightened his hold, experiencing a sudden thickness in his chest. Waiting for the contraction to ease, he slid his hand under her hair and grabbed the collar of her sweater, yanking. Taking the cue, she lifted her arms and he pulled it off. She looked up at him, a trace of wry humor in her voice, "I'm not sure that's what your boss had in mind."

"I'm sure it isn't," he said, giving her an unsteady laugh.

"This feels like we're breaking the rules instead of being cautious."

He pulled her closer, the smile fading from his face. He agreed. This didn't feel like being careful at all. Not a damn bit. "No," he murmured, being completely honest. "This feels like falling."

Her voice, husky and full of uncertainty, hit him hard in the heart. "As long as you catch me, I think I'll be okay."

His throat suddenly tight, he spoke, his voice barely a whisper. "I will, babe. I promise."

He watched her eyes soften even more, the air between them heating and so damn intimate it was making his head swim. A peculiar soft feeling filling up his chest. His hands slipped over her shoulders to her bra straps. With a flick of his wrist and a gasp from her, it was off.

The first time she had taken the initiative had caught him by surprise, but he was sure she wasn't used to seducing a man outright. She softly brushed her mouth against his, the warmth and moistness of the kiss making his pulse erratic. She licked his bottom lip slowly—very slowly. Opening his mouth to her seduction, Austin pressed in just enough to deepen the kiss, resolutely keeping his hands loosely on her hips. He wondered how far she would take it this time.

She changed the angle of her head, perfecting the seal of her mouth against his, then she smoothed her hand down his chest, dragging her thumbnail across his nipple. Austin jerked, her touch sending a sharp current of sensation through him, and his heart went into overdrive when she lightly rolled the hardened nub under her fingers.

He wanted to grab her and drag her against him, but this was her show. With a wild flurry of excitement building in him, Austin tightened his muscles against her tormenting touch, yielding his mouth to hers as she deepened the kiss. Just as she pushed her tongue into his mouth, she trailed her fingernails down his abdomen to his waistband. His breathing turned heavy, and it took every ounce of control he had to remain still and unmoving beneath her lightly exploring hands.

This wasn't sex or seduction, this was… He closed his eyes against the bump his heart made. Love. He loved her. He was involved here and as she grabbed hold of his waistband, he knew he couldn't deny her a thing.

Case or no case, he wanted to be with Jenna for the long haul, but there were definitely obstacles to cross. As her mouth became more ardent, he lost the thread of his thoughts, his chest filling with something fuller than he'd ever felt.

Yeah, he was freaking in love with her.

His thoughts fragmented as she cupped his hard, thick arousal. He sucked in a ragged breath, releasing a guttural sound against her mouth when she trailed her fingernails between his legs and down the sensitive base.

Working her mouth slowly against his, she shifted slightly, then used both hands to undo his belt. Austin stood there without moving as she pulled the belt free of the loops and dropped it on the floor, then slid her long fingers beneath his waistband. Her intimate touch electrified him, and he lifted his head and drew her tongue deeply into his mouth, the pulsating hardness in his groin nearly exploding as she carefully drew his zipper down. With the same slow care, she freed him, and Austin abruptly ceased to breathe.

Unable to remain passive one second longer, he caught her by the back of the head and ground his mouth hungrily against hers, heat searing through him as she lightly smoothed her thumb over the moist, slick tip of his arousal.

Grasping her face between his hands, he gazed at her, his breathing labored. Her eyes dark and heavy-lidded, her full, sensual mouth swollen from the urgency of his kiss, she was his weakness, his future, just *his*.

She caught his face between her hands and stared at him, then she leaned into him and gave him a soft, comforting kiss. The feel of her hands against his face, the absolute comfort in her touch, made his throat cramp up and he closed his eyes, experiencing such a surge of emotion that he was damned near upended by it. Opening his mouth against hers, he cupped her breast, rubbing her velvet nipple with his thumb.

Dragging her mouth lower, she kissed her way down his body, sinking to her knees, sending another jolt of sensation through him. Bracing himself for what was coming, he twisted his head to one side and straightened his hips to give her access, his face contorting in an agony of sensation, his whole body going rigid as she lowered her head. He closed his eyes and ground his teeth together, her touch setting off a chain reaction that made him stiffen and groan. And with a blinding surge of sensation, he gave himself up to her moist, questing mouth.

Twenty minutes later, they ate their warmed-up meal at the table. Jenna was quiet, almost as if she were giving him a breather. He'd always had the ocean and surfing when the winds blew and he could work out the excess physical energy on the waves. Jenna's seduction went a long way to helping with that, but now she was the one who seemed edgy. He'd been locked up inside all day. Maybe it was her turn.

He didn't like the idea that she was keeping the peace for him. Her past was full of men taking care of her. That wasn't a bad thing, but he wouldn't want to control her like her ex-husband. He wanted that to stop with him. But the circumstances set him in that role. Jenna wasn't big on confrontation, and given the choice, he suspected she would still skirt one if at all possible. He figured it was tied up with vulnerability and self-doubt and a nearly disabling insecurity that came from her father and ex-husband. That would leave deep and indelible scars. Was she too afraid of risking emotional exposure, where her personal insecurity was on the line? It was just too big a risk. He understood it, but he didn't like it. He didn't want any kind of power over her decisions.

"Would you like some more?"

Shifting his gaze from the swirling winds, he glanced at his plate, then at her. He shook his head. "No, thanks."

She stood up and reached for his empty plate, and Austin saw the misery in her eyes. He reached out and caught her wrist, taking her dish from her and setting it on top of his. Pushing the plates aside, he exerted a steady pressure on her arm and went to the couch.

She gave him a forced smile and tried to pull free. "I'll go get us some coffee and dessert."

He tightened his hold. "That can wait."

Her smile was a little more genuine the second time around. "But I made brownies." His eyes didn't waver. "With chocolate chips. Just the way you like them."

He knew what she was doing, and he wanted to shake her. He didn't argue with her. He simply caught her behind the knees and gave her arm a sharp tug, tumbling her across him. Before she had time to get untangled, he shifted her legs, then locked her up in a tight embrace. "You make me lose control. Just let's sit still for a moment."

She remained rigid in his arms for an instant, then the tension went out of her. Pressing her face against his neck, she slid one arm around his back. As soon as she wrapped both arms around him, he let go of her.

Her hair smelled like rain-washed flowers. He buried his nose in her shiny curls, leaned back and closed his eyes, a sudden tightness in his chest. It wasn't just the weather that was closing in on him. It was hard, cold reality. With the way he felt, he couldn't let her go, but he also couldn't make her stay. That was her decision.

Maybe it was the hormones, the adrenaline, the desperation of being under the threat of death talking. He just didn't know.

What he did know was their future hung in the balance. He hoped like hell she found the courage to take what she wanted. If she didn't, they would both suffer.

Chapter 15

Jenna stood at the sliding glass door, waiting for the kettle to boil, her arms wrapped around herself, the belt of her robe pulled tight. All the self-doubts, uncertainties and anxieties had swamped her when she'd woken from a dream of a man looming over her, the threat realized as his hands reached for her. Even the comfort of Austin's body wasn't enough to belay her fears.

To make matters worse, the ache in the small of her back made her head for the bathroom, quietly so she wouldn't disturb Austin. The light from the small room seemed piercingly bright, and the heaviness in her belly made her feel slightly dizzy. But what finally broke her was the visual confirmation that her period had started.

She shook her head with a small sound of pain. It wasn't every time she got her cycle she thought about it, but tonight, for some reason it was hard on her mind.

She was thirty-two years old, divorced, *childless*. The awful sensation of being disconnected from everything familiar left her feeling shaky and unsure, oddly exposed. And memories—disturbing memories—had begun floating to the surface of her mind, shadowy, indistinct memories that had no shape. But they weren't memories of things or places. They were memories of feelings. And in some ways, those were even worse.

She felt haunted, and it was nearly impossible for her to stay focused on anything. And Austin never made any reference to what had happened before they went to bed. He didn't ask about what was bothering her, and that made her feel even more vulnerable.

She had come here to be with her only living relative, but she bit her lip. Had she really been delaying the inevitable? The decisions she needed to make to move forward.

Now there was an even bigger layer of confusion thrown over everything since she had reconnected to Austin. In a way he reminded her of what she had almost done back then at the embassy. She hated that she had been so unhappy and hated that she only had herself to blame for it.

She'd married Robert when deep down she'd known he couldn't really make her happy. She'd given in to her father's tyrannical need to see her safe. Then he'd died and she'd been trapped in the prison she'd made because if she was being honest with herself, she'd gone in knowing that Robert would take care of her like her father had. He would make sure she was cared for. It was her own folly in thinking that there would be love and children, cherishing and family, fulfillment and bounty.

Instead there was nothing but loneliness, condescension and cold. Bitter cold.

The kettle was about to whistle, and she headed for the stove at a quick pace to cut it off before it woke Austin up. She pulled it from the burner just as she heard, "Are you all right?"

She was so far away in her thoughts and the sound of his voice was so unexpected that Jenna jumped, her heart slamming into high gear as adrenaline shot through her. Closing her eyes, she clutched her hand against her chest, not quite able to disconnect from the memories and her self-exploration—self-condemnation.

Austin came over to where she was standing and caught her under the chin, forcing her to look at him. He winced when he saw her face, then caught her by the neck and pulled her into his embrace—a warm, safe embrace. Jenna turned her face against him and fought the feelings of abandonment, of fear, of shame. She had been so young when her mom died and her father had been so devastated. He hadn't even realized how he'd abandoned her, becoming more her protector than her father, especially when she needed him.

She didn't want to feel what that child had felt. She didn't want to cry.

Austin tucked his head down against hers, tightening his hold, then slowly rubbed his hand up and down her back. "It's okay, babe. I'm here for you."

Of all the things he could have said, nothing could have been more devastating, more wrenching. It was as if he knew exactly what kind of emotional trauma she was experiencing right then and was there to lift her out of that nightmare morass. She shivered and pressed against his chest, and Austin tightened his hold.

"You want to talk about it?"

Her teeth clamped against the well of unshed tears, she shook her head. He rubbed his cheek against hers, and snuggled her closer. "Do you want to go back to bed?"

She shook her head again, and he smoothed his hand up and down her back, but he didn't say anything more; he just held her, his face tucked against hers. His warmth and physical closeness diffused the disturbing images, and Jenna clung to the solidness of him, her eyes tightly closed and her jaw clenched. It had come out of nowhere, that realization. Without warning it was just there.

"With a little music, we could have ourselves a nice little waltz here."

There was something so endearing in the inflection in his voice, and she turned her head to his shoulder. "You have a second life as a ballroom dancer that I don't know about, surfer boy?" she said, her tone uneven.

She felt him grin, and he gave one of her curls a tug. "I'm a veritable Fred Astaire."

She smiled again. "I'm afraid I'm no Ginger Rogers." Feeling oddly vulnerable, she pulled out of his hold and removed the kettle from the burner. Fighting against the feeling in her chest, she opened the cupboard door and reached for the tea canister. "Do you want some tea?"

There was a brief pause then he said, "Why can't you be one of those midnight margarita types?" He grinned. "Yeah, I'll have a cup."

She fixed a pot of tea and got two mugs out of the cupboard, then carried them to the table. Austin was leaning against the stove watching her, his unbuttoned pants riding low on his hips, his arms folded across his bare chest. He had an odd, intent look in his eyes, as if he were disassembling her piece by piece.

She set the teapot on a placemat and put the cups down beside it, knowing he was scrutinizing her and not liking the feeling. Finally he spoke, his tone off-hand. "You really don't want to talk about it?"

She shot him a quick glance, then began filling the mugs.

She had never learned how to take care of herself. She'd come down here because—she swallowed hard—she had hoped Sarah would take the burden off her hands for a while.

Still feeling the first moment when she'd looked at herself without any illusions, she was just too ashamed. Especially about the bit where she was a little mad at Austin.

He had been this confident, exciting marine with a killer grin and those sexy eyes. He had been passion, heat, *life*. And her universe had shifted. Right from the beginning, Austin Beck had made her feel special. He made her feel beautiful, smart, courageous and daring. She hadn't wanted him ever to see her as weak, ineffectual, delusional. It had been easy to be reckless with him, to take crazy chances, because he made it so obvious that her daring pleased him. That he was proud of her. And it was the first time in her whole life that anybody had felt that way about her. There was no pride in weakness and fear.

"Jenna?"

She looked at him, his steady perusal making her edgy. She shook her head and looked away. "No, I just got my period," she said, her voice uneven. "Nothing really to talk about, unless you're interested in the whole menstrual cycle and my cramps."

He didn't react but came over to the table, pulled out a chair at the end and sat down. Bracing his elbows on the tabletop, he laced his fingers together, his thumbs resting against his mouth as he continued to watch her. Her hands not quite steady, she set a steaming cup of tea in front of him, then sat down and cupped her hands around the hot mug. He watched her for a moment, then took a sip from his mug and set it on the placemat in front of him. He fingered the handle for a moment, then looked at her, his expression mild. "When I first saw you at the embassy, I knew you were going to hurt me and hurt me bad."

She had her mug halfway to her mouth, and she abruptly set it down, tea slopping over the edge. She stared at him, her heart lurching in her chest. She held his gaze for a moment, then abruptly looked at her hands, caught so off guard that she couldn't even think. "Austin—"

"I wanted you like I've never wanted a woman before. You looked so sad, so unhappy, and all I wanted to do was put a smile on your face and light in your eyes. So freaking beautiful."

She looked at him, trying to recover her equilibrium. "Austin—"

"For years I wondered what would have happened if I'd gone with my instinct and taken you right there, the moment you were ripe for it. You wanted me. I know that, but I couldn't be sure it wasn't because you wanted to escape from your reality. I had no idea how much you turned mine upside down...until now."

"Austin—"

"You were married, but I didn't care. I might have felt a bit guilty afterward when I got home and had to face Melanie, but not then, when I was holding you. I know you've got things to work out for yourself. I'm not completely clueless. I just don't know if you're going to kill me this time."

"I'm sorry," she whispered. "I'm so sorry." She waited, a nervous flutter in her stomach, expecting a whole host of questions. But he didn't say anything at all, and finally she looked at him, certain she had lost every speck of color from her face.

He was slouched down in his chair, watching her, his head tipped to one side, his arms folded across his chest, and Jenna looked away again. The silence stretched out between them, and she fidgeted with the corner of the table, trying to blink away the burning sensation in her eyes.

Finally he said, his voice quiet, "I accept your apology if you'll accept mine. I'm sorry I didn't freaking track you down to see what we had was real. I'm really sorry about that because, babe, I'm pretty sure this is as freaking real as it gets."

His words struck her an almost physical blow. It wasn't as if she hadn't wanted the same thing and now she was sick she had never acted on it, as well. She lifted her head and stared at him, her expression numb.

"Oh, God, Austin. I'm sorry about that, too."

He gave her a small half smile, his gaze dark and penetrating. "Yeah, we're two sorry people." He paused, his eyes still fixed on her. "So tell me," he said softly, "what are we going to do about it?"

Jenna didn't know where the sudden spasm of unbearable desolation came from, and she didn't know why that little girl had come out of hiding now, but suddenly her eyes filled and she sat there staring at him, hurting so much for the child she had been. How could she answer that question when she was so confused? She had only made her discovery just a few moments ago. Tears spilled over, and she turned away, and quickly wiped them, feeling ashamed and exposed.

Bracing his hands on the table, Austin rose, then reached across and caught her face. Tipping her head back, he leaned over and kissed her with such immeasurable care that more tears spilled over. Tightening his hold on her face, he slowly withdrew, then trailed his knuckles down her cheek. "When you figure it out and you're ready to talk, let me know, babe," he said huskily. He kissed her again, then straightened, giving her shoulder a little squeeze. "I've changed my mind about the tea. I'm going back to bed."

Badly shaken by the shifting, disturbing images in her mind, she stared after him, his open communication sending reverberations of a shadowy, half-remembered fear through her. It was as though her supports had abruptly crumbled away, and she was suddenly standing on unstable foundations.

Resting her forehead on her upraised knees, she closed her eyes and locked her arms around her legs, trying to quell the heart-racing panic. She had never been good at facing ghosts or at self-analysis because she had never wanted to look back—looking back meant facing all that fear and hurt and shame. It was like a huge hand clutching her chest. Maybe this time there was no escape. Maybe this time she was going to have to go back into the past before she could effectively move forward into her future.

Wiping at her tears that continued to stream, she

abandoned her tea and went into the bedroom. She dropped her robe and slid in beside Austin, curling her naked body around his. He stirred and caught her arm, drawing it around him, then sighed and tucked her hand against his chest. It was such a small, unconscious gesture, but somehow momentous, and Jenna molded herself against him and closed her eyes. This was the kind of comfort she had always been looking for and now she wasn't sure how she was going to handle anything…not herself, not Austin, not her hopes, fears or uncertainty.

Austin was just pulling up to Billy Dyer's house when he heard the gunshot. He had been lost in his musings about last night and his totally honest confession of what was in his heart. He and Jenna had skirted each other that morning after his outburst. He'd gotten Jack out of bed and over to Jenna's while Austin spent his time looking into Mitch Campbell. But throughout the day, away from Jenna, he'd found out the guy had no evidence of mental health problems, had a good relationship with his family and friends, and had never been arrested or convicted of stalking. His gut was telling him he wasn't a suspect. But that left him with no one.

But all that was blown away by the chilling sound. Billy had called him about half an hour ago, just before dusk. Austin was about to head back to Jenna's. He'd said he'd remembered something. Something important. Austin had to come right away. Billy couldn't go to Jenna's apartment and he didn't want to be outside right now.

Austin jumped out of his vehicle without even closing the door and when he got to Billy's front door, it was ajar. He went inside and found Billy on the floor, his eyes open and fixed, blood pooling around his head.

Then he heard a metallic sound from behind the house, and he sprinted to the back door. He saw someone jump Billy's fence and Austin blew through the back door. Keeping close to the sides of the overgrown alley, he ran past the next two houses. As soon as he hit another fence, he vaulted it, catching another glimpse of a fleeing man, big and tall.

Dogs were barking, lights coming on all over the neighborhood. He kept running, dodging trash cans and jumping over children's toys and around swings.

At the end of the block, he crossed another street. A hedge on the other side acted as a barrier. He darted around it and stopped cold. A crowd of people barred his way on the street. A farmer's market stretched along the road, people looking over carrots, radishes and beets along with heads of broccoli and cauliflower.

He swore softly and ran through the crowd anyway, but he had to accept the fact that he'd lost the man. He pulled out his cell phone as he walked back to Billy's house, notifying Jack, who must have worked quickly— he heard the sirens as he jumped the fence in Billy's backyard and entered the house.

A few minutes later, the place was crawling with cops and the crime scene techs. Austin was crouched near the body, regret flowing through him. Jenna had been right. Billy wouldn't have hurt a fly, but someone had been worried he'd known something that could implicate them and had taken him out.

"I want to know the caliber of the weapon as soon as you can get the bullet back to the lab for testing."

"Will do, sir," the guy said.

There was nothing else for Austin to do. He hadn't gotten a good look at the guy, so couldn't give a description. This frustrating case was now officially his most hated he'd ever worked.

He felt as if he was being led around by his nose, and he didn't like that damn feeling one bit.

An hour later, he had time to kill while Jack convinced a judge to give them a warrant to search Campbell's residence for a Beretta. The bullet came from a Px4 Compact, a small, easily concealed Beretta, and Campbell had one registered in his name. But Austin was like a cat on a hot tin roof, spending more time on his computer, checking into every aspect of Mitch Campbell's life. He would know the color of the man's underwear when he was done.

Jenna had settled on the couch with a book, but had fallen asleep, the smell of freshly brewed coffee brought her awake, the aroma tickling her nose.

She opened her eyes, fighting through the sludge in her mind. Heaving a sigh, she threw back the throw that Austin must have covered her with after she fell asleep. She found Austin sitting at the table still on his laptop. He must have moved so as not to wake her.

"Hey," she said, her voice still thick with sleep. There was deep regret that Billy was dead. Austin had told her when he'd returned. He might have been a nuisance, but he was harmless. She'd given Austin a hard time about it, but then realized from his tight expression he was feeling guilty about Billy's death. He had said he was sorry about the whole thing, but he'd had to follow up on it.

He lifted his head and looked at her, a smile appearing in his eyes. "Hello, Sleeping Beauty. About time you woke up."

She hunched her shoulders and tightened her arms in front of her. "Wasn't it your job to wake me with a kiss, Prince Slacker?"

The glint in his eyes intensified. "Someone got up on the wrong side of the couch."

"You're so cute and clever, aren't you?"

He watched her as she sat down adjacent to him, clearly amused by her irritability. "I so am. I'm thinking of changing my name to Cute and Clever Beck. What do you think?"

She pushed his shoulder, and he got up and went to the counter and poured another cup of coffee. He sat down again and went back to his screen. She didn't want to be ignored. But she didn't want to talk, either, so she settled for coffee. She couldn't remember ever being so contrary. Maybe she was just losing it.

She sipped her way through a cup of coffee, then drew up her knees and rested her cheek on them, her mind adrift, still more asleep than awake. She focused on Austin.

"You need a haircut."

He ignored her.

"And a shave."

"You're pushing your luck, babe."

That made her smile. "What are you cooking for dinner?"

He raised his head and responded with a long, steady stare.

She held his gaze, smiling at him. "I cooked spaghetti. It's your turn."

"We're taking turns, are we?"

"You're living here."

Studying her with a mixture of tolerance and amusement, he rocked back in his chair and hooked his thumbs in the pockets of his jeans. "Temporarily."

It caught her off guard. The jolt of pain went right through her heart. She didn't want to be reminded about what it would be like when he was gone. It hurt too much.

Austin's eyes narrowed a fraction, and he stared at her, his gaze suddenly dark and serious. He leaned forward and rested his arms on the table. "Are you ready to talk to me?" he said.

Jenna stared at him, a feeling of apprehension unfolding in her belly. Then he reached across the table and caught her by the wrist, silently urging her to her feet. He didn't say anything as they stood there, staring at each other as if they were going to take their last breaths.

When his laptop chimed that he had an incoming call, he answered. It wasn't Drea, but his boss.

"How is it going? I haven't heard from you in two days." The sound of her voice over the computer speakers was loud and her words were concise.

"That's because I have nothing to report. I'm working on doing up a profile of Mitch Campbell, the next-door neighbor, and waiting for the ballistics report and any other forensic evidence I can go on from the El Centro Police Department." He was staring at the screen, but Jenna could tell his attention was on her.

"Do you want me to light a fire under them? I can have the director call them."

"No, they're working on it. It's just time-consuming."

"Austin. I really need you back here. You have to wrap this up in the next few days. Don't let me down. I'm up to my eyeballs in cases." That made the jolt that went through her feel ten times worse. Kai was pressuring him to come back, and Jenna wasn't ready. Jenna was just about to tell him that she was still working it out in her head. She didn't have any answers yet.

"I need to make sure that Jenna is safe," he said, looking at her then, his eyes full of defiance.

"I understand," Kai said, her voice getting softer and gentler. Jenna figured she would like this woman a lot. "But she isn't your only priority and there's been no overt threat to her in a week. We just had a former suspect shot. Hit this harder."

"Yes, ma'am," he said, his voice anything but cordial. Kai didn't respond, just disconnected the call.

"She really wants you back," Jenna said, her voice subdued.

"Yeah," he said. "She's pushing hard for my return."

"I'm sure she values you very much, Austin. I'm sorry this is such a frustrating case."

He turned to her and there must have been something of her inner turmoil and guilt in her eyes because he went to her, pulling her into his arms. "This isn't your fault," he whispered. "Whoever is behind it is at fault. I'm not going to leave you alone to fend for yourself against a killer, Jenna."

She nodded, then looked up at him. Her eyes told him what she was thinking. Would he leave her alone after this was over if she asked him to? Would he walk away if she decided that's what she needed to be the independent woman she'd never been given the chance to be? His cell rang and he answered. She could hear Jack's deep voice.

Austin's face hardened. He looked at her. "He has the warrant for Campbell's place. He's on his way."

"After I leave, lock the door and don't open it for anyone but me," he said, pulling out his gun, and Jenna's heart jumped into overdrive.

"Be careful."

"I will," he said.

Jenna, feeling her face draining of color, followed him to the door. But she couldn't seem to turn the lock. Instead, she opened the door a crack. Austin walked over to Mitch's apartment. She only had to wait a short time for Jack, who came through the door to the complex with two uniforms. Jack walked up to the door and nodded to Austin. He knocked on the door. "Mr. Campbell, this is Detective Morton with the El Centro Police Department. Open the door."

No answer and no movement in the apartment.

"Mr. Campbell, open the door. I have a warrant and am prepared to break down the door if you don't comply."

Still no answer. Finally, Jack nodded to the officer with the door breacher. He swung the tool against the door, and it banged open. Jack and Austin moved inside with purpose, their guns drawn and ready.

Jenna was consumed with curiosity and she couldn't stop herself as she opened the door and crossed the hall into Mitch's apartment. Had he been the man who'd killed her cousin? She wanted to face him. She saw Austin, Jack and the two uniforms drop their weapons as they entered a back bedroom. Jenna entered the room, her hand flying to her mouth. On the floor before a closet lay Mitch Campbell, a gunshot to the head, a pillow and a gun next to him.

But it wasn't Campbell's body that Jenna was staring at. It was the open closet door where every possible surface was covered with pictures of…her.

Chapter 16

It was over. The man who killed Sarah was now dead and there was nothing left but the mopping up. She was once again in the background while people filled her apartment and moved in and out of Mitch's. Austin and Jack talked together but she heard bits and pieces, especially how the gun matched the firearm that had killed Billy and the pictures plastered all over the wall showed that her neighbor, kind, hardworking and gentle Mitch Campbell, had been stalking her. The eagle necklace that Sarah had been wearing was found among his possessions. His suicide note said it all. *Forgive me. I love you.*

How could he have loved her? He didn't know her except for the occasional greeting, borrowing a cup of sugar or helping her unload her groceries. She'd seen Mitch and Tina together and he had been so affectionate with her. It seemed so surreal to Jenna, who hadn't spoken to him about anything important. But the word *erotomania* was bandied about by Detective Morgan; Mitch had apparently been determined to maintain the delusion that she was in love with him even though they were strangers.

Feeling dull, having had no sleep since his body had been discovered, Jenna stared out at the wispy clouds on the western horizon still undercoated with slate gray, while the eastern ones were burnished with orange, gold and deep blushing coral. Soft purple wisps trailed out behind those clouds like the wake of a boat, painting the sky with slashes of color. On most mornings like this, she felt like if she could take a deep enough breath, she would be able to absorb all the colors, all the open-sky beauty. She would miss the wide-open spaces of the desert that possessed their own dry, dusty beauty.

She opened the back door and stepped outside. The air was heavy, as if the Santa Anas were gathering for one last buzzy episode before they finally moved off. She wrapped her arms around herself as she slipped through the gate and started walking out into the open area behind the complex, an uneasiness dogging her footsteps.

She wasn't sure if it was because she'd made up her mind about what she had to do, the best choice for her own personal growth. Her discovery that she had "let" people take care of her galvanized her to face the truth. She had to stand on her own two feet without some-one in her life paving the way or making it easier. Her throat tightened.

That included Austin.

It included accepting confrontation and saying no. It included making her own plans and decisions. It meant going back to DC, burying her cousin and deciding for the first time in her life what she was going to do with it.

"Babe?"

She turned from the spectacular sunrise to the sight of a spectacular man. The wind tossed his unique hair around, the color of his eyes matching the slate gray on the underbellies of the clouds. He looked tired and just as uneasy as she felt. It had to be because this was it. What he had told her he was waiting for. Her moment to talk about them.

Shivering in the glow of light and the hot blast of the wind, she closed her eyes. This cold had nothing to do with the external and everything to do with her internal revelations. She was going to leave Austin voluntarily when she had been the one to coerce him into a relationship he'd fought against for professional and personal reasons. Ever the guardian, ever the protector who looked out for the weak and downtrodden. A man to die for.

Her feelings for him were incomprehensible, jumbled, locked somewhere deep inside her for fear if she let herself feel them now, she would be right back where she started, letting a man take care of her, losing herself all over again. She climbed onto a picnic table, sitting on the surface and bracing her feet on the seat.

"You're going back to DC." He looked away. "When?"

"Tomorrow. I've already booked my flight." There was silence. "Please don't be angry about it."

"Angry? I'm not angry, Jenna. Why would you think that?"

"Because that's what happens when I want to do something that doesn't fit with people's plans. They get angry."

"You have to do what is the best thing for you. I would never hold that against you. Am I disappointed that you're not staying, that you don't want to discuss a future with me? Damn right. But I'm not going to hold that against you. You are in control of your own life."

"I just have to find out for myself. I need to plan this funeral without your help or anyone's. Sarah died because of me. I owe her that at least."

He looked uncomfortable for a moment. "Jenna, she died because someone killed her in your place. That doesn't make you responsible."

"I feel responsible."

He nodded. "I get that."

Feeling as if she was too close to a precipice, his tone set off warning bells. Tension was radiating off him, and Jenna's insides shrank into a hard, cold knot. Experiencing an almost strangling sensation of dread unfolding in her, she clenched her arms around her knees and watched him, every muscle in her body braced for a blow. "Someone? Don't you mean Mitch?"

He looked away and his posture told her that he'd been disagreeing with his boss, and he hadn't won the argument. "I don't like the way this panned out, and Campbell? He had no evidence of any symptoms of a disorder. I'm not convinced, but I'm told that the disease can manifest in a man in his late twenties. He could have been developing schizophrenia and it hadn't fully surfaced yet. I'm just not convinced. But I've been overruled and with the damning evidence, my words are falling on deaf ears."

Unsettled, she shivered against a sudden internal chill. "He had Sarah's necklace. The one she was wearing that night."

He remained immobile for a second, then he made a small, abrupt gesture with his hand. "Yeah, he did. Why did he keep it if it was you he focused on? He may have gotten the tickets, made the phone call to get Sarah out of the house, but why were the lights off? Why did he kill her if he thought it was you? Schizophrenics are not usually violent. The suicide, I can understand, stemming from his unrequited love. But he never approached you, and I can't see him locking you inside the library. Other than the head wound, there were no other marks on him. You said you stabbed your attacker." It was obvious he had more questions that didn't have answers. But she figured in this type of bizarre case maybe they would never know all the answers. He shrugged. "I could be wrong." He looked out to the brightening sky. "It doesn't matter. Kai wants me back at Pendleton tomorrow."

The heaviness in Jenna's chest increased as dread settled in, and she felt as if she were at the edge of a deep dark hole. "That means you're leaving…tonight?"

Jenna could feel the reluctance in him across the gap that separated them. When he finally answered her, his voice was barely audible. "Yes. I need to stay to wrap this up, but once that's done, I'll be heading out. We can have dinner together before I go."

This was what she wanted, what she had to do. "Okay, you're cooking."

He chuckled, then sobered. "All right. Agreed." They stared at each other with the full knowledge that hours from now they would be saying goodbye.

Feeling as if every bit of warmth had been sucked out of her, she lifted her head and looked at him, her stomach in knots. He was standing as he was before, but he was so focused on her; his body language was painful to see and so was the ache in his eyes. His face was like stone. But what wrenched at her heart was that beneath that rigidly controlled surface, she saw his absolute commitment to her. Just like at the embassy. Experiencing such a rush of feeling for that man, and for the man he had become, Jenna slipped from the picnic table and crossed to him. Her throat so full she didn't dare unlock her jaws, she put her arms around him, pulling his head against her shoulder, easing in a careful, constricted breath so he wouldn't know she was so close to tears.

For an instant he simply stood there in her arms, then he let his breath go and put his arms around her. Jenna closed her eyes and cradled his head against her, blinking furiously.

Jenna swallowed hard, struggling to achieve a degree of self-control, an outward calm. "I don't like Brussels sprouts."

Through the turmoil in his eyes, a tiny glimmer of humor appeared. "Oh, that's too bad. That's exactly what I was making."

"Beck!" Jack called from the back door and he turned.

He dropped his arms and stepped back. Reaching out, he snagged a curl, wrapping it around his finger, his expression drawn. He shook his head and let the curl go. "Duty calls, babe. I'll see you later."

Refusing to give in to the churning inside her, she smoothed down his shirt, then stepped back and let him go.

After a few more minutes, she went back into the house. Even before she entered, she knew it was empty. She found a note from Austin on the counter, saying he'd gone to the precinct and that he'd be back later on.

She listlessly slid the note into a slot by the telephone, then headed toward the bedroom, rolling her head to ease the tension in her shoulders. Time to get some sleep. She had to get packed up tonight and get ready to leave. She supposed since Sarah was deceased, so was the lease, but the rent had been paid up to the last day of next month. She contacted the power company and put in an order to cancel service; cable was part of the rent, so she just had to schedule the cancelation of phone service. The last thing she did was go online to cancel forwarding her mail. She picked up her cell phone and called the super. When he answered, she said, "Scott, I'm leaving tomorrow, but I will be back to pack up and take care of all Sarah's things."

"Now that everything is settled, you heading back home?"

"Yes, Austin is leaving tonight, and I'll be out tomorrow morning. I'll keep the key until I handle everything in the apartment."

"The rent is paid up until next month, so you're good. Have a safe trip."

"Thank you." She hung up and got up and pulled her two suitcases and carry-on out of the closet. One was large, the other midsize. But the thought of packing made her even more tired. She went and brushed her teeth and then lay down, dropping into sleep.

The feel of someone pulling the comforter up around her woke her, and she tried to swim through the gray weight of unconsciousness, her mind thick with sleep. It vaguely registered that she was huddled in bed with her hands under her face, trying to ward off the chill, her oversize T-shirt twisted up around her waist. Feeling as if she weighed a ton, she slowly opened her eyes, her body so heavy she couldn't move. Austin was sitting on the bed beside her, his hand on her shoulder, gazing down at her. "I'm sorry I woke you. You looked cold."

She stared at him, feeling almost drugged. "I was." She rubbed her hand over her face. "What time is it?"

"Only two. I need a little nap myself. Shove over."

She made room for him and he pulled the comforter over both of them. He turned to face her. He stared into her face, as if he was memorizing her features, and her heart did a funny little catch in her chest. He took a ragged breath and pulled her against him, burying his face in her neck. She felt raw and desperate at the way he held her with such absolute tenderness, and it made her throat close up all over again. He could turn her inside out, and God, how she… Oh God, oh God, oh God…she couldn't say the word to herself because if she did there would be no leaving him. And she had to go. Had to do this on her own.

His gazed fixed on her, he continued to stare at her, his gray eyes now a somber dark charcoal. The expression in his eyes softened, got warmer and more intimate. "I'm going to miss this…and you, babe."

Something in his tone, something in his eyes, set off a fierce ache in Jenna's chest, and her throat got so tight that she wasn't sure she could swallow.

He cupped her face, then with a heavy sigh, he lowered his head and gave her the sweetest, softest kiss. Releasing another sigh, he lifted his head and gazed at her, something in his eyes making her shiver. She smoothed her hands up his back and murmured against his mouth. "I'm going to miss you, too." She ran her hands over his stubble, then into his silky hair. "Go to sleep. You've got a drive to make and it would be better if you had some sleep under your belt."

He closed his eyes, but dragged her closer, and she couldn't stop the burn of tears that finally let loose as she cried silently against his shoulder.

The next time she woke up, a heavenly smell was coming from the kitchen. She got up and slipped a sweatshirt over her T-shirt and dragged on a pair of jeans. Her stomach took a nosedive as she saw Austin's open suitcase at the end of the bed. When she came out of her room, she found him in the kitchen.

"Whatever you made, it smells delicious."

"Good timing, lady. It's almost ready. I was about to wake you up." She took a deep breath as he dished out two steaks, potatoes and green beans. He offered her the plates as he went to the fridge and poured them each a cup of iced tea.

At the table they started eating. "I see you're not packed yet."

"I took the liberty of throwing some stuff in the washing machine. It's almost dry."

She nodded. Twilight settled into darkness, and they sat in companionable silence as the wind that seemed to have picked up moaned at the window sash. They talked about where he lived in San Clemente and how close his very nice apartment was to the beach.

"I could teach you to surf if you come to San Clemente."

She smiled and nodded. "I would love that."

After they finished their dinner, Jenna cleaned up, and Austin went to pack. She worked at trying to disconnect from the cold, hard reality that Austin was minutes away from leaving. She had the dishes in the dishwasher and everything wiped up by the time he rolled his suitcase out of the bedroom to the front door.

He stood there, and she caught her breath, wavering for a minute, then realized how disappointed she'd be in herself if she caved in and let people take care of her. She had to find her own footing. She had to do it without Austin's wonderful presence.

She tried to brace herself for what was coming, but nothing could soften this reality. He was leaving, and she had to let him.

"You going to give me a hug and one last kiss before I go?"

She was across the kitchen in seconds, her arms around his neck, the chill of being without him already settling into her bones. She closed her eyes against it, her heart suddenly too big for her chest. As if he sensed her reaction, or felt the same way, he tightened his hold.

She hugged him hard, hanging on to him for as long as she dared, then she physically pulled herself together. She wasn't going to make a scene, and she wasn't going to make it any harder on them than it already was. She had made her choice. Now she had to learn to live with it.

Then he kissed her, his mouth fiercely gentle. "Keep in touch, Jenna. I owe you a surfing lesson."

This was the second time she was saying goodbye to him. Hugging herself, her throat so tight she couldn't answer, she nodded.

He stared at her for an instant, the muscles of his jaw bunching. Then he was gone, the door closing behind him.

She stood there for a moment, not sure what to do. At a total loss. She wanted to run out the door, chase him down and beg him to stay. But he had a job to get back to, and she had her life to figure out. Instead of doing something foolish, she went into the bedroom and packed up all her clothing except her nightclothes and what she was wearing tomorrow. Then she went into the bathroom and ran a bath.

Settling into the tub, she lit some candles and leaned back to let the heat work at the pain of having to say goodbye to the one man on this earth she never wanted to let go.

When she was ready to get out, she reached for a towel, rising from the tub as water sluiced off her body. She stepped out and dried off.

As she reached for her robe, the lights went out.

Chapter 17

Jenna stood frozen in the semi-darkness, her gaze darting to the bathroom door. The wind outside swelled, the moaning getting under her skin and making it buzz with pinpricks of uneasiness. It must be the wind. It had knocked down a power line, caused a transponder to explode.

She tightened the belt around her waist and went into her bedroom, planning on grabbing her phone and calling Scott to find out. But when she got to her bedroom, she realized she'd left her phone on the counter in the kitchen.

That was where the flashlight was, as well. Going back into the bathroom, she picked up a candle, careful not to spill the wax that had accumulated on top as she'd soaked. She swallowed hard. What had Sarah thought when the lights had gone out for her? She hadn't had the benefit of a candle to light her way when she'd gone to retrieve the flashlight.

When she came out of her bedroom, she stopped dead. A man was standing in her kitchen and he was talking on the phone. She glanced at the front door and started to move toward it.

Then she recognized his voice. It was Scott. He was already here? She frowned. She got close enough to hear what he was saying.

"Yes, this is Jenna Webb calling. The power has gone out in my apartment—again. Could you come and fix it?" he said in a falsetto voice. Then he started talking in a normal voice. "I'm sorry, Ms. Webb. You're not going to need any light where you're going."

His face looked cold and empty even in the glow of the candlelight. She backed up. "What is this about?"

He chuckled. "I'm here to finish the job I was paid to do." He pulled a Bluetooth mic away from his ear.

"You called your own phone and answered with the Bluetooth. That was that alibi."

"Yeah, pretty effective. This thing has an amazing reach."

Tucking it in his pocket, he pulled out some flex cuffs. "I made a mistake. First time in my life by the way. Usually when I'm hired to snuff someone out, I get it right the first time. You caused me a big mess, Jenna. But I believe in second chances, don't you?"

He advanced on her and Jenna reacted. She threw the lit candle at his face. He screamed as she reached for a lamp and clobbered him across the face with the base. Then she was running for the door, but before she could get there, it burst open, the bright light from the hall illuminating several uniforms, Jack and…Austin. All of them had their guns drawn, but there was no need to subdue Scott Posner, her super.

He was out cold on the floor.

Austin holstered his weapon as Jack and the uniforms headed for Scott. She headed for Austin and he wrapped her up in a strong embrace.

Ambassador Robert Webb's Residence
Washington, DC

Hours later, Jenna stood outside what had once been her home, alongside Austin and Agent Beau Jerrott. Austin glanced at her and she took a big breath. He knocked. Marta opened the door, her face as dour as usual.

All the way to DC, Jenna had stewed over everything. Austin hadn't believed that Mitch Campbell was Sarah's killer. He hadn't spent the time at the precinct at all. Of course, Austin hadn't wanted to alarm her. If it turned out that Mitch had been the killer, he wouldn't have had to get involved at all. But if the killer was someone else, he would be prepared. He'd bought a security camera, a very small one, and positioned it across the hall from her, up on the ceiling to monitor her apartment door. He'd put a plainclothes El Centro policeman on Scott, convinced that he was the man who had killed Sarah. He knew the phone call from Sarah's phone to him could have been staged. He'd been betting it was. With no way to prove Scott had been present in the apartment, Austin had set a trap for him. He had apologized to Jenna, wanting her to know, but not wanting to worry her. He needed her genuine responses when setting Scott up.

After Austin interrogated Scott for most of the night, he confessed that her ex-husband had paid him to kill her. He'd had no choice but to confess; his blood, collected at the library where he'd attacked Jenna, would match, as well as the indentation from his ring that had left a distinct bruise on Sarah's face. The thin latex gloves couldn't mask the distinct impression. The call from his colleague Drea had confirmed he'd been on the right track. The medical examiner had matched the ring to the bruise. Scott said Jenna's ex-husband's instructions had been succinct. He'd wanted Jenna to die in the dark through strangulation, in the kitchen where she belonged. No other way would suffice and the second half of Scott's payment hinged on his instructions being followed to the letter. Robert had hired an assassin to pose as the super to gain access to the apartment to kill her.

She felt sick to her stomach. Scott had confessed that he had mistaken Sarah for Jenna. He'd sent Sarah the tickets, expecting her to be thrilled to get to go see her favorite artist, but he'd underestimated how much she'd been dedicated to the Blue Angels.

Billy died because Posner couldn't take the chance that Billy could identify him. Scott had been on the phone to himself to set up his alibi when Billy's peeping caught him in the glow of Sarah's phone. Austin had already put it together that Scott had called his own phone, using Sarah's.

Poor Mitch. He had been totally innocent. Scott told Austin that he had knocked the guy out and tied him up. Then he'd gone to Billy's house and killed him with Mitch's gun. Then once back at his apartment, he'd forced the man to kill himself. If he didn't, Scott would make sure that Tina died as horribly as he could manage it. They'd never find her body. Mitch's autopsy revealed that he'd been struck on the back of the head. The suicide note was written to Tina, not Jenna. Scott hadn't realized the note was meant for Tina, since it wasn't addressed to her and he didn't really care. But Mitch's self-sacrifice at least wouldn't be in vain.

Now they were back at her ex-husband's, and Jenna couldn't seem to contain the overwhelming rage that surged within her. Agent Beau Jerrott was with them from the DC Office, as the law dictated only law enforcement from the resident state could make an arrest of the suspect.

When Marta saw Jenna, her eyes widened. "Mrs. Webb."

She had plans to change back to her maiden name but hadn't quite done it yet. She was determined to start the process as soon as possible. "Don't address me that way, Marta. I'm not Mrs. Webb anymore, and thank God. Is Robert home?"

"He's having his breakfast."

"Oh, good. He's not busy." She breezed past the woman and ignored her strident protests. Robert looked up at the commotion, his eyes narrowing and his mouth pinching. "What are you doing here, Jenna?"

"You son of a bitch," she said, her tone low and fierce. She pulled out a cell phone and pressed a number. A phone began to ring.

He glanced at his suitcoat, his eyes wide. "Aren't you going to answer it?" she said with a cold, twisted smile.

He closed his eyes, his face going pale, disappointment and hatred in his expression. "I want my lawyer."

Austin stepped close to Jenna. "You're going to need one, Ambassador." He squeezed her arm, then went around the table and hauled her ex-husband to his feet. Austin cuffed him and started to read him his rights.

Agent Jerrott said, "You're under arrest Mr. Webb."

Something broke in her, and something cold and deadly started to unfold. She stared at her ex-husband, her eyes unwavering. Jenna marched forward and drew her hand back and slapped him across the face as hard as she could. The pain from the blow reverberated up her arm into her shoulder, her palm stinging. Her tone deadly quiet, she said, "You killed Sarah. I hope when they shove you into that cell, they throw away the key."

She slapped him again and turned away in distaste, the muscles of her jaw rigid. God, he made her sick. She gripped the table, then bent over and clenched her jaw so hard, her muscles cramped.

Minutes later Austin was back. He reached for her, but she stepped back. "Thank you for letting me come along. I'm sorry. I've got to go. I appreciate everything," she said, her gut full of ice and bitterness.

She brushed past Austin and left the house that had been the host of so much unhappiness. She got behind the wheel of her car, blindly drove to her town house and went inside. She was safe now. Safe, but Sarah was dead and it was all her fault. She clutched her stomach and sunk down against the front door, reliving the awful feeling that had churned through her when Austin had come out of the interrogation room and told her that Robert had hired a hitman to kill her. Scott had had strict orders to make sure it was in the dark, helpless with her hands bound. He was supposed to deliver a message. *I will always be your master. I will take your life and leave you alone in the dark like you left me.*

But because of a twist of fate, Sarah had died in her place, her young life snuffed out. Jenna braced her head against the back of the door, finally giving in to the intolerable pressure in her chest. It was also the accumulated strain of years of worry and moments of heart-stopping unhappiness. For years, she had shoved constant anxiety to the back of her mind, refusing to give in to it. But now, bereft, guilty and alone, huddled on the floor, it took her under, as if, after months of stockpiling the fear and the panic and the frightening uncertainty, her own internal dam had broken.

It seemed like an eternity before she cried herself out, her harsh sobs dwindling to the occasional ragged one. Pressing the heels of her hands against her throbbing, swollen eyes, she forced herself to dredge up some control, then she pushed up from the floor, went to the bathroom and doused her face with cold water. She wiped it, blew her nose, then closed her eyes and tipped her head back, waiting for her emotions to settle. Her cell rang, and she pulled it out of her purse, but when she saw it was Austin's number, she couldn't bear to talk to him. She shoved her phone back into her purse.

She spent a terrible, fitful night and in the morning after she'd unpacked, her eyes still swollen, she started working on Sarah's funeral. Her body would be arriving at Reagan Airport in two days. When Jenna ran into red tape at Arlington Cemetery, she got so angry she couldn't see straight. Without hesitation, she called one of her friends on the Hill and unabashedly pulled strings.

After that phone call, things flowed smoothly and

two weeks later, Jenna went out to Arlington, turning down Elise and Tom's invitation to drive her. When she arrived, a lump in her throat at all the white grave markers, she almost lost it again. But today, she owed Sarah her courage and her commitment. She was going to get through this with dignity. Spring was erupting all over the DC area, the promise of the cherry blossoms adding a pink glow to the trees in the cemetery as they prepared to burst into vibrant color. Sarah's final resting place would be beneath one of those magnificent trees.

As she arrived at the chapel at Joint Base Myer-Henderson Hall, where she met with the funeral director, many guests arrived and filled the pews. Sarah's flag-draped coffin was to her right and before she sat down, she touched it, saying a soft goodbye to her wonderful cousin. A man came up behind her and she turned toward him. He wore navy dress blues, his eyes swollen, red-rimmed and moist. Behind him Commander Henry J. Washington and several of the Blue Angels saluted her in unison. She nodded to them.

"Hello, Ms. Webb. I'm Lieutenant Ben Torres. I was—" his voice broke as he looked at the coffin "—in love with her. I know she didn't tell you about me, but she mentioned you. She was so thrilled to have you in her life. I hope that brings you peace. Thank you for arranging all of this. She deserved it."

Jenna wrapped her arms around him as he broke into sobs, hugging him tight. She was glad he came. She had notified everyone on Sarah's contact list to let them know when the funeral would be.

She kept herself together during the beautiful service, performed by a chaplain, and Sarah's casket was moved back into the hearse by eight sailors in dress whites.

Music sounded as the navy band in front of the hearse began to play. Elise slipped her arm through Jenna's right and Tom took her left as they filed behind the white hearse. She longed to have Austin here to support her, but she hadn't returned any of his calls—she'd been so raw with guilt and worried she would beg him to come to DC. She had to stand on her own two feet.

They walked at a moderate pace to the gravesite, where chairs were available for comfort. As Sarah's casket was unloaded, the chaplain, Commander Washington and the rest of the officers saluted, and the pallbearers brought the casket to the burial site, lowering it to the ground. All saluted again. The chaplain said a few words while the pallbearers held the flag above the coffin. The cemetery official asked them to rise for the presentation of military honors and Commander Washington saluted, shouting loudly in the quiet of the grounds, "Present arms!"

Once the sharp, staccato sound of the Twenty-One Gun Salute echoed away, the sound of taps filled the air. Elise squeezed her arm and Jenna looked up. Austin, a bugle to his lips, stood in his dress marine uniform—black coat with red piping, his medals, white belt and cover on his head. He looked so official.

Her eyes met his, and she couldn't hold on to her numbness. Pain seeped in and before she knew it, tears streamed down her face. How could she have been so blind? She didn't have to go through this grieving alone. Austin would never treat her like Robert. He was her rock, her support, and she needed him in her life. But she had so many things to do before she could even think about making that a reality.

From a distance, the sound of jet engines drowned out other sounds for a moment as four planes screamed above them, Jenna's throat and chest tight as one of the blue-and-yellow Hornets broke off and rose above, disappearing into the clouds. "Goodbye, Sarah. Rest in peace," Jenna whispered.

With the last mournful note of the bugle, the wind swelled and a rain of pink blossoms fell like snow onto the casket and Jenna's hair. The flag was folded and passed to Commander Washington. He knelt down in front of Jenna and set it in her hands, murmuring words of condolences and thanks for Sarah's service. Jenna thanked him. Shortly after, the Arlington Lady, a representative from Arlington Cemetery, offered Sarah a card of condolences and added her best wishes for peace in her trying time.

After the reception, she looked for Austin, but couldn't find him. It was clear he must have already left. She thought about calling him, but didn't know what to say, how to tell him how much she appreciated that he had attended the funeral.

When she got home, she had never felt so energized in her entire life. She'd laid her cousin to rest and now it was time for Jenna to move forward with her own life.

She reached for a piece of paper Elise had given her and dialed the numbers. As soon as the woman on the other end of the line answered, Jenna said, "Piper Kaczewski, this is Jenna We— Reed." She smiled at the sound of her maiden name. She was no longer associated with Robert at all. "I'd like to talk to you about a project I have in mind."

Camp Pendleton, California
NCIS Headquarters
Two weeks later

"Hey, you going to win tomorrow?" Drea said, giving Amber a wink.

Austin smiled and shot their enthusiastic probie a look. "Why? How much money did you bet on me?" He frowned. "Or against me?"

Drea opened her eyes really wide and smiled innocently. "What? Bet against my coworker? I would never."

"A hundred bucks," Derrick said, his face straight and unreadable.

Austin's brows rose. "Really?"

"That you'd wipe out on the first wave." Derrick laughed and looked over at Amber.

Austin shook his head. "You don't have faith in me, brah. That cuts me deep."

Amber gave Derrick a chastising look. "She did not. She bet you'd place. So did Derrick. He's kidding."

Austin had signed up for the Camp Pendleton Surf Competition taking place tomorrow on Camp Del Mar Beach. Everyone from the office was coming to watch him surf, even Kai.

He was closing out Lieutenant Sarah Taylor's murder investigation, finishing up his final report. Former Ambassador Robert Webb had confessed to soliciting a murder-for-hire in the case of his ex-wife, Jenna Webb.

He and Richard Somers, AKA Scott Posner, had been charged with multiple counts of first-degree murder in the deaths of Lieutenant Sarah Taylor, William Dyer and Mitchell Campbell. Jenna's ex-husband was due to be extradited from Washington, DC to San Diego, California to stand trial. Extradition from one state to another wasn't automatic and to transport her ex-husband would require going through state judicial channels. An email popped into his account while Derrick, Drea and Amber argued about his surfing prowess. Austin just smirked when Derrick said, "He's going to smoke the competition."

He opened the email from Beau Jerrott and read the short message. He sat back in his chair and Amber said, "Bad news?"

"No, not really. Robert Webb is dead, heart attack. He's not even going to serve his sentence." Austin felt nothing but relief. "Can't say I'm sorry about that. I wouldn't put it past the bastard to put another hit out on Jenna."

Derrick gave him a knowing look, and Austin flipped him off. "You should go after her."

Austin ignored him. "I'm out of here," he said, grabbing his travel bag. "I'll see you guys in the surf tomorrow. Derrick, bring your money."

Amber and Drea laughed as Austin headed for the parking lot and soon was leaving base. He picked up some seafood from The Shack, his stomach grumbling all the way to his apartment. Once inside he set the food down on the kitchen counter, went into his bedroom, stripped down and jumped in the shower, then dried off, leaving his hair wet. In board shorts, he opened the fridge, grabbing a beer. He took a swig, snagged the food and sat down by the window, eating while watching the surf. The Santa Anas had blown out to sea, but the projected surf for tomorrow's competition was going to be radical.

He couldn't wait.

The waves started to pick up and he grinned, taking another swallow of his beer. So Webb was dead. Good riddance. For the umpteenth time, he thought about Jenna and his chest tightened at the memory of the last time he'd seen her. He'd made sure when he was notified of the funeral date and time to volunteer to play taps. He'd wanted to stay and comfort Jenna, but he knew she didn't want to talk to him, which hurt like freaking hell, but he had to honor her wishes. She wanted to go this alone, and no matter how much he disagreed with that, he would stay away. She would have to come to him, and he rubbed his breastbone. God, he hoped like hell she would come to him. He was still deeply in love with her, and it was killing him to remain passive. But she'd asked him to let her handle things. Not that he wouldn't have if he'd been with her—that was the problem. If she'd wanted to do this under her own steam, he would have stepped aside and minded his own business. He just wanted her in his life.

After finishing half of his meal, he sat back and sent his hands over his face and into his hair. He rose and grabbed his board and some wax. To fill the time before he went to bed, he gave the board several coats, then set it back in its brackets on the wall. He checked his competitor's entry packet to make sure everything was inside, including his number, and set it on the dining room table.

He answered some personal emails, then got ready

for bed, opening one of the windows before settling under the covers. Austin lay there, wishing Jenna was here in his arms, listening to the soft crash of the surf. He turned to his side and stared out at the moonlight, so bright that it made eerie shadows on the rolling waves. He closed his eyes, remembering how he had absently fondled her hair, thinking it would be the perfect night for surfing—or for watching the stars.

He thought about her soft skin and the way she gasped when he entered her. He got hard, cursing for torturing himself, thought about how they'd parted, how he had burst in to find out she'd dispatched Posner/Somers with candle wax and a lamp. She was amazing. But then she had closed down when he'd told her what Posner/Somers had said, who was behind her murder-for-hire and that three people had died as a direct result.

She had gone so cold and distant.

It was even worse than their goodbye in Ja'arbah. So much worse. She had never once tracked him down, never once phoned him or sent him a letter or visited him at Walter Reed when he'd been wounded. He remembered how he kept expecting her to come through his hospital room door, but she hadn't. But he hadn't realized back then that she would have come to him if she had known. He was sick at the years they had wasted.

He had been resigned back then, kidding himself that she didn't matter, but now he was pretty torn up. In fact, it had hurt pretty bad when she had left him after the ambassador's arrest.

It was as if they had suffered some kind of strange destiny, and they each had their own paths—but every once in a while, those isolated paths would bring them together, and for a brief time they could bask in each other's lights. Then they would both move on. He sometimes wondered what his life would have been like if he'd never met her at all. The thought disturbed him more than he liked. Just knowing that she was living and breathing somewhere had kept him going more than once, and he could not imagine his life without her in it. He didn't want to think what it would be like to never see her again.

His throat got thick, and he closed his eyes, aching to cradle her tight against him. He pushed away from the board and grabbed his guitar. Strumming it, he settled on the couch and played a song that said everything that was in his heart. He sang to her, across the distance and time, waiting and praying for a chance to bask in her light again. He gave himself up to the music. He wasn't going to think about it. Not tonight. Not while there was still hope, not while she had settled like a beautiful weight on his heart.

Camp Pendleton, California
Camp Del Mar Beach
Two days later

Austin shaded his eyes. The waves were rushing to shore in a sound that always made his surfer heart sing.

"Hey, surfer boy," Derrick said and they bumped knuckles. "You ready to take some of these breakers and show them who's boss?"

"Cowabunga, dude," Austin said, grinning. "Bring it on." The talent present was exceptional and these guys were in great shape, several from the coast guard, navy and of course, marine corps. So, it wasn't going to be a ride in the park. But Austin had been surfing every day possible since he was old enough to stand on a board. Even with all that competition, he was on top.

The event was organized by the Pendleton Surf Club, of which Austin was a member; he was considered by necessity a retired marine, but anyone who served knew that you couldn't retire: *Semper Fi*. It was in every service member's bones.

It was the last day of the championship, and he intended to show some of these guys what he was made of. He was second in the race and he needed a good ride to win this finals heat and the competition. Surfers had to surf serveral heats to actually win a competition, with the competition lasting two days on average. He'd already advanced through the semi-finals and was now in the final. His heat was called and he picked up his board and headed for the water.

Paddling for all he was worth, he duck-dived below a wave and was up and paddling again. As the ocean heaved against the board, Austin's honed instincts crested. Yeah, the one he wanted was just swelling. It was his wave. He prepared to pop and ride as it started to break. He slipped down the crest slick as you please and continued to ride until the wave broke up. Tons of water foaming around him, he knew that his score would be high. He moved along a medium wave, trailing his hand through the water on top of the wave. He heard whistling and clapping from the beach and grinned as he guided the board over the top of the crest.

When the heat was over, he rode a wave to shore and rose out of the water. Kai, Drea and Amber were jumping up and down in the crowd and people were clapping. Amber's husband, Tristan, and Derrick and his wife, Emma, were hooting and hollering. He shook his head like a dog, droplets flying everywhere. He reached back and unzipped his wet suit and peeled the top off, leaving it hanging from his hips. When he looked up the beach, he stopped cold.

Jenna was standing there in a blue-and-white-flower-print sleeveless dress, a white sweater over her arm, white sandals on her feet. She looked so good that for a moment, he thought he was dreaming.

He jammed his board in the sand and stared, sure he was just conjuring her up. Derrick gave him a shove in the back. "Man, what are you waiting for."

He started walking, and she shielded her beautiful blue eyes from the sun, her expression going soft when she saw him making his way through the crowd to her. The scores were being announced and people were cheering, but the competition faded into the background. All he could see was Jenna.

"Babe," he said as he reached her, and she looked up into his eyes.

"Austin, you were...amazing."

"I can't believe you're here," he said gruffly. He watched her, a sudden ache jamming up his throat.

She tried to smile, the worry in her eyes evident in the bright light. "I am. Here to stay."

His heart jerked hard in his chest. "What?" He looked away, trying to handle the sudden stinging in his eyes. God, but she could turn him inside out. Finally managing to get a shaky breath past the lump in his throat, he looked at her, aware of how pensive she was, aware of the dark uncertainty in her eyes. That uncertainty stripped him to the quick, and he walked the rest of the way across the sand toward her. "Come here," he whispered gruffly.

With a choked sound, she came into his arms, and he gathered her up in a tight embrace, roughly tucking her face against the curve of his neck. Austin felt her take a deep breath, then she pressed her face tighter against him as she slid her arms around his waist. He could feel her trembling, as if she hadn't been sure about how he would welcome her.

He pressed a kiss to her temple, then slid his fingers along her scalp, cradling her head in his firm grip. The sweet feel of her curls tangled around his fingers, their loose fall like satin against her neck and shoulders. Austin closed his eyes and hugged her hard, a swell of emotion making his chest tighten. Damn but she felt so freaking good.

He felt her take another heavy breath, and he smoothed one hand across her hips and up her back, molding her tightly against him. Easing in a tight breath of his own, he brushed a kiss against her ear, then spoke, his voice gruff and uneven. "You did say you were here to stay. I didn't hear that wrong, right?"

A tremor coursed through her, and Jenna dragged her arms free and slipped them around his neck, the shift intimately and fully aligning her body against his. Austin drew an unsteady breath and angled her head back, making a low, indistinguishable sound as he covered her mouth in a kiss that was raw, governed by the need to comfort and reassure. Jenna went still. Then, with a soft exhalation, she clutched at him and yielded to his deep, comforting kiss. Austin slid his hand along her jaw, his fingers snagging in the warm strands of her hair as he altered the angle of her head. She kissed him back just as deeply, pressing herself against him, a fever of emotions sluicing through him. He was so thankful she was here, knowing that he was going to keep her there forever.

Dragging his mouth away from hers, he trailed a string of kisses down her neck, then caught her head again and gave her another hot, wet kiss. His breath ragged, he tightened his hold on her face and drew back, holding her against his chest. He held her like that, his hand cupping the back of her neck, until his breathing evened out.

He stared down into her now luminous eyes, the uncertainty gone. "Oh, Austin, I wasn't sure how you were going to react. I've been trying to do all this alone, all this grieving, and I was wrong, so totally wrong. You would only have stood by me and supported me through it all. And it was okay if I leaned. That's what a woman does when she's so deeply in love with the man she wants to be forever in her life. Can you forgive me for not seeing that?"

She was shaking like a leaf.

"Yes, of course I can. All of that is true."

"But you honored my wishes and that was so courageous and valiant of you, to come back here and wait until I was ready. I should have known and never expected less of a marine. I'll never forget that." She stared at him, then she swallowed hard and looked away. "Robert's dead. Did you know that?"

"Yes, Beau emailed me two days ago. I can't say I'm sorry. I didn't trust him to try again to hurt you even behind bars."

She nodded. "That crossed my mind, as well. I had no idea he was such a control freak. I should have, with his micromanaging, his obsessively pointing out things I needed to change in the guise of *helping* me. His silent judgment as a passive-aggressive way to make me see how *wrong* I was, describing worst-case scenarios in an attempt to deter me from certain behaviors, and his unsolicited, thinly veiled attempts to direct me with his insufferable 'constructive' criticism." She wiped at a tear that slid out of the corner of her eye. "He invalidated my emotions and he tried to drive a wedge between me and the people who didn't see it his way."

He kept his eyes on hers, giving her silent support in voicing her feelings.

"I should have talked to you about these things, but I was ashamed at how weak I had been."

"You were innocent, and he got you at a young age. It was what you knew."

"That's right, until you came along and became my catalyst, showed me true passion, unending courage, and didn't leave me in the embassy to fend for myself while Robert flew off without a backward glance. You were life to me, and I held the memories of your kiss and your kindness with me until I couldn't bear him one more day. It took me a while but I was finally able to break free."

"You can tell me anything, Jenna. I would never judge you," he said quietly. Meeting her gaze, his expression serious, he continued. "I love you, Jenna. Unconditionally and without boundaries. I don't want to contemplate another moment without you in my life permanently."

"I want that, too. So much." She took a breath and her eyes grew moist. "After my mother's death, I had been so afraid, and my father used that fear to crush my independence. He meant well, but his overprotective need to shelter me, to keep me safe, had terrible consequences." She held his gaze a moment, then she bent her head and clasped his hand, started rubbing her thumb back and forth across the back of it. "As a young woman, I was ill-prepared to deal with an over-bearing older man. Robert subverted my will, lied to me outright, all in the name of protecting me, but he'd wanted my father's society and government contacts. He especially wanted me for my looks. It stroked his overinflated ego." Her touch not quite steady, she swallowed, then took a deep, unsteady breath. "After my divorce, I'm ashamed to say I was clueless as to how to handle my own life, so Tom and Elise stepped in. Tom took over paying my bills and handling my finances. Elise coddled me and pampered me. They had been a safe haven."

Feeling as if he'd just been let out of a tight, dark place, he closed his eyes, absorbing her words, hugging her hard, feeling as if he could take his first deep breath in days. He pressed a kiss to her brow, then hugged her again. She was opening up to him, and it was clear she had done some major soul-searching, making sense of what had happened in her past to leave her susceptible to Robert's proclivities.

"I'm so glad you've worked this all out and we can start fresh here."

"I would never have met you again if it wasn't for Sarah." Her voice broke and her words trailed off. "Sarah was so independent, so strong and confident. There was something in her that called to me. I came to El Centro on a mission that had only begun with starts and spurts. My volunteer job where I asserted myself, and my idea of fund-raising, which I can now say is well under way, was the beginning for me. Sarah gave me that. Even though I had gone there to allow some-one to take care of me again, she really showed me who I was and what I was capable of." Her voice was soft. "I'm going to be working with Piper Kaczewski in her San Diego office. She's a fund-raiser and I'm going to learn the ropes from her. We're going to be partners. I kinda need a place to stay."

"You can stay with me if you're not going to hang your girlie things over my shower rod."

"I'm so going to hang all my girlie things every-where, and I know that you're going to grumble about it, but secretively you'll love it."

He pressed his lips together, trying his damnedest not to smile.

"Yeah, I see the way you're working at not smiling." Her grin faded and she said, her voice breathless, "In case you missed it, I said that I love you, Austin, and I want to be with you forever."

His heart was so full as he said, "I didn't miss it. I love you, too, Jenna. In case you missed it."

Releasing a pent-up breath in a rush, Jenna slid her arms around his neck. Closing his eyes against the on-slaught of sensation, Austin turned his face against her and wrapped her in a hold, lifting her off the sand, won-dering how he had ever managed without her. Grasping a handful of hair, he clenched his jaw and turned his head against hers, something joyous and wild expanding inside him. Inhaling raggedly, he clutched her against him. A tremor coursed through her, and he leaned back. "I can feel the stares of my friends, coworkers and boss behind me. Would you like to meet them?"

"Very much. I am dying to meet Kai and ask where she shops. Her clothes are to die for."

He chuckled and clasped her hand. He turned around and everyone cheered. At first he thought it had to do with his reunion with Jenna, but with a jolt he realized they were all waiting to congratulate him—he'd won the competition.

With a laugh, he went through the crowd fist-bumping, shaking hands and getting his back slapped. When he reached his friends, he said, "Everyone, this is Jenna."

With a wry smile on his face, Derrick said, "Jenna who?"

Everyone laughed, and Austin introduced her to each of his friends one at a time until he got to Kai. "It's good to meet you finally," Kai said with welcome in her voice. "You got lucky with this one."

Beaming at her, Jenna turned to look at him. "Don't I know it."

They went out to celebrate with good food, good company and alcohol; Austin had bragging rights after his win, the trophy sitting in the middle of the table. Afterward, he took her home to his apartment on the beach.

Once inside, she took her time looking around. "You're very neat. I like that. Love the architecture and the windows are glorious. Can you hear the surf?" She knelt down and sent her fingers across the strings of his guitar on a stand by the "glorious" windows. The sound was deep and well-tuned, just like their love.

He pulled her down to the couch and picked up his guitar. "I've been practicing this for you." He strummed the strings and sang "Once Upon A Dream."

She smiled, wiping now and then at her tears as he

came to a close. She rose and went to the window as he set the guitar aside. "I'm so happy," she whispered.

"Yeah," he said, stepping up to her, turning her, his hands gasping the fabric of her dress and pulling it off over her head, displacing those curls and making them bounce back to her shoulders. Her tantalizing mouth turned up at the corners and he made a low sound when he found her in nothing but her panties.

She pushed his clothes off his body with eager hands, and they fell together on his bed with questing hands and delving tongues. He fit himself to her and it felt like coming home.

Afterward, they lay together in each other's arms and Austin looked out the window. "Look at those stars."

She turned her head and sighed. "And the surf. It's hard to decide which is more breathtaking."

He looked down into her face and said huskily, "That would be you." He searched her eyes. "You have everything worked out then? For sure. No more doubts?"

She went still in his arms, then she turned her face to his and tightened her arm around his waist. "No more. Six years ago I fell head over heels in love with you. It didn't have to do with adrenaline, hormones or the danger we were in. It was all about you. Our chemistry, our deep and intense connection. We were always meant to be and fate brought us together in a terrible way for a second chance at love. You taught me what courage was all about. I love you so much, Austin."

Pressing a kiss against her hair, he began slowly stroking his hand up and down her back. His expression softening, he said, "I love you, Jenna."

She pursed her lips and gave him a cheeky grin.

"So," she said, running her finger over his stubble, "I remember someone making a promise to me."

He frowned. "Oh, yeah?"

"Yeah, surfer boy. Lessons? You know, in the water with a board and everything. Do you think you can handle that?"

He gave her a sensuous look. "I sure can, especially the clothing part. You'll look amazing in a wet suit."

She slipped her finger under his chin and dragged his eyes to hers. "Good thing there's no naked surfing or I'd never get any lessons."

"Oh, you'd get plenty of lessons," he murmured, rolling on top of her, and her soft laughter echoed in the fullness of his chest and the confines of his apartment, pushing out the darkness and filling it with light.

Epilogue

Austin and Jenna walked into the Blue Angels administration building, and Commander Washington walked up to meet them.

"Hello, Jenna, it's good to see you again. You ready to do this?"

She smiled. "Yes, and thank you for the invitation to ride."

"Of course. There isn't a day that goes by that we don't all remember Sarah and her contributions to the navy and this team. Let's get you suited up." First she was taught to breathe—the technique would keep her from blacking out at the effect of g-force. After the lesson, she was led to a room where they gave her a black coverall that she put on.

As she was tying up the boots, Austin said, "You nervous?"

She shook her head. "No, not at all. I'm excited."

"I'm proud of you, Jenna." She rose and wrapped her arms around his waist, clinging to him, thinking about Sarah and her lifelong dream.

When they came out of the room, the public relations pilot, Lieutenant Michael Jordan, smiled and said, "You set to go?"

"Ready."

She walked out of the building and onto the runway, the weather idyllic, not a cloud in the sky, the temperature mild for March. She passed jet number one, then two, and she paused at jet number three. Lieutenant Benjamin Torres stood near his F-18, his name lettered in gold just beneath the cockpit. He had been chosen for the team to replace Sarah, and he beamed at Jenna. She faced him and gave him a crisp salute. She had been practicing, with Austin giving her very good pointers. Benjamin's face contorted, and he saluted her back. The muscles in his throat contracted as he held the salute and the desolation in his eyes softened ever so slightly as he tried to smile.

Protocol be damned, she marched up to him and hugged him hard. He hugged her back just as hard. For a moment, they stood there in silent remembrance. Then Austin touched her shoulder, and they moved on to jet number seven, a crew member standing by. He helped her up the stairs and into the cockpit right behind Lieutenant Jordan. The crewman helped her into the harness, then the helmet, as Austin looked on.

The pilot settled in, as well, going through the same process. The crewman shook his hand, wishing him a safe flight, then hers, as well.

"How you doing back there, Jenna?" Lieutenant Jordan said through the mic as the canopy started to close.

"A-okay," she responded.

"All right. Then let's get this show on the road."

She turned to see Austin standing there, and she waved to him, then blew him a kiss. He pretended to catch it and brought his hand to his lips. *I love you*, he mouthed.

She mouthed it, too, and he stepped back as the jet started to move, jockeying onto the runway.

With a tremendous force against her body, it accelerated until they lifted off, the world outside the canopy dropping away at an alarming speed. Before she could catch her breath, six planes were above her and beside her as they flew in perfect formation. She turned her head and saw Ben and her heart swelled at the sight of him. When he'd been chosen, he'd called her and she had been so happy for him.

He said over the mic, "I'm doing this for the team, but most especially for Sarah. I'll fly her plane with pride and honor her every moment I'm in the sky and in the cockpit."

She was lucky that he had known Sarah so well. He'd filled Jenna in on all the stuff she hadn't gotten a chance to find out about Sarah. Up here with the blue all around her, she felt close to her cousin, and she could imagine as she experienced the barrel rolls and the sharp maneuvers that Sarah rode along with her, laughing and enjoying every moment of the flight.

Right before they landed, jet number three trailed out pink smoke, and Jenna closed her eyes against the tears welling and the emotion clogging her chest. Pink had been Sarah's favorite color.

"Thank you for that," she said softly into the microphone.

"You're welcome, Jenna," Lieutenant Jordan said.

After they landed, Jordan and Washington presented her with several mementoes, pictures of Sarah—one as she flew a training mission, another of her next to her aircraft—then one of Jenna in the cockpit of the recent flight, wearing a blue-and-gold pin and a Blue Angels Hornet patch depicting the insect in white.

"Take these for our first air show of the season next weekend. We'd love for you to be our guests. There's plenty of tickets there for friends you'd like to invite."

"Thank you for taking me up. It was an honor to fly with you. I'll cherish it forever." She clutched the gifts to her, and she and Austin went home.

The following Saturday, they were back on base sitting in the stands as F-18s screamed across a cloudless sky, six blue-and-yellow aircraft aligned in perfect formation, flashing over the crowd of thousands of upturned faces, people gasping in astonishment.

Jenna's was one of those upturned faces, sitting next to Austin as they watched all six planes aiming for a preestablished reference point on the ground, appearing to come together for a split second, then angling off in gut-wrenching climbs, trailing white smoke to mark their paths.

Kai was next to her; they had become fast friends just as Jenna had expected, along with Amber and Tristan, Derrick and Emma, Dexter—and Piper, her new business partner. And last but not least, their probie, Andrea Hall.

"Thanks for inviting us. I've always wanted to come out here and see the Blue Angels in action," Drea said.

"They are quite something to see," Jenna said. She

was thrilled with her new partnership with Piper Kacze-wski. They were already making strides in fund-raising for libraries in California and organizing literacy events.

She'd moved into Austin's wonderful apartment on the beach and they made love, laughed, ate and surfed. She couldn't be more content.

Later that night, wearing their wet suits and sitting on their boards in the rolling surf, Austin leaned over and grasped her arm, pulling them together. The moon was full and illuminated the water until it was a swath of glistening, gently ebbing and flowing light. A breeze blew her hair around her face and even though she so enjoyed night surfing with her man, she couldn't wait to snuggle with him up in that warm bed.

Suddenly he reached into his wet suit and pulled out something on a chain and when he turned his hand, light flashed brilliantly off something in the darkness.

Her breath caught and she stared at him. He took her hand and placed the ring onto her palm, still grasp-ing the chain. "Jenna, I lost you, then found you again. We overcame complications and obstacles to pledge ourselves to each other. Would you do me the honor of marrying me and becoming my wife, my lady love, my forever?"

She couldn't say she was surprised. She really be-lieved that they were meant to be together for the forever he promised. There was no doubt in her mind that he was the right man for her, one who would support her, but at the same time, let her be free to make her own choices, confident that Austin would be completely open to her opinion. He was the man of her dreams and she was thrilled. One could say she was head over heels in love with him. She picked up the ring and handed it back to him, offering her left hand. "On a few conditions."

"Conditions? What conditions?"

"That you be my husband, my guardian and my forever—"

"Yes, agreed." He started to slip the ring on her finger.

"Wait, I wasn't finished."

"There's more?"

"Yes. How do you feel about teaching our children to surf when they're babies?"

He smiled. "You don't need to be subtle about children, Jenna. I'm all for the rug rats, and teaching them to surf is required in this family. My mom will have them up there, anyway."

"She's a classy, beautiful lady, by the way, and your sisters are very sweet. You can tell they love you very much."

His gaze beamed. "Okay, here we go." He began to slide the ring on again, but she said, "Not so fast."

"This has been anything but fast. What now?"

"Hey, I don't want a grumpy proposal."

"Then stop saying 'wait' then," he grumbled, removing the chain.

"But there's more." She giggled at his put-upon expression. "I get a lifetime of lessons."

He cocked his head, a smile tugging at the corners of his mouth. "You think you need a lifetime of surfing lessons?"

She smiled and reached down, guiding his fingers as together they slipped the ring on. With a quick shove, she knocked him off his board, and he splashed into the water with a satisfying plop.

Giggling harder and with an unbridled glee, she paddled away, tossing over her shoulder, "Who said anything about surfing?"

He sputtered and swore, and his laughter chased her out into the waves, embedding itself deep in her heart.

Austin. Her forever.

* * * * *

If you loved this story, don't miss the other thrilling romances in Karen Anders's
TO PROTECT AND SERVE *miniseries:*

THE AGENT'S COVERT AFFAIR
HER ALPHA MARINE
A SEAL TO SAVE HER
HER MASTER DEFENDER
JOINT ENGAGEMENT
DESIGNATED TARGET
AT HIS COMMAND

All available now from
Harlequin Romantic Suspense!